Nighbert, David F.
    Squeezeplay.   St. Martin's Press,
1992.
    263 p.

I. Title.

SQUEEZEPLAY

Novels by David F. Nighbert

TIMELAPSE
STRIKEZONE
CLOUDS OF MAGELLAN

SQUEEZEPLAY

DAVID F. NIGHBERT

(ST. MARTIN'S PRESS) NEW YORK

1992.

M
C.2

SQUEEZEPLAY. Copyright © 1992 by David F. Nighbert. All rights reserved. Printed in the United States of America. No part of this book may be used or reproduced in any manner whatsoever without written permission except in the case of brief quotations embodied in critical articles or reviews. For information, address St. Martin's Press, 175 Fifth Avenue, New York, N.Y. 10010.

Design by Tanya M. Pérez

Library of Congress Cataloging-in-Publication Data
Nighbert, David F.
        Squeezeplay / David F. Nighbert.
                p.   cm.
        ISBN 0-312-07847-1
        I. Title.
PS3564.I363S68   1992
        813'.54—dc20   92-7612
                                                                         CIP

First Edition: August 1992

10 9 8 7 6 5 4 3 2 1

To my brothers

ACKNOWLEDGMENTS

I want to thank Diane Wonio, my Houston guide and driver, and the real Bubba Lusby, who bears no resemblance to his fictional namesake. Special thanks also go to Richard J. Retz, media/liaison officer for the Houston Police Department; Bruce Koger, chief arson investigator for the Houston Fire Department; Rob Matwick, director of public relations for the Houston Astros; Helen Conyne of the Houston Garden Club; and Dan Ogea of the Houston Garden Center. Any inaccuracies, liberties, or exaggerations are entirely my own responsibility.

If we could just love each other the way we say we love Him, there wouldn't be all the bother in the world there is.

From the film Resurrection,
written by Lewis John Carlino

There's no good way to get the news of a friend's death, but hearing about it on the radio while driving at high speed in heavy traffic has to be one of the worst.

I was on my way up to Houston that white-hot Saturday morning, just passing the Baybrook Mall on the Gulf Freeway, when a country-western deejay dedicated his next song to "the late great Holy Joe Ahern, a Christian gentleman and one of the finest pitchers ever to grace the diamond."

I went blank for a moment. I was on my way up to see Joe. *How could he be dead?*

I came out of my daze as I was about to slam into the back of a stationwagon, then jerked the wheel hard to the right and shifted blindly into the next lane. To the blare of horns, I kept going, swerving out of traffic onto the verge, and skidding to a stop.

For a moment, I sat there trying to kickstart my brain, wondering if I'd really heard what I thought I'd heard. I cut off Gary Morris in the opening bars of "Wind Beneath My Wings," switched to AM, and turned to KTRH. After catching the tail end of a report on a robbery at a Houston church and a commercial for mobile homes featuring an LBJ impersonator, I heard, "Recapping

1

our top story: Joseph Michael Ahern, star pitcher for the Astros, was found shot to death this morning in a South Houston apartment."

There it was. He *was* dead. And not just dead, *shot to death.*

"A second body in the room," the broadcaster continued, "has been identified as that of Cordelia Mae Oliver, age thirty-two, an employee of Goodtimes Executive Escorts. The bodies were found in Ms. Oliver's apartment by a neighbor at nine-fifteen this morning. Each apparently died of a single gunshot wound to the head. Police report that an Austrian-made Glock nine-millimeter automatic was found at the scene, but they have not yet established that it was the murder weapon. Robbery, they say, could have been the motive."

I was having a hard enough time believing that Joe was dead, but that he would pick up a prostitute was inconceivable to me. I couldn't picture him sleeping around on Peggy Ann, but if he *had,* he could have had his pick of eager amateurs. Why go for a pro, especially in this day of AIDS? A cynical part of me suggested that discretion might have been his motive, but I flatly rejected the idea.

Sound bites followed.

The Astros' general manager said, "This is a terrible loss, and more than just to the team. It's a loss to Houston, a loss to baseball, and most of all, a loss to anyone who ever had the pleasure of knowing the man."

Joe's closest friend on the team, Dwight Samson, the third baseman, said in his Kentucky twang, "I'm still so damned bewildered by it all, I can't think straight. To tell you the truth, I'm not even sure I believe it. I mean," he said in confusion, "how can Joe be dead?"

. . . .

When it comes right down to it, most of us don't believe in death, at least not when it applies to us or the people we know. That's why we so often respond to the news of a friend's death by saying, "But I talked to him only yesterday," or last week, or last month. Our friend was all right then; how can he be dead now?

I talked to Joe on Thursday evening. He called me during the seventh-inning stretch of a game in which he held the San Diego Padres to three hits and no runs in eight and a third innings.

I was working on my novel with the TV on in my study, glancing up now and then to admire his performance, when he called. Most writers would probably find this distracting, but I actually found it easier to write with a ball game playing in the background. My agent says I need the reminder of who I was to help me become who I *can* be. To me, that smacks too strongly of an Army recruiting ad, and my theory is simpler. The sounds of a ball game make me feel at home. That's all.

"Talk about weird," I said to Joe, when he identified himself. "Just saw you strike out Tony Guinn on three pitches. Some slider."

"Thanks," he said. "Only have a minute, but we need to talk."

"Sure. What's up?"

"I have a story for you."

"Fiction or non?"

"Non, I'm afraid. There're some bad people out there, Bull."

"Bad people make a good story," I said.

"Guess they do," he agreed. "I don't have time to talk about it now. Gotta get back to the dugout. Why don't you drive up Saturday and catch the game. Bring Molly and make it a day. If you get here about one, we can talk about it before I head out to the Dome."

I had planned to spend Saturday and Sunday on the climactic scene of the novel. I had some ideas I wanted to try. And even though Joe was a friend, I probably would have begged off if he hadn't also been a valuable contact, the kind you didn't say no to without a very good reason.

With him dead, I couldn't help feeling a little guilty about my attitude. On the other hand, he hadn't actually asked for help; he'd just said he had a story for me. And whatever my motive, I'd said yes, so I wasn't sure why I was feeling guilty.

Joe and I had spent most of one minor league season together back in '78—him on the way up, me on the way out. We'd moved in different circles, and had rarely seen each other outside the ballpark, but we'd often talked in the dugout or the bullpen. As a rule, I avoided the company of self-proclaimed Christians, but Joe was the exception. He was smart and easy to talk to, never smug or overbearing, never preachy or judgmental. He'd chosen to witness by quiet example, and I'd never seen a better one.

Joe was there that night, thirteen years ago, when I played my last game—the night I killed Domingo Sanchez with a fastball. Joe was in the locker room afterward, when everybody else, including my best friend Juice Hanzlik, was keeping their distance. It was Joe who saw me floundering and came over to talk to me. I don't remember what he said—doubt I heard much of it at the time—but the sound of his voice was the only comfort I can recall from that evening. Later that night, when Juice and I were thrown in jail for a drunken bar fight over which of us was more responsible for the pitch that killed Domingo—me for throwing it, or Juice for calling it—it was Joe who bailed us out. Because Domingo and I were known to be enemies, with a long history of fights, a coroner's inquest was called to investigate the circumstances of his death, and it was Joe's testimony I remembered from that inquest. Speaking with the authority of a fellow pitcher, he explained that all of us *had* to throw inside to win—it was an axiom of the game—and pitching inside necessarily entailed the risk of hitting somebody. Batting helmets were developed to guard against this, he said, but the designers failed to account for the possibility of a batter accidentally dislodging his helmet just before the ball hit him. The next afternoon, after the inquest rendered a verdict of accidental death, it was Joe who drove me to the airport.

1

Houston sprawls over 620 square miles of South Texas real estate, occupying large chunks of Harris, Fort Bend, Montgomery, and Galveston Counties. It's a vast spider of highways, with a very limited public transportation system and almost three million people in the metropolitan area. A land where the automobile is king. Interstate 610, called the Loop, forms a lumpy square around the heart of the city, with the Pasadena and the East Freeways bringing people in from the east; the Eastex Freeway, the Hardy Toll Road, and the North Freeway from the north; the Northwest, the Katy, and the Southwest Freeways from the west; and the South and Gulf Freeways from the south.

Because I know Houston just well enough to know how easy it is to get lost there, I always carry a Key Map. But I know the Gulf Freeway well, the stretch of I-45 that sweeps up from Galveston Island, through the coastal wetlands, past the blinding stench of the Texas City refineries, fifty miles to the city.

I-45 intersects the 610 Loop at the southeast corner, then cuts through the lower half of the square at a sharp diagonal and makes a sweeping turn to the north at the western edge of downtown. The elevated highway banks around the skyscrapers, with walls of mirrored and colored glass and steel rising to the right, almost close enough to touch.

After the S curve finished with another sweep back to the northwest, I got off onto I-10, which is called the Katy Freeway as it heads west. It runs through a light industrial area, then skirts the wooded edge of posh Memorial Park. Just before you pass under the West Loop, you can catch a glimpse of an emerald-green polo field off to the left.

Joe and Peg lived more than a dozen miles from downtown and better than fifty from the point where I'd heard that Joe was dead. They lived beyond the small independent townships of Spring Valley and Hunters Creek, past the Sam Houston Tollway, in a wooded area off Memorial Drive, on the banks of the Buffalo Bayou.

. . . .

The wrought-iron gates to Shady Lane had been slammed shut, and two Columbia blue-and-white police cruisers sat nose to nose, blocking access. TV vans flanked the police cars, and a small crowd had gathered. Such crowds are held down in size in Houston by the heat and the general lack of sidewalks, and the popular local equivalent is a drive-by. Two policemen were waving carloads of gawkers past, so I had to find a place down the road to stash my pickup.

It had been an unusually mild summer, with more rain than heat, but today was more typical of July in Houston. The temperature and humidity were both in the nineties, and I'd sweated through everything I was wearing by the time I made it back to the gate.

Press and public alike looked wilted, standing in loose clusters in front of the police cars. I nodded at Floyd Malcovitch, the columnist for the *Chronicle,* then squeezed between two couples in wet trunks and string bikinis and walked up to one of the policemen. I told him I was a close friend of the family and wanted to express my condolences.

He was a big kid, with a sweet smile and the rosy overfed look of a small college middle-lineman. He was sweating, too, of course, but he didn't seem to mind. "I'm sorry, sir," he said, "but nobody gets through here without permission from Ms. Ahern or another resident."

"Is there any way you could let her know I'm out here?"

"You'll have to call her on the telephone, sir, and have her call the guard on the gate."

"Could I speak to the guard?" I asked. "Maybe he could call her for me."

Still smiling, he said, "I'm not supposed to let nobody get past, sir."

"I only want to talk to the guard and see if he can call Ms. Ahern for me. Isn't that what he's there for?"

I had him there. "Maybe so," he conceded, smile unwavering, "but we was told not to let—"

"Nobody get past," I finished for him.

"That's right," he cheerfully agreed, pleased that I had finally comprehended his orders.

I turned to the older officer, whose car formed the other half of the barrier. He was leaning on the door of his cruiser, arms crossed and a tired expression on his face. "Can you see any way out of this?"

He sighed and pushed himself off the car. "Name?" he asked. I told him, and he said to wait there.

I wasn't sure that sending Peg a message would do any good, since I didn't know if I really qualified as a close family friend. Joe and I had lost contact after I'd left baseball, and we hadn't seen each other for ten years. But he'd called me after reading my book about Juice's murder, and we'd gotten together for dinner. Since then, I'd spent a good many offseason afternoons at his house or on his sailboat, getting to know him and Peg. Some people might find it odd that a friendship should develop between a born-again Christian and an unreconstructed atheist. But, in spite of our religious differences, I enjoyed their company, and they appeared to consider my lack of faith to be no more than a minor eccentricity, readily subject to change. Still, I had some doubt that Peg would want to be bothered by me at a time like this.

"What're *you* doin' up here?" a raspy voice drawled, and I turned to look down at Floyd Malcovitch. He was a skinny little man with an incongruous pot belly and nose hair long enough to braid, who smoked fetid cigars and wrote a viciously witty column for the *Houston Chronicle*. We'd met a couple of times at press functions the summer before, when I was writing a weekly baseball column for the *Galveston Daily News*. Floyd asked, "You haven't gone back to the rag trade, have you?"

"Nope, I learned my lesson."

"Glad to hear it," he said. "You a friend of the Aherns?"

"An acquaintance."

"That's not what you told the patrolman."

"Eavesdropping?"

"Of course," he said. "What'n hell ya think I get paid for?"

"I've wondered."

"So, how well do you know the Aherns?"

"Well enough."

"Uh huh." He used a soggy handkerchief to push the sweat around on his face. "You were a ballplayer, weren't you?"

"You'll get some argument on that."

"Ever play with Joe?"

"Teammates in the minors."

"How long?"

"Most of one season."

Showing me his discolored teeth, he asked, "Think Peg'll invite you in?"

"Maybe."

"Worth a try, anyway?"

"Something like that."

"Uh huh."

His smirk vanished when the older cop walked over to say that Mrs. Ahern had asked him to send me through.

"What about me?" Malcovitch complained.

"No reporters," said the officer, "only friends."

"Friends." The columnist eyed me sourly, as though I'd tricked him somehow. "Yeah, I get it."

3

Shady Lane was originally the private drive to the home of Lord Francis Evelyn Fitz-Williams—an Englishman who'd made a killing in Texas oil back in the twenties. In 1979, the place was bought by a Houston real-estate *wunderkind* named Jerry Lamp, who moved his entourage into his Lordship's Mediterranean villa, claimed twenty-five acres as his private estate, and turned the rest into the most exclusive new development in town.

Great live oaks lined the drive, their topmost limbs creating a cool, green-shaded tunnel. I rolled down the window to smell mown grass, tree mulch, and the scent of late-blooming jasmine.

Only one house was visible from the lane: a white-columned, plantation-style colonial, no bigger than the Library of Congress, seen through a lushly wooded landscape off to the left. The lane wound to the right and back to the left, then crossed over a brook on a wooden bridge, from which I caught a glimpse of Joe's house between two towering oaks dead ahead. A handsome Tudor in bleached cypress and old brick.

The view from the front was blocked by a high wall, and another blue-and-white was parked at the gate. A silver Sedan de Ville pulled in next to the police car as the cop waved me through, but

9

the sun glaring off the Caddy's windshield kept me from seeing the driver.

As I cleared the gate, I was hit with a whiff of Peg's rose bushes. The blossoms made shocking splashes of color against the quiet green shadows.

An unmarked police car was parked in front of the house, but Dwight Samson's wife, Margie, opened the door. Margie was a little brunette with a perky figure and a wicked tongue. She was the only one of the players' wives, other than Peg, whom I knew on a first name basis. Back when I was writing my column, Margie used to call with something juicy every week or two. She was usually good for a quote because she spoke her mind, but today, she just said hi and led me across the entry hall into Joe's mahogany-paneled study.

Peg stood and came to meet me. She'd been crying, but it was under control now. If anything, she seemed almost too bright and composed.

Giving me a hug, she said, "Good to see you, Bull."

I didn't usually like to be called "Bull." It was the nickname given to me as a hot young pitching prospect and no longer seemed appropriate, but Peg could get away with it.

"Where's Molly?" she asked.

"Couldn't make it," I said. "Work kept her on the island."

"Too bad," she said. "I'd like to have seen her. But thank God you and Margie are here. I need familiar faces around me right now."

Peg had the freshly scrubbed look, the perfect skin, and the natural suntanned beauty of an Ivory Girl—Texas-size. The former Peggy Ann Sanders of Carthage, Texas, and daughter of State Supreme Court Justice Walter Matlock Sanders, stood nearly six feet tall. In her middle thirties, she still possessed the slender, broad-shouldered build of a former competitive swimmer, and she could pass for ten years younger, if you weren't close enough to see the fine lines at the corners of her mouth and eyes.

When Margie asked if I wanted anything, I said, "No, thanks."

But Peg told her, "He just doesn't want to put us to any trouble,

10

Margie. Why don't you bring in the iced tea? I'm sure Bill could use something cool."

We sat down; Margie left, and Peg said, "They think he killed her, then killed himself."

I just stared at her. Not knowing what to say, I said the first thing that came to mind. "I don't believe it."

"Good!" she said with unexpected force. "You don't know what a relief it is to hear somebody else say that. The police've made it clear what they think. And Margie . . ." Her shrug said she believed Margie sided with the police on this, which sounded unlikely to me. "Why don't *you* believe he did it?" she asked.

"Why would he call and say he had something to tell me, then kill himself before I got here? And with a record of seventeen and three, he was only a few wins away from icing the Cy Young. There's no way any pitcher would kill himself with that on the line." She stared at me openmouthed. "Plus, I never saw Joe give in to a batter, and I can't picture him giving in to suicide."

"No," she whispered, and looked away, "he *couldn't* have. And we have to let people know that." Turning back, she asked, "What did he call you about?"

"Said he had a story for me, but he didn't have time to talk about it."

"Of course not," she said. "If he couldn't trust *me* with it, he couldn't risk it on the phone."

"Then he didn't tell *you* about it, either?"

"No, but he told me he'd invited you up, and I knew he was worried about something."

"No hints about what?"

"None I noticed."

"No intuitions?"

"I think it had something to do with an investment."

"In what?"

She shrugged. "I don't know."

"Why do you think it was an investment?"

"Because of something he said to me one night as we were getting ready for bed. He went on about how trouble always started with money. That sounded pretty funny to me, coming from a man

11

who'd just fought so hard for an eight million dollar contract, but he was serious."

"Are you having any kind of money trouble?"

"Far from it," she insisted. "I handle the books, and I know our accounts are healthy. And we always discussed any large expenditures. I didn't really think much of it when he said it. Joe was prone to occasional late-night sermons," she explained. "But now I think he was trying to tell me something." She rocked forward and reached out to touch my knee. "I'd like you to find out what it was, Bill."

Before I could voice any reservations, Margie showed up with the iced tea, and the three of us sipped silently until two plain-clothes officers appeared.

4

One officer was large, red-faced, and sweaty, one medium, pale, and dry. The big one followed his partner into the room, taking it all in, a slow-moving bear of a man in his late forties, with quick eyes and powerful sloping shoulders. The smaller one was maybe five years younger and considerably less impressive, but he led the way. He was a skinny fellow about five-ten, with a narrow face, an anemic complexion, and thin sandy hair. He reminded me of one of those guys employed by banks, whose job it is to say no to people. They're usually balding and have several ballpoint pens in their pockets. This one had the hairline and the row of pens, but he wasn't dealing with an ordinary depositor today, and I could see him putting on his best face for Peg.

"I'm Sergeant Cobb," he said to her, "and this is Sergeant Puckett."

The big man nodded to her. "Ma'am."

"Sorry to intrude," Cobb went on, "but we have just one or two questions for you."

Peg made a face, then sat up straight and gestured for him to proceed.

"When did you last see your husband alive?" he asked.

13

"I've answered that question several times," she said.

His mouth tightened. "I'm sure you have, ma'am, but it sometimes helps to have fresh ears. So would you mind answering it just one more time?"

"I last saw Joe around midnight last night, when he dropped me off here. He told me he needed to talk to somebody and said he would be home late."

"Did he often come home late?"

"Never."

"Never?"

"Never," she declared, with such conviction that Cobb didn't challenge her.

"Who was he going to meet?"

"He didn't say."

"Did you guess?"

"No."

"Did you know Cordelia Mae Oliver?"

"No."

"Did your husband ever speak of her?"

"No," she said, then decided that wasn't strong enough. "Never."

He nodded and asked abruptly, "Did you know your husband used prostitutes?"

A muscle jumped in Peg's jaw, and I thought for a moment she was going to lose it. But she reined in her anger and said with all the precision of a former debating-team captain, "No, I didn't know my husband used prostitutes. I still don't *know* it. I only know what you've told me. And you only know what you want to believe—what you think will make your job *easier.*"

Cobb shrank under her onslaught, and Puckett rubbed his mouth to wipe away what might have been a grin.

"I promise you," Cobb said defensively, "that we won't be satisfied until the truth is known."

Peg made a skeptical noise, and Cobb uncomfortably shifted his gaze to me, then Margie. "Would you mind giving us your names, please?"

"Margery Samson."

14

"Wife of Dwight Samson?"

She nodded.

"And you, sir?"

"Bill Cochran."

"Member of the family?"

"Just a friend."

"Mister Ahern's friend?"

"And his wife's."

"You live in town, Mister Cochran?"

"Galveston."

"What brings you up to Houston?"

"Joe invited me up. Said he had a story for me."

"About what?"

"He didn't say. But it doesn't make sense that he should kill himself before he got a chance to tell me about it."

"Suicides," said Cobb, "aren't in a sensible frame of mind."

"I don't believe it *was* suicide," I insisted. "He said there were bad people out there, and I believe he was killed to keep him from revealing what he knew."

"Did he give you any names?"

"No, he said we'd talk about it when I got here."

"I see," said Cobb, dismissing it. "And when did you learn about his death?"

"Heard about it on the radio as I was driving up."

He jotted something down and said, "That'll be all for now, but we may want to speak with both of you again later on."

"Are you telling us not to leave town?" I asked.

Cobb didn't care for my attitude. "In your case, Mister Cochran, I suppose we'd have to allow you to return to Galveston. But I'd like your address and phone number, just in case we need to get in touch."

As he scribbled them down, Peg said, "You'll be seeing him around anyway, Sergeant, since I've asked him to look into this for me."

It would have been better, I thought, if she hadn't sprung it on them like that, especially since it wasn't yet settled that I was doing it.

As Margie, Puckett, and Cobb turned to me, I admitted, "We've discussed it."

Cobb glared. "You with the Galveston police, Mister Cochran?"

"No, sir, I'm not."

"Private investigator?"

"Just a friend."

He chewed that over and didn't care for the taste. Then he nodded to Peg and Margie, gave me one last resentful glare, and headed for the door.

Sergeant Puckett stepped in and said gently to Peg, "I'm sorry about your loss, ma'am. I always thought your husband was a good man, and I'll sure miss seeing him pitch." With that and nods to Margie and me, he turned and followed his partner out the door.

Margie said, "What a pair," then checked her watch and got to her feet. "I have to pick up the kids. Will you be all right, Peg?"

"I'll make it, Margie. Thanks for coming. You were a rock."

Margie smiled, gave her a pat, then told me goodbye and left us alone.

With her gone, I suddenly felt out of place. "Guess I should be going, too."

"You can't," said Peg. "You still haven't promised to help me."

I took a deep breath. "I *want* to help you, Peg, and I want to find out what happened to Joe. But I'm no detective, and my advice is that you tell the police about your suspicions."

"I did," she said. "Not to those two. I hadn't seen them before. But the others had the same attitude. You heard them. They think they *know* what happened."

"You could go to their superiors."

"No."

"Then I'd recommend a good private detective."

"I don't want some greasy redneck poking his nose into this."

"They're not all greasy," I said, "or redneck."

"*No,*" she said firmly. When I shrugged, she added, "You came up for a story, didn't you?"

"That, and because Joe asked me to."

"Doesn't his death prove he really had something?"

16

"*If* he was murdered."

"You're the one who said it couldn't have been suicide."

"I still believe that, but . . ." I took a deep breath and laid it out for her. "The last time I got involved in something like this, it nearly killed me." I didn't have to add that I had the scars to prove it. She could see the knife-thin slash of shiny pink tissue that ran from the right corner of my mouth to the left corner of my chin, and the other, less noticeable scars on my cheeks and forehead. I got them hunting for the man who shot Juice Hanzlik in front of me, but Juice was my best friend, and his killer was after me, too, so I was given little choice in the matter. Here, the choice was mine. I knew what I might be in for, and I knew that no smart man would volunteer for a second round.

Peg said gently, "I have no right to ask this of you, Bull, and I'll think no less of you if you refuse. I just didn't know who else to turn to."

On the other hand, whoever said I was smart? "Did the police take anything from this room?"

"Then you *will* help?"

"I can try."

Peg rocked forward and squeezed my hand. "Joe picked you for this because he trusted you. And so do I."

How could I argue with that? "To do what you want, I'm going to need your help."

"Of course," she agreed eagerly. "How?"

"You must know something, even if you don't *know* you know it."

"Like what?"

"Something he said, something you sensed, something you found in his pockets. *Did* he use prostitutes?"

"*No!*"

"I had to ask that. The police think he did, and I need to know if they're right."

"No," she said firmly, "he did *not* use prostitutes."

Not pushing the point, I asked, "What was Joe like last night?"

"Like?"

"His mood," I said. "Was he nervous, jittery, depressed?"

17

"No," she said, "he was *not* depressed. Suicidally or otherwise."

"I've already said I don't believe it was suicide, but I need to know about his frame of mind."

She thought for a moment. "He was quiet. Unusually quiet, now that I think about it. Like he had something on his mind."

"Like before a game?"

"Sort of, but . . . Wait!" she remembered. "He snapped at me."

"When?"

"On the way home. He told me to shut up. And he never did *that* before."

"Why did he snap at you?"

"I don't know." She shook her head. "Believe it or not, I'd forgotten about it until just now. Guess it went out of my head after they told me he was dead. That was only"—she glanced at her watch—"three hours ago now. I had to go down and identify him, you know."

"I know."

She shivered. "The place was so cold, and he was only covered with a sheet."

I repeated, "I know." What else could I say? "Going back to last night, what was happening when he snapped at you?"

"Nothing. We were just driving along."

"Were you talking?"

"*I* was."

"What did he do right afterward?"

She shook her head.

"Think back," I said. "Was he driving?"

"Yes."

"So, he was in the driver's seat, and he snapped at you to shut up. And then what did he do?"

She covered her eyes with a hand. "He leaned forward." Her other hand went out. "And . . . I think he did something to the radio."

"Like what?"

She shrugged.

"Turned up the volume, maybe?"

18

She uncovered her eyes. "You know, that may have been it."

"Then maybe there was something he wanted to hear. Maybe that's why he snapped at you. Any idea what it was?"

She shook her head. "No."

"What station was he listening to?"

"I don't know."

"Music or talk?"

She thought hard, but said, "I really don't remember."

"Did he have a favorite station?"

"Not really. He'd drive along with one hand, switching stations with the other, until he found something he liked. It was a nervous habit he had."

"Too bad," I said. "If we knew which station he was listening to, we might be able to find out what they were talking about at the time. Any late-breaking news stories, or whatever. Think there's a chance it's still set on the same station?"

"I doubt it."

"I'll check it out anyway. Was it right after that that he told you he'd be dropping you at home?"

"It might've been," she said, trying to remember. "That sounds right."

"Before last night, how was he?"

"I guess he's been quiet a lot lately."

"How was it between you?"

She blushed and examined the palms of her hands. After a moment, she said in a girlish voice, "It wasn't the same."

"For how long?"

"Three weeks or more. Since before that short road trip."

"What was different?"

"He didn't want me," she said matter-of-factly, but tears were flowing now.

I wished I had a handkerchief to offer her, but I never carried one. My father had carried *two* handkerchiefs, freshly laundered and pressed, every day of his life. But I was one of the people who bought those little packets of Kleenex you found in drugstores, the ones with the tiny tissues, never big enough for the job.

"I know three weeks isn't a long time to be worried about," she

19

said. "And I know all couples go through periods when one or both are preoccupied. But it happened very rarely with us. We were like teenagers most of the time. We couldn't get enough of each other. We'd be someplace public—even in church—and he'd catch my eye, and I'd feel a warm tingle all over."

"But not lately?"

"Not in the last few weeks."

"And you never suspected he might be involved with another woman?"

"Of course I suspected it," she said. "When your husband stops making love to you, the first thing you think of is another woman. But I don't think it *now*. Now I think there was something else bothering him."

"Like an investment."

"Something like that."

I went back to my original question. "Did the police take anything from this room?"

"A couple of things from his desk—his appointment calendar and his Rolodex—but they didn't seem very interested. I told the first policeman I thought Joe might have been killed over an investment, and I offered to let him look at our financial records. But he said he didn't think that would be necessary."

I nodded toward the PC on the desk. "He kept his records on disk?"

"And paper copies on file." She gestured at the row of two-drawer mahogany filing cabinets that sat below the bookshelves behind the desk.

"Would you print out what he has on disk?"

"Of course," she said.

"Did he keep copies of his correspondence?"

"Always."

"I'll need to see that, too."

"Of course."

"And if you could arrange for me to see the police reports, that would be great, too."

"I'll talk to Daddy tomorrow. He's flying in at noon."

"Mind if I look around?"

20

"Please." As I headed for the desk, she asked, "Care for a sandwich?"

"I don't want to—"

"To be a bother," she said. "I know. But I need to do *something*. So, let me make you a sandwich."

I smiled. "What do you have?"

"Will ham and Swiss do?"

"Perfect."

Joe's desk was similar to the one in my study, a nineteenth-century mahogany kneehole. On top, there was a green-shaded desk lamp, a leather blotter, a marble-based pen set, a phone, a fancy wooden tissue box, and a well-worn Bible. On the right, there was Joe's IBM PC, monitor, keyboard, and mouse. I had an IBM of my own and could have accessed his files, but I didn't feel comfortable with the idea. It was all right for Peg to print out the files for me, but for some reason, it felt like prying to go digging for them myself.

That feeling didn't transfer to his desk drawers, but they contained little of a personal nature. In the middle drawer, I found pens, pencils, erasers, a box of paper clips, a pocket knife, and an Astros schedule, while the others were filled with equally unrevealing items like boxes of printer paper, empty legal pads, and refills for the tissue box.

My only interesting discovery was a battered brown fielder's glove with a baseball nesting in the pocket, which I found in the bottom left-hand drawer. With the Bible and Peg, they constituted the three pillars of Joe's existence.

Knowing that some of these old desks had secret compartments in the kneeholes, I started feeling around under the center drawer.

Finding nothing, I got down and crawled into the kneehole for a closer look. I began tapping the panels to right and left, working my way from top to bottom. I was feeling underneath the narrow gap at the base of the left panel when Peg called my name.

I poked my head up and said, "Hi."

"What're you doing?" she asked.

"Looking for something."

"What?"

"Would you believe a secret compartment?"

"Find one?"

"Nope."

"Have something to eat," she said and handed me a sandwich on a plate with potato chips and bread-and-butter pickles.

"Thanks," I said with a grin. "Maybe I'm hungrier than I thought."

I nibbled the snack as I walked around the room. I looked through Joe's books, examined his photos, opened his drawers and cabinets, but found nothing of obvious importance.

"Is there a safe?" I asked.

Peg nodded and walked behind the desk, where the bookcases were interrupted by a long niche in which Joe had hung a few of the awards and honors he'd picked up over the years. There were several prestigious civic awards, the certificate for the Cy Young he'd earned his third season, and a congratulatory note from President Ronald Reagan, but the safe was concealed behind the framed, yellowed copy of the first contract he'd signed in professional baseball.

Inside it was a fat envelope containing five thousand dollars in twenties. "Joe always kept cash on hand in case of emergencies," Peg explained. "Why don't you take out a thousand for yourself?"

"A thousand dollars?"

"As a retainer."

"I couldn't take a fee for this."

"Why not?"

"I wouldn't feel right about it," I said. "And I still don't know if I can help you."

"Well, it's just not right that you should have to pay for it all yourself," she declared. "I have more money than I need, and you're doing this for me, so at least let me cover your expenses."

I'd long ago spent my advance for the novel; I wasn't making much off the moving company these days, and the money my father had left me would be running out soon enough as it was. So, I said, "All right, I'll let you reimburse me for my expenses."

"Good," she said, satisfied with the arrangement.

Turning back to the safe, I took out a brown accordion file folder full of deeds and contracts, including his current one with the Astros.

"Mind if I take a look?"

She smiled. "Go ahead."

I had to shake my head in wonder. Joe had incentive clauses for more money than most people would earn in a lifetime. Yet, in the market of contemporary baseball, he was worth every cent of it.

Other items in the safe included an old Hamilton wristwatch in a box wrapped in white tissue paper; a small leather portfolio of very old, very valuable autographed baseball cards; and a packet of letters.

"Whose?" I asked.

She took them from me, her voice growing husky as she said, "Mine to him, from when we were dating."

Under it all was a red paper tube that looked like a fat firecracker. It was about three inches long and an inch thick, with two short wires trailing from one end, instead of a fuse.

Peg asked, "What is it?"

"Some kind of electrical component, I think. Ever seen it before?"

"No. You think it means anything?"

"Maybe. We should definitely report it to the police?"

She said angrily, "I would have shown them the safe, too, if they'd asked. But they didn't ask because they didn't think it was worth the trouble."

"It was just luck that I found it myself," I said.

"Maybe so," she agreed, "but before we hand it over to them, I think we should try to find out more about it. Maybe it's important."

24

She was only asking me to do what I wanted to do, so I didn't put up much of a fight. I knew it was bad form to conceal evidence from the police, but as I rationalized it to myself, we didn't *know* it was evidence.

After I'd seen all there was to see in the study, she showed me the rest of the house. With fifteen rooms to cover, I was forced to concentrate on those in which Peg said Joe spent most of his time.

In the master bedroom, I searched through his chest of drawers and rifled his closet, looking for something out of place. All I found was a small address book in one pocket of a windbreaker and, in the other, a bent and flattened pack of Tiparillos—cheap cigars with plastic mouthpieces. The pack was open with two cigars missing, and a book of matches was slipped under the plastic on the back.

"I didn't know he smoked," I said.

"What?" She was sitting on the bed, lost in thought.

"Did Joe smoke Tiparillos?"

She turned. "Joe didn't smoke, and he couldn't stand the smell of cigars."

"Then whose are these?"

"I don't know."

"Does any of the help smoke?"

She shook her head. "There's only Mr. and Mrs. Dorsey in the house and Mr. Whittaker who comes in to help me with the yard. They've been with us for years, and I'm sure none of them smoke."

"How about guests?"

"They usually understand that smoking isn't allowed in our house. And if they have to smoke, we ask them to step outside."

"Then maybe these were left outside."

"It's possible," she agreed.

I slipped the Tiparillos back into the jacket pocket but kept the address book. "Mind if I take this? Maybe make a copy of the pages?"

"Take it."

It was more potential evidence we were concealing from the police, but the same rationalization worked for this one. We didn't *know* it was evidence.

Joe's private gym was equipped with state-of-the-art exercise machines, a sauna, and a whirlpool, while his recreation room contained a pinball machine, a pool table, a Ping-Pong table, a table for cards and board games, a built-in entertainment center, and a bar that supplied Coke and Sprite on tap, but no alcoholic beverages.

Leaning on the bar, I asked Peg, "Can you think of any place else I should look?"

"His pickup."

I nodded. "Have to check out the radio."

"And his observatory."

"Right, I forgot about that. He took me up there once to show me his telescope."

"When things got to be too much, he'd go up and look at Mars or the Moon."

"Was he up there much lately?"

"Yes," she said. "Even more than usual. He was up there Thursday morning."

"He was?"

"Went out early, came back about nine-thirty, and went up there for a couple of hours before going to the Dome."

"How do you know he was up there?"

"Because he told me that's where he was going."

"You said he was out early that morning."

"About seven-thirty."

"Do you know where he went?"

"No."

"I'd like to see his observatory."

• • • • • • • • • • • • •

We spoke to Mr. Dorsey on the second-floor landing. He was vacuuming the carpets, while his wife manned one of the downstairs phones, answering the stream of sympathy calls coming in for Peg. The Dorseys were a quiet, ghostly couple in their fifties, who looked more like twins than husband and wife. They stood about five-eight, had the same slender build, and moved with identical grace. They often went hand in hand, and you almost never saw one without the other, but you rarely saw them at all. When I questioned them later, neither seemed to have any idea what had been bothering Joe.

Peg took the stairs with ease, but I was puffing and blowing by the time we reached the third floor.

Walking past gilt-framed portraits of stern-faced elders in nineteenth-century garb, I asked, "Whose relatives are these?"

She grinned. "They were a sort of private joke. None of Joe's relatives had been able to afford formal portraits, but he said no castle was complete without a gallery of ancestors. So, we spent a few weeks traveling around the country, attending estate auctions, and buying these."

We went through the last door on the left and climbed a black iron spiral staircase to another door that opened into a square room about twenty feet on a side. It had short brick walls to left and right, a cathedral ceiling, and French doors straight ahead that opened onto a balcony. The wall behind us was rough brick, and the floors were bare hardwood, but the room was air-conditioned like the rest of the house. Without it, the place would have been a sweatbox, not a retreat.

It was furnished with a desk, a desk chair, a worn leather armchair, and a reading lamp. The brick wall was covered with a giant star map, photos of nebulae and other astronomical objects, and large blowups of the Moon in all its phases. Joe's telescope was set up out on the balcony, covered with a sheet of transparent plastic. It was a big, expensive instrument, with a barrel a foot in diameter and about four feet long, supported on a heavy-duty tripod, with a complex balance and alignment mechanism.

Peg told me, "Joe took those pictures of the Moon through his telescope."

"He was really into this, wasn't he?"

She nodded. "Much as he loved baseball, he would have given it all up to be an astronaut."

6

I stayed with Peg until some of her church friends came over. She offered to put me up in one of the spare bedrooms, but I explained that I needed a more central location. I also didn't think it would look good for her to have a man move in with her at this time.

Before I left the house, I made two phone calls. One to the Wyndham-Warwick Hotel to reserve a room and one to Goodtimes Executive Escorts.

The woman who answered my call at the escort service asked seductively how she could help me, but I explained that I needed to talk to the manager. "As you wish," she said. "Would you hold please?"

After a few seconds, a husky voice with an Ivy League accent said, "This is Cleo Speaks. Can I help you?"

The name sounded like a stage direction, but I liked it. "Hope so," I said, "but I would prefer to talk to you in person."

"A consultation could be arranged," she said.

Consultation. I liked that, too. Made it sound like I was getting a second opinion on the condition of my spleen.

"Would you mind telling me who referred you to us?" she asked.

"I'd prefer to discuss that in person as well, if you don't mind."

"A bit mysterious," she said, "but then I'm fond of mysteries. When would you like to come?"

"Now," I said, "if that's possible."

A throaty chuckle came down the wire. "Eager, too. Then, by all means, come ahead. Do you know where to find us?"

I didn't, so she gave me directions. "I'll be there in half an hour or so, depending on traffic."

"Of course," she said with amusement. "Drive safely."

As I cleared the gates of Shady Lane, I turned on the radio again. A few more facts were now available. The 9-millimeter automatic was found on the floor between the two bodies, and the police had now established that it was the murder weapon. For the first time, they were publicly acknowledging that the evidence indicated the possibility of murder-suicide.

I took I-10 back into the downtown area and got off at Studemont heading south, then I made a right onto West Gray directly into a low hanging sun and followed directions to a neat little rose-trellised bungalow in the Cherryhurst area, on the edge of River Oaks. River Oaks was one of the town's most exclusive urban residential developments, built up over the last century, as new money had elbowed a place for itself among the old.

There was no sign on the minuscule lawn, just a polished bronze plaque beside the door, saying in virtually unreadable antique script *Goodtimes Executive Escorts*.

· · · · · · · · · · · · ·

Cleo Speaks was in her thirties, five-eight or so, and big boned, with an Amerindian look to her dark, smooth complexion and high cheekbones. She wasn't pretty—her features were too strong for that—but she was damn close to being beautiful. Dressed all in black. Skintight black leather pants, roomy black silk blouse like a pajama top—leaving plenty of room for her ample and unsheathed bosom to roam—black nail polish on the toes of the naked feet she had propped on her desk, and a thick mane of black hair coiled over her shoulder like a serpent.

Her office occupied the back half of the house and was decorated like a English drawing room, with paintings of foxhunts and land-scapes on the papered walls.

I'd thought about trying to pass myself off as a potential client, but after one look at Cleo Speaks, I figured she'd see right through my bullshit and probably toss me out on my ear. So, I introduced myself and told her who I represented.

She asked, "Don't the police think Ahern did it?"

"They're only saying that's a possibility."

"Wouldn't anybody else have taken the gun with them?"

"Not if they wanted it to look like murder-suicide."

She steepled her hands under her chin and gave it some thought. Finally, she said, "She told me to call her Dee-Dee, and that was about as personal as it got. I didn't know her well enough to call her a friend, but I liked her. She was also one of my girls, and if somebody other than Joe Ahern killed her, then I'd like to see them pay for it."

"That's what I'm after."

She'd come to a decision. "So, what do you need to know?"

"First of all," I said. "Do you happen to have a picture of her? I don't even know what she looked like."

Cleo put her feet down, pulled out one of the drawers in her desk, and thumbed through it for a moment. She came out with an 8-by-10 photo and slid it across the desk.

The first thing you noticed was the woman's beauty. You didn't have to think about it. It was there. The teeth were perfect, the skin flawless, the eyes cornsilk-blue, the hair buttery blonde. But it was the tilted grin and the knowing look that gave her character. She seemed to be laughing at the game and laughing at me for playing it.

Looking up, I said, "Maybe you could tell me something about your business."

Suddenly suspicious, she asked, "How will that help you?"

"I'm trying to find out who killed her, and how she earned her living could be important."

She examined me for a moment. "You're not wearing a wire, are you?"

"You think I'm here to bust you?"

"You *could* be."

"You want to frisk me?"

She smiled. "Perhaps another time. For now, opening your shirt will do."

I stood and unbuttoned my shirt, tugged it out of my jeans, and turned to show her that there was nothing strapped to my torso.

"Not bad," she said with amusement. "You can put it back on now."

As I sat down, she said, "First of all, we're very expensive."

"I can believe that."

"The price is part of the attraction, of course, as we're aiming at people with too much money. And even in these times, there are still plenty of those around, if you operate in the right circles. Such people simply can't appreciate something unless it's overpriced, so we do our best to accommodate them. Whenever possible, we provide transportation as well as an escort, which further adds to both the cost and the attraction. We offer a package deal with a limo service, and the drivers are paid extra to serve as bodyguards for the girls."

"What if a client insists on providing his own transportation?"

"Then the girl's on her own," she said. "But they know I'm only a phone call away. The limos have cellular phones, and they all come running if one of the girls lets out a squeal. Truthfully," she added, "such problems are rare. You have to understand what we offer here." Catching my smirk, she said, "No, that's only what you *think* we offer. We provide an evening out with a highly decorative, polished, and well-educated young woman. One who can talk, if that's what the client wants. Who can understand his jokes, if he chooses to tell them, and even laugh, if it seems called for. A woman guaranteed not to embarrass, regardless of the occasion. And since image and appearance are generally more important to these men than sex, this is of primary consideration."

"But there *is* sex involved, isn't there?" I asked. "I mean, these guys do expect their escorts to go to bed with them, don't they?"

"I'd say it ends up in bed no more than thirty percent of the time. The drivers tell me it's much more often consummated in the back of the limo." I laughed. "I should add that our girls are

31

certified free of any social disease, and twice a year, each is tested for AIDS, the results of which can be provided to the prospective client on demand. I also try to protect the girls by insisting that our clients wear condoms, since we don't know where *they've* been."

"What did you think of Dee-Dee?" I asked.

"The best," she said. "If I had ten more like her, I could retire in five years."

"How did you meet her?"

"She called me and asked for a job."

"Do you know where she worked before she came to you?"

"She was at an escort service in San Antonio. I talked to the manager, and she told me to hire her on the spot. She said Dee-Dee was very special and would make me scads of money."

"What made her special?"

"Other than being a knockout, you mean?"

"Yeah, other than that."

She chuckled to herself, as she threw her pretty feet back up on the desk.

"What is it?" I asked.

"In many ways, she was wrong for the job. Too old to start with. Our clients usually prefer women in their early twenties, younger if they can get them. But Dee-Dee asked for a tryout and promised I'd never regret it. And I didn't. She wasn't *easy,* in any sense, and I'll wager that she didn't offer more than a kiss and a feel or a handjob to fifty percent of her clients. Yet she always got the biggest tips and the most repeat customers."

"How'd she manage that?"

"She knew how to manage *them,*" she said. "How to make them feel good about themselves, make them feel special, with a minimum of physical contact. With one, she would be the ice princess, unreachable, untouchable, unworldly. With another, she would be wounded and slightly sad. Whatever it took to bring out the gentleman in the john."

"She never had *any* trouble?" I asked. "Not one bad customer in all that time. Not one who beat her up or tried to rape her?"

"As a matter of fact, there was one, not long after she came to work for me, who gave her a black eye. When I saw it, I asked her

32

what had happened, but she said not to worry about it. She told me *he* got the worst of it, and I believed her. After that, it never happened again. But twice, she cancelled on a client. After taking a look at him, she called me from the nearest phone and said she couldn't do it. Both times, she told me I shouldn't let any of the other girls date this guy, either.

"And I'll tell you something," she said, putting her feet down and leaning forward. "The lady had great instincts. The first time, I was ticked off at her for leaving me in the lurch like that, and I ignored her advice. I sent somebody to fill in for her, and the girl got roughed up. The next time it happened, I simply explained to the gentleman that we wouldn't be able to accept his business."

"What about the guy who beat Dee-Dee up? Do you have his name and know where I might find him?"

"I have his name," she said, "but you don't need it."

"Why not?"

"He just went to prison for murdering his wife."

"Guess that lets him out."

"Guess so."

"Can you think of anybody who had a reason for wanting to kill Dee-Dee?"

She shook her head. "Nobody. Even the other girls liked her."

"Did you ever make a date for her with Joe Ahern?"

"No."

"Ever see them together?"

"Never."

"Did you have any reason to think they might be involved?"

"None. But I knew very little about her private life."

"Have you arranged dates for any of the Astros?"

"No. As I say, we specialize in the executive set. The board-room, not the clubhouse."

"How do you screen your clients?"

"They're either recommended by another client, or they come in for a consultation, so I can get a look at them."

"Do you know if she was involved with anybody?"

She shook her head. "She never mentioned anyone, and I never saw her with a man who wasn't a client."

I thanked her.

"You look disappointed," she said.

"I was hoping you could give me the name of a jealous boyfriend or disgruntled client, somebody who might want to kill Dee-Dee. Because I can't think of anybody who'd want to do it to Joe."

"Even if I gave you a name, you'd still have to explain why Ahern was there."

"I know," I said. "Joe called me Thursday night and said he had a story for me, and I was thinking that maybe he got it from Dee-Dee. Your clients are corporate types, so maybe she picked up some dirt on a powerful executive, who had them killed to avoid exposure."

"Why would she take the story to Ahern?" she asked. "Why not go to the newspapers or the cops?"

"I don't know," I admitted. "That's what I have to find out. Here's my hotel number and the one at home." I scribbled them down on a sheet from my pad. "If you think of anything else, I'd appreciate it if you'd give me a call."

"I'll do that," she promised. "Whoever the sonofabitch was, he killed a good person."

"*Two* of them," I said.

For eight years, I was partnered with Juice Hanzlik in a moving-and-storage business in Galveston. I still owned half, but it was now operated by a former employee who'd bought Juice's 50 percent. Back when I was running the business, I never knew when I'd have to spend a night or two away from home, and I got into the habit of carrying a bag with a couple of changes of clothing and toiletries in the lockbox of my pickup.

I checked into the Warwick Hotel about seven o'clock, then made a call to Detective Flanagan of the Galveston police and caught her at home. "It's me," I said.

"Hey, you," said Molly. "You back?"

"Still in Houston."

"Oh." I couldn't help being pleased by the disappointment in her voice. "You driving down tonight?"

"I don't think so."

"Oh." More gratifying disappointment.

"How are you?"

"I'm okay," she said. "Question is: how are you?"

"Still reeling."

"I can imagine. It's all they can talk about down here."

"What're they saying?"

"That he did her, then himself."

"How'd they come to that conclusion?"

"From the description of the scene Parkinson got from Houston. When you have a man and a woman dead in a room with the gun laying between them, it sure sounds like murder-suicide."

"What do *you* think?"

"I'm a cop," she said. "You know you're all guilty in our eyes."

"C'mon," I said. "What does your gut tell you?"

She answered without hesitation, "That somebody killed them and made it look like murder-suicide."

"Whew!"

"Sound like you were starting to doubt it."

"Tough to swim against the tide."

"Tell *me,*" she said. "Truth is, I'd probably be siding with the rest if I didn't know Joe."

"Cops up here seem pretty sure of themselves."

"That's part of what you pay us for," she replied. "But until they get the autopsy and lab results, nobody *knows* anything. If there's no gunpowder on his hand, they'll have to look for another explanation."

"I hadn't thought of that."

"That's why you have me," she said.

"Among other reasons."

"That, too," she agreed with a smug chuckle. "How's Peg?"

"She goes along okay for a while, then it suddenly catches up with her."

"Angry?"

"Yeah, at the police, especially."

"Good," she said. "It just might get her through this."

"She wants to clear Joe's name."

"And she wants you to help her do it?"

"You're pretty smart."

"Middlin'," she conceded. "Does she have anybody staying with her?"

"One of her church friends promised to spend the night."

"No relatives?"

36

"Her father's flying down tomorrow."

"Where're you?"

"At the Warwick." I gave her the number. "You working tomorrow?"

"No, Parkinson gave us the day off. So, what're you going to do?"

"I told Peg I'd try to find out the truth. That's all I promised."

"Oh, *that's* all?"

"You don't think I can do it?"

"I didn't say that. But it'd be a lot safer for everybody—especially *you*—if you let the police handle this."

"What if they *don't* handle it?" I asked. "They're convinced it's murder-suicide—another good man brought low by lust—and everybody's happy about it. The cops don't have a murderer running around loose; the news people sell lots of papers and airtime, and the rest of us get to see another paragon stumble."

"And you figure it's up to you to see justice done?"

"Something like that."

"Well, I know better than to try to argue you out of it. But you should remember what happened the last time."

"I haven't forgotten."

"At least be careful," she said. "If you won't carry a gun, maybe you should hire somebody who does."

"A backup?"

"Why not?" she asked. "It could save your life."

"I'll think about it. But my instinct says two people will only be more conspicuous than one."

"How do you expect to be inconspicuous, if you go around asking questions?"

"I said I'd think about it."

"Okay," she said, tabling the matter. "So, where do you start?"

"I talk to people, find out about the girl, look into Joe's investments."

"Investments?"

"An idea Peg has. Also, I need to examine the police reports and, if they'll let me, take a look at the scene of the crime."

"You shouldn't have any trouble with the scene. They're probably finished with it by now. But I wouldn't count on looking at the reports."

"Even if Peg's father pulls some strings?"

"Reports are strictly confidential," she said. "Police business only. I could ask Parkinson to give them a call, but I doubt it'd help."

"Think he would?"

"Sure. He likes you."

"He *does?*"

She laughed. "I'll ask him."

"Thanks," I said. "As for the rest, I thought maybe you could drive up tomorrow and give me the inestimable benefit of your training and experience."

"What do I get in return?" she asked.

"Custody of my body for the evening?"

"How can I turn down a bargain like that?"

"I can't imagine."

She chuckled. "I have some errands to run in the morning, but I should be able to make it by one. We'll brunch."

"Yum."

8

During our season together in the minors, I once overheard Joe tell a reporter that he had God to thank for his success. Later, when I asked Joe what God had against the rest of us, he laughed and apologized. He said he'd meant to say that it was his *faith* in God that was responsible for his success, not any direct intervention from the object of that faith. He assured me that he didn't believe anymore than I did that God took sides in sporting events. He said I should feel free to call him on it whenever I caught him being self-righteous, but the truth is I rarely got the chance. Unlike most born-agains, Joe usually knew when he went too far.

I could have resented his stardom. He'd succeeded where I had failed, becoming one of the best in the game, one of the best ever. Number six in all-time winning percentage, number nine in lifetime earned run average, and an eventual shoo-in for the Hall of Fame. But believe it or not, I'd actually had more natural talent.

My curve was tighter and sharper than anything he'd ever produced, and my fastball was once clocked at ninety-eight miles per hour. True, it was on the fast speedgun, with a slight tail wind, but Joe couldn't have broken ninety-two with Hurricane Carla on the assist. But he also had the splitter, the straight change, and The

Slider. His best pitch. A diving, darting, demon of a slider that, after eleven years in the bigs, still left batters shaking their helmets. But it wasn't his impressive arsenal that earned a thirty-eight-year-old righty a two-year, eight million dollar contract from one of the tightest wallets in the sport. It was Joe's command that did that.

Command took Joe to the All-Star game eight times in eleven years, just as the lack of it took me into the moving-and-storage business. In spite of my high-octane "stuff," I had very little idea where either of my pitches were going, while Joe could put all five of his anywhere he wanted them. I struck batters out; Joe just kept them off balance. He knew how hard it was to hit a baseball, and he never gave batters more credit than they deserved. Joe could maintain his command for seven or eight innings almost every time out, while I rarely made it into the fourth before losing the strike zone. Over and over again, I'd walk a couple of hitters, give up an infield single or hit a batter to load the bases, then fall behind the next guy and have to groove one to keep from walking in a run. With Joe, they'd swing over the ball, or under it, start their swing too early, or wait too late, and end up grounding weakly to second, or popping up, or striking out. With me, the smart hitters would just sit back and wait for a mistake and then smack the living shit out of it.

After three years in the minors, Joe was the hottest prospect in the Red Sox organization. After five years in the minors and one brief, disastrous stint in the majors, *I* was just looking for an excuse to quit. Killing Domingo Sanchez wasn't what I'd had in mind, of course, but when it came to excuses, I couldn't have asked for a better one. A year later, I was out of baseball, and Joe was pitching in Fenway Park.

I *did* resent his success at the time, of course, but I hadn't felt that way in years. I'd grown to respect him too much to resent him, and this year in particular, I'd just enjoyed watching him work. It was a case of a good man and a great pitcher having a dream season, the kind of season that made for baseball legend. The kind of season that wasn't meant to be cut short. That it should end in humiliation was flat out incomprehensible.

I decided that my novel could wait. Even with as much as a

month's delay, I should still have a draft ready for the publisher by the end of the summer. That was soon enough.

Kicking off my boots, I stretched out on the bedspread and started going through Joe's address book. It included numbers for places like Domino's Pizza, Zimm's Body Work, and Paxton's Ford Trucks. I also recognized the names of ballplayers, Joe's agent, a few politicians, a couple of prominent businessmen, and some church people I'd met through Joe, while other numbers were plainly labeled as those of "B. Smithers—UNICEF" or of "J. Hayes—ABC News."

I copied down ten numbers that had only first or last names or initials beside them, plus an 800 number labeled "Emergency—Willis." The latter turned out to be a twenty-four-hour emergency number for a travel agency Joe had used, and one of the supervisors—off-duty when I called—was named Willis.

Three of the numbers were answered by machines, and three didn't answer at all. One number was answered by a Spanish-speaking woman. When I asked to speak to Paco (the name next to the number), she started talking very fast, far too fast for my rudimentary grasp of the language. After sixty seconds of mutual unintelligibility, I said *gracias* and hung up. I spoke to a woman named Gloria Adams, who cooked dinner while we talked. After only slight coaxing, Gloria confided in a whisper that she'd been Joe's high-school sweetheart. She'd called him when she and her husband had moved to Houston a few years ago, and they'd gotten together with Joe and Peg for dinner a time or two. She told me she was "all torn up about Joe dying," and I believed her. One was the home number of a casting agent who'd hired Joe for several commercials. And one was answered by a gruff-voiced man, who read the number back to me. When I asked for Wilmer, he repeated the number. When I tried to introduce myself, he hung up. I didn't know if Wilmer was a first name or last, but I made a note to check it out.

I got about halfway through the book a second time, then decided I needed something to drink. I slid the book under the pillow to hold my place and went to get a cold drink and a bucket of ice.

The ice maker was down the corridor, in an alcove with the soft-drink machine. The scoop wasn't inside, and I was using the bucket to scoop out some ice when I heard a step behind me.

The blow caught me as I turned, glanced off the side of my head and bounced me off the front of the ice machine. On my hands and knees, I caught a glimpse of the pointed toe of a fancy red and black cowboy boot. Then a second blow put me under.

9

I awoke with my head drumming, cheek pressed to the carpet, staring in exaggerated close-up at what I eventually recognized as a heavy metal ice scoop. The cowboy's blunt object, I assumed.

A male voice asked, "You okay?"

Beyond the scoop, I caught a sideways view of a man and a woman at the opening to the alcove.

"Hey, mister, you okay?" the young man repeated, sounding nervous.

I sat up too quickly and almost keeled over. Hanging onto consciousness by my fingernails, I rasped out, "You see anybody else?"

He glanced around. "In here?"

Carefully searching my head with my fingers, I said, "Somebody hit me." The left side was swollen and tender, but the biggest bump was near the crown, where the last blow had landed. "You didn't happen to see who did it?"

"No, sir," he said. "I don't think so."

"See anybody wearing fancy boots—red and black?"

Sounding cooler than her boyfriend, the girl said, "We haven't seen anybody at all except you since we got off the elevator. You want us to call the police?"

43

"No, I'll do it. Thanks."

I made it to my feet by crawling up the wall, then lurched sideways past the couple into the corridor. Wincing at every excruciating step, I wove my way down to my room.

The door was standing open, with the keycard in the lock, and I stumbled inside to find that my bag had vanished. My ring of keys and wallet were on the bedside table, but all my cash was gone. The mysterious electrical component had disappeared from the top of the dresser, but the address book and my notes were still under the pillow. That was something.

. . . .

I reported the attack to the front desk, and the clerk said he'd call the cops. After that, I phoned Homicide and left a message for Cobb or Puckett to call me. Having lost what might have been evidence, I thought it was time to admit that I'd been concealing it. I knew they weren't going to be happy about it, but I figured the sooner I got it out of the way the better. Besides, they needed to know about the attack. If it wasn't just a robbery, then somebody was afraid I'd found something, which meant there had to be *something* to find.

But who knew or had reason to suspect that I might be involved in this? The cops, Peg, and Molly, of course. Also Margie, the Dorseys, Cleo Speaks, the people in the crowd outside the gates to Shady Lane, including Floyd Malcovitch, and whoever was in the silver Sedan de Ville that drove up as I pulled into Joe's driveway. Too bad I didn't see a face.

The hotel manager came up to apologize for the treatment I'd received in his establishment and to promise immediate compensation for any losses or medical expenses. After I'd allayed his fear of a lawsuit, he asked me to let the house physician examine me. The doctor decided I probably didn't have a cracked skull or a concussion, but he recommended that I go to the hospital for precautionary X rays. I promised I would, after I talked to the police, but I didn't actually plan on spending the evening in the emergency room, if I could avoid it.

A uniform cop arrived while I was being examined. After the

doctor left, I told the cop about the attack. He looked to be in his middle twenties and couldn't have been at this long, but he already seemed bored by the routine question-and-answer of another unsolvable robbery.

"What'd he get?" he asked.

"My bag was still packed, and he took it, along with all my cash."

"How much were you carrying?"

"Couple hundred."

"One man?"

"That's all I saw."

"Could you describe him?"

"Only saw his boots. One boot, actually. The toe. Had a fancy design on it in red and black."

After he left, a woman detective from robbery came by. She asked basically the same questions, got basically the same answers, then took the keycard and explained that it would be dusted for prints. She asked me to drop by the South Central Patrol Station the next day to be fingerprinted, so my prints could be eliminated, but she warned me not to get my hopes up about recovering my property. Finding identifiable prints of the robber would be a long shot.

The management sent up a replacement for my keycard, and I'd just laid down on the bed again and picked up the notebook when there was a knock on the door. I walked over, looked through the peephole, and saw Sergeant Puckett.

As he moseyed into the room, I asked, "Where's your partner?"

"At a birthday shindig for his daddy," he said. "They tell me you been bushwhacked and burgled."

"Yeah."

"Hurt?"

"Only my head," I said, "and the doctor gave me something for that."

"What'd they get?"

"Something I found in Joe's safe."

He pulled out the desk chair and sat down. "What was it?"

45

"A fat red paper tube. Looked like an overgrown firecracker, but with wires coming out of one end instead of a fuse."

"And you didn't think we'd be interested in hearing about it?"

"Ms. Ahern wanted me to find out what it was before telling you about it."

"She's grieving her husband's death," he said, "and not exactly responsible for her behavior. You, on the other hand, don't have that excuse."

"Well, I—"

"Concealing evidence is a class A misdemeanor, you know."

"For Christ's sake," I snapped. "I found something in the dead man's safe, something *you* could have found if you'd looked for it. And we didn't *know* it was evidence."

"That's not for you to decide," he said. "If you don't mind my askin', what's your interest in this?"

"I'm a friend."

"I hear you wrote a book about a killing down in Galveston."

"That's right."

"You plannin' to write about this one, too?"

"I might."

"So, you're up here diggin' up a story?"

I didn't like the sound of that. "Ms. Ahern thinks you've already made up your mind about what happened, and she was afraid you might choose to ignore something that didn't support your premise."

"And what did *you* say?"

"I warned her that we should go to you with it."

He nodded, then leaned in and said quietly, "I'll tell you something, Mister Cochran. If I find out that you're concealing any more evidence, I'll see to it that you spend the next few months doing your writing behind bars. You understand me on that?"

It was at that point that I decided to show him the address book.

10

I awoke at eight o'clock Sunday morning with a pounding head, a raw scalp, and an overinflated skull, but I knew I was lucky to be waking up at all. I'd researched the results of blows to the head for my novel and knew they were far more dangerous than books and movies generally implied—as likely to kill or permanently disable as they were merely to knock a person out.

After a shower and three Extra Strength Tylenols, I called the Astros' PR director to make an appointment with the manager, Stick Hillerman. Then I got dressed and went out to do some detecting. The team was flying to San Diego after today's game, and if I wanted to talk to them, it had to be this morning.

The parking garage is across Fannin from the hotel, which stands on the narrow green esplanade between Fannin and Main. I got onto Main and headed south, swerving around the Mecom Fountain, which sits in the middle of the intersection with Montrose.

Beyond the fountain, live oaks shaded the boulevard. Mansions sprawled behind high walls to my right, and across the esplanade, on the other side of Fannin, was the great lawn of Hermann Park. The mansions gave way to the colleges, dorms, and playing fields of Rice University, as Hermann Park gave way to the Texas Medical Center—a city of hospitals, behind a gray wall of parking garages.

The trees reappeared for a stretch, with smaller houses behind walls to the right and restaurants to the left. Then Main crossed Brays Bayou into the strip of restaurants and hotels that fed off AstroWorld, and I could see the snowy cap of the Dome rising over trees to the left. After making the turn onto Murworth, I still couldn't see all of it. The opening at the end of the street wasn't wide enough. It wasn't until I reached Kirby that I got a clear view of the Harris County Domed Stadium, known to the world as the Houston Astrodome. As big as it looked, I knew you really couldn't appreciate the size of the place until you got inside.

I crossed Kirby Drive to the West Ticket Gate and stopped at one of the row of booths. I gave my name to the guard and told him I had an appointment with Stick Hillerman. He made a call, then directed me to the W1 parking lot at the top of the press ramp.

The press was everywhere. Broadcast vans were setting up; equipment was being checked; cables were being run. People stood in clusters, drinking coffee and Cokes, eating donuts and granola bars, waving their hands.

The guard stationed in the box at the top of the ramp glared at my identification and grimly allowed me to pass, saying that I should wait for Mr. Monday down on the dock.

Mr. Monday was Eddie Monday, the Astros' PR director. He arrived in a couple of minutes to shake my hand and lead me inside. When I mentioned that I didn't usually get this kind of personal service, he said sadly, "No, but Joe Ahern's widow does."

Monday was a small man, about five-five, known as "Fast Eddie" because of his usual headlong dash and speedy patter. But today his energy seemed spent. He didn't dawdle, but neither did he dash. And as for patter, there wasn't any. What talk there was, I had to drag out of him.

He led me through double doors into an elevator.

As the doors slid closed, I asked, "How you holding up, Eddie?"

He sighed. "I tell you, Bull, I don't know if I'll ever get over it."

"I know what you mean."

"It's just the saddest, most impossible thing I ever heard of in my life."

That pretty much said it. "Do you believe it was murder-suicide?"

"Not for a minute," he declared. "And if that's really what the police think, then they got their heads up their collective ass."

As we stepped off the elevator, I asked, "Did you ever hear of Cordelia Mae Oliver before this?"

"Never."

"What about Dee-Dee?"

"Nope."

"Have you seen pictures of her?"

He nodded. "The police showed me some, and I saw the ones in the papers and on TV."

"Did you ever see her with Joe?"

"Never saw her at all," he said firmly, "with anybody. I'd remember if I had."

"I was thinking she might have been a team groupie."

"Not one that I saw. She's pretty enough but a little older than most of them."

He led me past the entrance to the clubhouse, around the corner to the back door, which he unlocked by slipping an ID card into the slot and punching a combination into the key pad. The manager's office was just inside, across from the trainer's room, so he could get the bad news first.

Stick Hillerman was just hanging up the phone. He stood and reached across the desk to shake my hand, then waved me into a chair.

Eddie said, "Good talking to you, Bull. See you around the barn." Then he nodded at the manager, said, "Stick," and took his leave, still moving at half his usual pace.

"Don't have long," Hillerman told me. "Gotta be in Pine's office in a few minutes." Willard Pine was the team's GM.

"Thanks for seeing me on such short notice," I said. "I know this is a bad time. As I told Eddie, I just need to ask you a couple of questions."

"Anything for Peggy Ann," he said. "How's she taking it?"

"She seems in control," I said, "but it has to be eating her up."

He nodded. "Talked to her last night. She sounded . . . I don't know—different. Older, maybe." He shook his head. "She's good people, and doesn't deserve any of this."

Stick was only a few years older than me and barely half a dozen years out of the major leagues, now managing the team on which he'd played most of his career. But the job aged a man fast, and Joe's death appeared to have tacked on another decade overnight.

I asked him the same questions I'd asked Eddie: had he ever heard of Cordelia Mae Oliver before this and had he ever seen her? To which the answers were no and no.

"Do you believe it was murder-suicide?" I asked.

"Hell, no," he said. "I don't care what the cops say, Joe was no killer."

"They're only saying that murder-suicide is a possibility."

"Not if you knew Joe, it wasn't. You can't convince me he'd murder anybody, let alone some helpless woman. And he'd never kill himself. I mean," he said in exasperation, "he had everything to *live for.*"

"Did you notice anything different about him over the last few weeks?"

He rubbed his face with his right hand. The ring finger looked a little strange because he'd snapped the tendon sliding into base back when he was a teenager. The damage had never been repaired, and when he held up his hand, the finger flopped into an S-shaped curve. But it hadn't prevented him from winning a gold glove his fifth season in the majors or from batting .287 for his thirteen-year career.

"No," he decided, "I can't say he seemed different to me. I mean, he had his ups and downs, just like anybody else. But since that off day he had in New York just after the All-Star break, he's been cruisin'." He shook his head. "If there was anything different about him, I sure didn't see it."

"Do you know of a ballplayer who'd want him dead?"

"No," he said, "not even Mussleman."

Kurt Mussleman was the Astros' All-Star right fielder and current National League RBI leader. He and Joe were the team's biggest stars, but that didn't make them bosom buddies. Joe had rarely showed anger on or off the field, but he and Kurt had been involved in a fistfight in the clubhouse three years earlier, shortly after Kurt had joined the team. Joe had been embarrassed by it and had never told me exactly what had started the fight, only that it was something Kurt had said. Since then, they'd kept their distance, with Joe mostly ignoring Kurt, while Kurt got in an occasional jab by complaining that Joe's do-gooder image gave him an unfair advantage with the press.

When Stick glanced at his watch, I realized my time was up.

I wrote down my numbers at home and at the hotel on a piece of paper and gave it to him. "If you think of anything else, give me a call. And thanks again for seeing me."

He got up and came around his desk to walk me to the door. With his hand on the knob, he said sadly, "Joe was bound for glory this year."

"I know," I said. "I was having a great time watching him."

He lifted his shoulders and let them fall. "The way he was goin', I thought we might finally take it all. And God *knows* this town could use a winner."

. . . .

The coaches' locker room was the next on the right, with the laundry room on the left. Then came the dining room–lounge area, where they put the postgame buffets, with the kitchen across from it. The equipment manager's office was at the corner, where you turned right to leave the clubhouse or went straight ahead into the dressing room.

The dressing room was empty except for two reporters whispering to each other. They dismissed me with the briefest of glances and returned to their conspiracy.

I heard a shower going, but I figured that was one place a man should be allowed his privacy, so I left the clubhouse. I took the corridor to the left, past the door to the home dugout, and on around the curving corridor to the wide tunnel that dips under the stands and out to the field.

The guard didn't want to let me out. But I caught Eddie Monday's eye, and he waved for the man to let me through.

The first sight of the place coming out of the tunnel is still a stunner. You look up forever to the dome, tall as an eighteen-story building, the painted Lucite panels glowing translucently in daylight.

Some people think of indoor baseball as a travesty. But for anybody who ever played baseball *outside* in the summer in south Texas, it was home sweet Dome. You missed the smell and feel of grass, but not the oppressive heat, the insufferable humidity, or the mosquitos, which along the Gulf Coast, grow to the size and ferocity of rabid hummingbirds.

Eddie introduced me to the team's traveling secretary. I asked my questions and got the same answers. About ten o'clock, I went back to the clubhouse and found the press in a full feeding frenzy. Most of the players were there by now, fielding questions. With so many cameras, several were even briefly turned on me.

Dwight Samson walked by with a towel around his waist, but when I tried to speak to him, he waved me off, saying he needed to see the trainer. Later, back out on the field, I caught him for a couple of minutes alone, as he waited for his turn in batting practice.

Dwight Malachi Samson was a tobacco-chewing Kentuckian from Pineville, working on his masters in economics at Rice. He was a long, lanky redhead, with a long, freckled face, a goofy grin, and a cheerful disposition, normally difficult to rile. But today he was convinced that somebody had killed his friend, and he was hot.

He talked about how much he'd admired Joe and how unjust he thought it was that he was dead. But in the end, he came to the same question I couldn't stop asking myself: "What was he doin' with that girl?"

"Then you don't think he was there for sex?" I asked.

"If it was anybody else, I'd say sure. But I'd *know* if Joe messed around, and he didn't. That's all there is to it."

"That means there's a murderer on the loose," I said.

He nodded. "One who not only killed Joe but tried to humiliate him. I hope somebody finds the sonofabitch and kills him."

52

"The perfect solution," I agreed.

For those who weren't Joe's personal friends, he was still their teammate, somebody they worked with and shared a dressing room with and joked with and lived with on the road. And their responses came, as you would expect, in two primary flavors: anger and bewilderment. The angry ones were generally more quotable than the bewildered ones, who were easily identified as the ones who kept shaking their heads and repeating, "I just can't believe it."

One thing both groups had in common was that neither believed Joe had had an affair with Cordelia Mae Oliver. None, that is, except for Kurt Mussleman.

Kurt slid through life with cleats high, and as one of the few self-confessed bigots in the game, he regularly led the league in racial slurs and public apologies. He wouldn't have been tolerated if he hadn't been so damn good at hitting the baseball. After six years in the majors, he was still putting between twenty-five and thirty balls over the fence every season. And that was with him playing half of the games over the last three years in the Dome, which was notoriously unkind to home-run hitters.

When I tried to intercept Kurt on his way in from the trainer's room, he stuck his craggy chin in my face as he passed and snapped, "The fuck do you want?"

"Just have a couple of questions," I said.

" 'Bout what?" he called back, heading for his locker.

"Did you ever see Joe with Cordelia Mae Oliver?"

He slammed down his gym bag and turned. "Nope, never did."

"Ever see her before at all?"

Peeling off his tee shirt, he said, "Never laid eyes on her."

"Were you surprised?"

" 'Bout him poppin' a piece a strange like that, you mean?"

I said, "They don't *know* that he did it."

"That's not what I hear," he replied. "And it wouldn't surprise me none if he did."

"It *wouldn't?*"

"No," he said, speaking to me, but playing the room. "Anybody with an ass that tight was bound to blow up sooner or later."

The locker room suddenly quieted, as players and press turned our way. After a few seconds, a voice called out, "You're an asshole, Mussleman."

"No, Cooney," he said, *"you're* the asshole."

Sorry I'd gotten myself into this, I said, "So, you figured it was only a matter of time?"

"Isn't that what I just said?"

"Can you think of anybody who'd want to kill him?"

He grinned. "I'd say there's players who won't miss steppin' into the box against him. The self-righteous sonofabitch could pitch. You had to give him that. And it's for damn sure this pissant crew ain't gonna win nothin' without him."

That evoked some disagreement, and I got out of there fast, before somebody remembered who'd started it.

11

I stopped by the South Central Patrol Station to be fingerprinted and was back at the Warwick by twelve-thirty. After buying copies of the *Post* and *Chronicle,* I got a cup of coffee from the Café Vienna, just off the lobby, then claimed an overstuffed chair with a good view of the revolving doors. Molly wasn't due until one o'clock, but I wanted to be sure of catching her entrance.

The hotel was built in '26, and the lobby reflected the ornate taste of the time. The floors were white marble, the walls paneled in oak, the oriental carpet richly patterned, the room dressed with a crystal chandelier, Chinese vases, and an embroidered tapestry over a marble sideboard.

As I sat down, a skinny old dandy in a navy-blue three-piece suit and a snazzy red bowtie looked up from his *New York Times* to give me a disapproving glance. I didn't know what he had against me, so I just winked at him and took a look at the papers.

Joe's and Cordelia Mae's pictures appeared in color above the fold on the front pages of both. Shots of Joe in uniform, one on the field and one in front of his locker, both showing a handsome, dark-haired man in his late thirties, with a direct look and a quirky grin. The *Chronicle* used the same head shot of Cordelia Mae that

55

Cleo Speaks had shown me, while the *Post* had her in a formal gown, looking like Rebecca of Sunnybrook Farm—innocence personified and a runaway winner for Miss Purity.

Both headlines ended in question marks. The *Chronicle* asked in inch-tall letters, MURDER-SUICIDE?, while the *Post* wondered in even larger capitals, DID HE? Both lead articles were built around a quote from Captain Brister, saying, "Given the evidence, murder-suicide would have to be considered a possibility."

It seemed to me that the descriptions of the scene in both papers were slanted to support that theory. On the other hand, maybe they didn't have to slant it; maybe the implication was already there in the sight of two bodies laying side by side, with the murder weapon on the floor between them. Of course, Dee-Dee *could* have done the shooting, but that didn't make as good a story.

Except for a rude column by Floyd Malcovitch, titled "Say It Ain't So," the related articles were mostly respectful of Joe, who was awfully well liked in this town. But the *Post* in particular had harsh things to report about Ms. Oliver. They'd tracked down an alleged former friend in San Antonio and a second cousin in Oklahoma, who between them, dished up oodles of rich dirt.

They told some juicy tales about her years on an Arizona commune during the seventies, her involvement with a former Black Panther, a failed marriage to a college professor who'd committed suicide, a child she'd put up for adoption, bouts with alcohol and drugs. But I noted that neither paper mentioned any arrests for prostitution.

· · · · · · · · · · · · ·

Molly was uncharacteristically late, and I was getting up to go for a second cup of coffee when I caught sight of her.

She pushed through the revolving door, coming out of the sunlight with her strong, purposeful stride, white blouse billowing, red hair bouncing, muscles flexing in her long legs. She was in her off-duty mode today, moving free and easy, with a garment bag full of my clothes slung over her shoulder. She glanced about with what appeared to be only casual interest, but I knew she was casing the joint behind her shades. Molly was the most beautiful cop I'd ever seen—five-ten, with auburn curls, eyes the green of old bottles, and freckles covering every square inch of creamy flesh—but she was still a cop. And off-duty or on, she did what cops do.

She was still doing it when her glance brushed past me, then panned back and settled. She gave me a slow, challenging once-over from toe to crown, then tilted her head, fingered the shades down her nose, and tossed me a sleepy sideways glance that said she didn't know me from Adam. But her cocked hip said she was willing to learn.

Before I could respond, the old dandy lowered his *Times* and asked her, "Could I, perhaps, be of some assistance, my dear?"

"Not in this lifetime," I muttered.

To which, the old guy replied without looking at me, "I heard that. But this young woman appears to be quite capable of declaring her own preference."

"That's telling him," said Molly.

"And surely," he went on, "a woman of such obvious beauty, discernment, and intelligence wouldn't allow herself to be swayed by the callow, shallow, short-lived, and shall we say *fleshly* advantages of youth. Certainly not when offered as an alternative the superior intellectual and shall we say *financial* opportunities that only advanced maturity and wise investments can provide."

"Financial?" she asked, clearly interested.

He gave me a smug squint and asked her, "Would you care to hear how much I'm worth, my dear?"

"Why not?" she said.

He motioned her closer, waited for her to lean in, and stage-whispered, "Would you believe seven million dollars?"

"You don't mean it."

"I do," he said. "My worth fluctuates with the markets, of course, day to day, often hour to hour, but even on the worst of those days, my liquifiable assets exceed seven million." Tossing me a disdainful glance, he asked, "Can you top that, young man?"

"Not this week."

He said, "I thought not." Then he concluded to Molly, "So, the choice is yours, my dear. Which will it be—immaturity or security?"

Molly left me hanging for a beat or two, milking the moment, but finally told him, "I suppose I'll have to give the young one first option, kind sir."

"A pity," he said.

"I may live to regret it."

"I'd say that was inevitable."

"But," she added, "there's something to be said for those fleshly advantages of youth."

He nodded, sighed, and reluctantly conceded, "Isn't it the truth." With a last wistful look at Molly, he settled back with his paper.

. . . .

"You believe that old buzzard?" I said on our way up in the elevator.

"I thought he was sweet," she said.

"*Sweet?* That dirty old man?"

"He wasn't dirty," she insisted. "Smelled very clean, in fact. A combination of talcum powder and Ben-Gay."

Later, with my head under the sheets, I asked, "Think *he* could do that?"

"Who?"

"Rip Van Rockefeller."

"Hmmm," she said. "Wonder what it would feel like without teeth."

I tried to make her pay for that, but she didn't seem to mind. We hadn't seen each other in two days, and we were doing our best to make up for lost time when I inadvertently hit the back of my head on the headboard.

Hearing my gasp, Molly naturally wanted to know what was the matter. And I naturally had to tell her.

"Why didn't you *call me?*"

"I didn't want to worry you," I said. "And I was planning to tell you when you got here."

"Why *didn't* you?"

"Gosh, I don't know. Guess I must have been distracted or something."

58

"Well, you should have at least gone to the hospital."

"Doctor said I didn't have a concussion."

"He said you *probably* didn't have a concussion."

"I'm all right, really."

"Let me feel it. In the back there? That it?"

"Yow!"

"Nice one," she said. "Make a man-size omelet out of that. And on the side, too? There?"

"Hey!"

"Well, I hope it at least knocked some sense into you."

"I doubt it."

"Me, too." She stroked the scar on my chin. "This didn't teach you much, did it?"

"Not much, I guess."

"So, what did Puckett say?"

"He didn't approve of my withholding evidence."

"Of course not."

"Told me he'd put me in jail the next time."

"And he'll do it, too, you know."

"I know. So I told him everything. I tried to make him see that the attack on me proved that Joe's death was more than simple murder-suicide, but he said there was no evidence that they were even related."

"And he's right," she said.

"What else could it have been?"

"Robbery," she said. "Thief saw you come in, liked the looks of your bag, and hit you over the head so he could steal it."

"My bag? With all the Gucci in this place?" She shrugged. "Besides, there was nothing in it except clothes and shaving stuff."

"The thief wouldn't know that, would he?"

"Why would he steal that electrical component?"

"Who knows? You said it was red. Maybe he took it because it went with his boots."

"You really think it was a coincidence that I happened to be examining possible evidence in a murder investigation when I was hit on the head and robbed?"

"No," she said, "but what I *think* doesn't matter. Puckett was talking about *evidence*, all of which so far points to murder-suicide. And if you actually had a clue that might have pointed him in a different direction, it may now be lost to him. No wonder he's hot."

"Okay," I said. "I was wrong, and I promise not do it again."

"Hmmph," she said, unconvinced.

12

The TV vans and patrol cars were gone from around the gates to Shady Lane, and the guard had been warned to expect us. After I identified myself, he opened the gates.

Justice Walter Matlock Sanders opened the front door. He was a tall, rawboned Westerner with a weathered, but still handsome face and curly silver hair, going a bit wispy on top. In his mid-sixties, he looked like he could still hogtie a steer if called upon, although he'd once admitted to me that he'd never even ridden a horse until he was in his forties. In spite of the frontier drawl, he was an educated man, who'd graduated near the top of his class from both the University of Texas and Harvard Law. He'd gone on to become a legendary trial attorney before being appointed to the state bench in 1981. His wife was dead now, and Peg was all the family he had left.

"Come in, come in," he repeated hospitably, as he pulled us inside and shut the door. But when he said, "Good to see you again, Bull," I had the feeling he didn't really see me at all.

"Good to see you, too, sir. Only wish it was another occasion."

He sighed and nodded. *"Any* occasion but this one."

"Yes, sir." I turned to Molly. "I don't think you've met Molly Flanagan."

"No, I haven't," he said and mustered a smile from somewhere. "And that's a shame." Gallantly, he took her hand and lowered his head over it. "I'm Walter Sanders, Miz Flanagan, and it's a sincere pleasure to make your acquaintance."

"The pleasure's mine, sir," she replied and almost curtsied.

"Peggy Ann's been looking forward to seeing you," he told her. "Do you know where the study is?"

"Yes, sir."

"Why don't you go on in? Tell her we'll be along in a few minutes."

As she walked away, Justice Sanders suggested that we step outside. He led me across the living room and opened French doors onto a flagstone patio. It was shaded but still hot, and I broke into a sweat as soon as we cleared the doors.

When he turned back, his customary charm was gone. In its place, I saw an angry, worried man. "Do you really think you can help her with this?" he asked.

"I don't know."

"What've you got so far?"

I told him.

"In other words, nothing," he said.

"Very little."

He nodded unhappily. "If you don't mind my saying so, that was a mighty dumb stunt you pulled with the police."

"I know," I said. "But how'd *you* know about it?"

"I spoke to Captain Brister," he explained. "From now on, if you get *anything,* you tell them about it immediately, you hear. I don't care what my daughter tells you."

"Yes, sir."

"Brister told me you were attacked last night."

"That's right," I said. "And I'm certain there's a connection between it and Joe's death."

"Why?"

"Too much of a coincidence, otherwise."

"Coincidences *do* happen," he informed me. "I don't believe

62

Joe was capable of murder, so I agree that an independent investigation is called for. However—"

"You're not sure I'm the right man to lead it."

"*Are* you?" he asked bluntly.

"To be honest, sir, I have my doubts. I told Peg that, but she insisted that I give it a try."

He nodded. "I tried to persuade her to let one of the bigger agencies take over, but it's *you* she wants. And I won't fight her on this, not while it's all that's holding her together. So," he concluded, "what're your plans?"

He didn't seem overly impressed by what I could tell him, but he graciously resisted saying anything critical. "I'll do what I can to see that you have the cooperation of the authorities," he assured me. "To accomplish anything on this, you're going to need all the help you can get."

I couldn't have agreed with him more. "Thank you, sir." I added, "I'd like to see the police reports if you could arrange it."

"So would I," he said. "I'll have a word with the Chief. But that woman's a hard case, so I wouldn't get my hopes up."

He handed me a card with a list of his phone numbers on it and concluded, "If you need anything, or just decide you can't handle the job, you give me a call, you hear?"

I said I heard him, and he took me in to see Peg.

She looked tired and more fragile than the day before, but she seemed genuinely happy to see me and Molly. She made an embarrassing fuss over my head injury and insisted that I let her Aunt Florence bring me a hot cup of camomile tea. Florence, her mother's sister, had flown in from Carthage to take over running the household, leaving Peg with nothing to do but mourn. So, any distraction Molly and I could offer was eagerly welcomed.

Peg presented me with a five-inch stack of computer printouts and two cardboard boxes full of letters and bills Joe had received over the last decade. "This doesn't include his fan mail, of course," she explained. "Joe tried to answer most of it, but he usually threw the letters away after he'd read them."

While we kept her occupied, Justice Sanders went into another room to make calls to Captain Brister and the Harris County

Medical Examiner. The news was bad. Very bad. The murder weapon was registered to a Dallas policeman, who'd reported it stolen from his home a few weeks earlier. Two partial prints had been lifted from the gun. Both were Joe's. Particles of gunpowder had been found under the skin of his right hand, and traces of metal from the butt of the gun had been found on his palm, proving beyond doubt that he had fired the weapon. The M.E. told the Justice he was sorry, but the evidence clearly dictated a ruling of murder-suicide.

When the Justice passed on this devastating news, Peg turned to Molly in disbelief. "How is that possible?" she asked.

"They've only proven that Joe fired the weapon," she said, "not that he was the murderer."

"I *know* he wasn't a murderer," said Peg. "I just don't see how they could say he fired that gun."

"Could he have?" Molly asked.

"No."

"Could it have been his?"

"No."

"Did he own a gun?"

"No, he hated guns," she insisted.

"Did he have any experience with them? Did he even know how to shoot one?"

"Well, yes, he did. His father used to take him hunting when he was a boy. But I'm sure he hadn't fired a gun in twenty years. He didn't believe in them and wouldn't have them around him."

Molly could only shake her head.

"So, what happens now?" Peg asked her.

"Without evidence to contradict the M.E. and no other suspects," she said regretfully, "my guess is that the police will accept the ruling."

"And then *what?*" asked Peg.

"They'll close the case?"

"Just like *that?*"

"I'm afraid so," Molly said gently. "They'd need evidence to keep it open."

Turning to her father, Peg pleaded, "Can't you *do* something?"

64

He turned to me helplessly and asked, "Are you staying with this?"

I could feel all of them looking at me. "Yes, sir, I am."

"Then I guess I better see if I can get you a look at those police reports."

B

The Medical Examiner's ruling broke on the Sunday evening news. The announcement was followed by shots of Captain Brister saying, "Our investigation has led us to agree that this appears to be a case of murder-suicide." When the Captain was asked if that meant the case was closed, he refused to comment further. But Monday morning's *Post* announced confidently, CASE CLOSED!, while the *Chronicle* settled for, M.E. RULES AHERN DID IT. The *Post* also had a front-page article playing up an analysis of the final autopsy report, concentrating on the pattern of five bruises found on Cordelia Mae's left shoulder.

The M.E. described them as "consistent with imprints left by pressure from the fingertips, those of the left hand, in this case." He went on to say that "the depth of the bruising indicates the application of considerable force, while the distance between the marks made by the thumb and the little finger suggests that her attacker had large hands and long fingers." When pressed on how Cordelia Mae could have received such bruises, the M.E. said, "I should remind you that this is purely speculative, but it is *possible* that her attacker could have had his arm around her, squeezing her by the shoulder to hold her still as he pressed the gun to her head."

It was a vivid image and did nothing for our cause, especially since Joe was a right-hander and well known for the long fingers that had made his split-fingered fastball such a deadly weapon. I could picture any lingering sympathy for him withering away.

Molly left for Galveston about eight A.M. After breakfast and a shower, I dressed, then called the six numbers from Joe's address book that I'd failed to reach Saturday night, plus the one that had been answered by the Spanish-speaking woman. I got her again and hung up. The other numbers connected me to a mechanic who worked on Joe's vehicles, an osteopath who treated his spine, and a counsellor at a drug treatment center he'd endowed. I also had a repeat visit with one answering machine, and two phones still failed to answer.

After that, I drove to the police station. Peg's father had worked wonders. Using all of his considerable influence and persuasiveness—aided by the fact that the police were about to close the case anyway—he'd finally talked the Chief of Police into letting me look at the case records.

I pulled into a visitor's slot in front of the Central Patrol Station and fed the meter a handful of quarters from the roll I kept in the glove compartment.

The front desk was a long black counter, with three uniformed officers behind it. I gave one of them my name, and he made a call. After hanging up, he gave me a blue visitor's sticker to paste on my shirt and told me to hold on a moment, explaining that somebody would be coming down to get me.

A minute later, an attractive young Hispanic woman in civilian dress got off the elevator and walked over to speak to one of the cops. When he nodded at me, she smiled and asked if I would follow her, please.

In the elevator, I introduced myself, and she told me her name was Magaly Ybarra, or Maggie, and that she worked in Public Affairs. We got off the elevator on the third floor and turned left just as Sergeant Cobb shoved through the double doors ahead.

He scuffed to a halt, not at all pleased to see me. "I had my way," he growled, "you wouldn't be here. But the Captain tells me I got no choice. I don't have to like it, he says; I just have to go along with it, so that's what I'm doing. But," he said with his coldest cop stare, "you conceal any more evidence from me, and I'll put your ass in jail."

"Yeah," I said, "Puckett warned me."

Cobb didn't want to hear about Puckett. "Just don't forget you heard it from me, too."

"No, sir, I won't forget. And thanks."

"For what?"

"Telling me where I stand."

He didn't like that, either, but he'd already said what he had to say. So, he gave me one last icy glare and walked on by, disappearing around the corner to Homicide.

I asked the woman, "He always like that?"

"So far," she said dryly.

She led me through the double doors, past the open door to the Public Affairs office, and down a quiet carpeted corridor to a smaller office, where she introduced me to another woman in civilian clothes. "Minnie, this is Bill Cochran. Bill, this is Sergeant Parkhill, known to her friends as Minnie."

Minnie was six-two in her stocking feet and a good three to four inches taller with her heels and the hive of teased, strawberry blonde hair on top. She was built on the scale of Rosie Grier but vamped like a barroom sweetie.

After my escort left, Minnie batted her mascaraed lashes and drawled, "Molly told me 'bout you. Said you were a hunk. But then she always was prone to exaggerate." She laughed and slipped me an elbow to show that she was only joshing, while blessing me with a whiff of strong and distinctly musky perfume. "So," she asked, "what can I do you for, sweetcakes?"

"I'd like to see everything you have on the Ahern death."

"You don't want much, do you?"

I winked. "No more than you can give."

She liked that. "Should be enough," she agreed with a laugh.

It was sometimes steep going with Sergeant Parkhill, but she was good at what she did, and with her help, I got to see it all:

The initial report by the first patrolmen on the scene. The questioning of the neighbor who discovered the bodies, the manager of the apartments, and the other tenants. The EMS report. The death certificate. The Medical Examiner's preliminary and final autopsy reports and his ruling. The lab reports. And a manila envelope full of photographs from the scene.

After two hours of reading, I'd gathered the following facts: the bodies were found by Ms. Nivia Gonzalez at approximately 9:15 A.M. in apartment 2-G of the Bayou View Apartments. The apartments were located in the Braeswood area of Southwest Houston, just below the point where the South Loop swings northward into the West Loop, not far from the Astrodome. According to Ms. Gonzalez and the first policemen on the scene, the apartment showed no signs of forced entry or a struggle. The autopsies placed the times of death between midnight and 2 A.M.. The Gonzalez woman, Homer Lusby (the manager of the apartments), and one other tenant reported hearing shots just before 1 A.M., but nobody saw anyone entering or leaving the apartment, either before or after the shots were fired. Nine other tenants were home at the time but claimed to have slept through the shootings. Of the three who admitted hearing them, only Ms. Gonzalez had called the police. She lived across a courtyard from Dee-Dee and couldn't tell the police where the shots had come from, whether inside or outside the complex. She wasn't even certain they were shots, so the police had only driven by for a look. *Three* shots had been fired, one putting a hole in a framed German map of Great Britain and shattering the glass. The autopsy reports reiterated that the deaths were from 9-millimeter gunshot wounds, both delivered from extremely close range, with the slugs entering just behind the victims' right ears. The one that killed Joe had left only a modest exit wound above the opposite ear, but the results were more gruesome in Dee-Dee's case. The slug had entered at a downward angle and had taken most of her left jaw on its way out. I saw pictures from the scene: Cordelia Mae collapsed in an uncomfort-able-looking twist; Joe in a more natural position on his back, as though resting after his stretching exercises. Photos had been taken from various angles and distances, including a dozen gory closeups of the entry and exit wounds. The lab reports left no doubt that Joe had fired the weapon, but I took comfort from the fact that the technician admitted it was impossible to say *how many times* Joe had fired it.

The partial prints lifted from the gun were a clear match with Joe's, down to the scar on his thumb, and it was easy to see why the police had pegged it as a murder-suicide. But it seemed to me that the absence of other prints on the gun was suspicious. Joe's fingers could have been pressed to the weapon to leave prints after he was dead, just as the bad guys always did in the movies. As for his having fired the gun, maybe there was an explanation for that, too. The third shot gave me an idea. The lab report said that the angle at which the slug entered the framed map had indicated that it was fired from a standing position. But what if the culprit had lifted Joe off the floor after he was dead, put the gun in his hand, and fired the shot into the map. That would have left the prints and the gunpowder traces, while making it look like Joe had done the shooting.

When I ran the idea past Minnie, she said, "I don't see why that wouldn't be possible, but you'd need a hell of a strong man to do it."

"Or woman," I said.

"She'd have to be *damn* strong," she said. "Doubt I could lift a dead weight of two hundred and ten pounds into a standing position. But the case is closed. All that's left is some paperwork and the announcement, and I can tell you now they won't reopen it on the basis of any theory. They're gonna need hard evidence for that."

"What about the third shot?" I asked. "Is it common for suicides to miss like that?"

"No, but it *is* fairly common for them to fire a 'test shot' before actually turning the gun on themselves."

"Oh," I said. "I didn't know that."

"That doesn't mean your theory isn't possible," she said, "just that it isn't evidence."

Peg had told me that Joe had dropped her at home around midnight, and it would have taken him at least forty-five minutes to drive from his house to Bayou View Apartments. If the reported timing on the shots was accurate, then they must have been fired only minutes after he arrived. That didn't leave much time for an argument to progress into a killing rage, so if Joe had done it, he had to have gone there with the premeditated intent of murdering Dee-Dee. If somebody else had done it, they must have either followed him into the apartment or have been waiting for him there. But if Joe didn't go there to kill her, why *did* he go there?

Minnie let me go through the Polk Directory with the list of numbers I'd copied down from Joe's address book. The Polk Directory is a reverse telephone book, used for finding a name and address when all you have is a telephone number. Two of the numbers weren't listed, including the one for the gruff-voiced man who'd answered by reading back his number and one of the two that still hadn't answered.

I asked Minnie, "How do you get the names and addresses for unlisted numbers?"

"We take a grand jury warrant to the phone company, but the department won't waste one on a closed case."

I figured she was probably right about that, and I decided I'd have to see what Peg's father could do.

14

I tried out a new Greek place in Montrose for lunch, then went back to the hotel and called Homer Lusby, the manager of Bayou View Apartments. The man's voice was unexpectedly high-pitched, almost girlish. After making an appointment to take a look at the crime scene the next morning, I started hitting the box files and the stack of printouts.

I quickly decided that Joe's financial records were over my head, so I called Pete Shirmer. My company had destroyed some expensive speakers while moving Pete into a beach house in Galveston a few summers before. After he'd called to complain, I'd gone out to assure him that our insurance would replace his property, and we'd ended up getting stoned together. Since then, he invited me out whenever he was down to the island, and his investment firm now handled the small portfolio of stocks my Aunt Helen had left me.

When I asked Pete to take a look at the records for me, he didn't need much convincing. The idea of peeking into Joe Ahern's personal finances clearly turned him on. He had a date this evening, but he said he would be home about seven, and I told him I'd drop by.

After that, I concentrated on Joe's correspondence, of which there was more than enough to keep me busy. I didn't know how it was arranged in the computer, but as it was printed out, his business and personal correspondence were all lumped together. Because Joe had a gift for making even the most utilitarian note seem personal, I had to read every entry through to the end to be sure of its purpose. And whenever he referred to a letter he'd received, I had to go hunting for that letter in the files, which were at least in some kind of order. I was looking for someone with a grudge against Joe, someone with a reason for wanting him dead. His correspondence had seemed like a good place to start, but the process was tedious.

I kept at it until about six o'clock, then got out the pickup and took Montrose north. After a few miles, Montrose changes to Studemont, then again to Studewood. Houston streets do that. I made a left onto the feeder for I-10 and took it over to Heights Boulevard.

Towering live oaks grew in the broad median and along both sides, offering shade to older, larger houses, many of them two and three stories, several of an elaborate Victorian gingerbread variety. Some of the houses were in sad shape, while others had been recently renovated, or were in the process of renovation, by folk who drove BMWs or Volvo stationwagons. Still, as with virtually every other neighborhood in the state, there were a few pickup trucks in sight.

Pete Shirmer's house sat on a large lot, with a lawn like a putting green and a scattering of oaks circled by beds of purple verbena and snowy canna lilies. The house was three stories tall, painted a pale yellow, with dark-green shutters and a cylindrical tower rising up one side like a decorative silo.

As the heir to one of the oldest banking families in the state, Pete could have built himself a mansion in Memorial, accepted a directorship at the family bank, and lived off his trust fund. But he was an independent cuss, who preferred to renovate his white elephant in the Heights, invest his trust allotments in his own business, and live off his personal wiles. The ease of his early success was probably due in part to the Shirmer wealth and name, but people continued to put their earnings in his hands not because he was a Shirmer, but because he gave them a good return for their money.

As I climbed the brick steps to his porch, he opened the door, wearing white linen trousers and nothing else, bare feet and hairy chest exposed to Heights Boulevard. Pete was two years younger than me at forty-one, half a head shorter at five-eight, and thanks to two sets of competitive tennis every day, in better condition than I was in my playing days.

"Turned gumshoe, have you?" he asked with a grin.

"No, but if I thought it'd help, I'd buy a pair."

He nodded at my armload of files and printouts. "That the stuff?"

"That's it."

He took it eagerly and led me into his study, where I sipped a cold Bass ale while he finished dressing. He was assisted in this by his trusty manservant, Jeeves. At least, that's what Pete was calling him this evening. It was a game they played, and I could never tell what Jeeves thought of it. Pete was as likely to call him Simons or Carruthers, or almost anything but Breedlove, which was his name. Mr. Breedlove tolerated this behavior in return for a sizeable weekly salary, an occasional stock tip, and a pleasant suite of rooms at the rear of the ground floor. He was a large, strong, easy-moving man of fifty, who served as Pete's valet, party bouncer, butler, and sometime driver. I preferred to believe that Breedlove was generally amused by his employer's antics, but I couldn't say that for a fact, since I'd never actually seen him crack a smile.

"I'd invite you to stay for dinner," Pete explained to me as he pulled on a sock, "but I have an engagement this evening with an exceedingly attractive young woman, and I don't need the competition."

"That's okay," I said. "I don't need the temptation. A man has to be careful when his sweetie carries a thirty-eight."

"Sounds kinky," he said with a leer. "How *is* Molly?"

"Still the scourge of the Galveston criminal set and the apple of my eye."

Speaking as a connoisseur, he said, "A red delicious, as I recall.

I'm having some people out to the beach house on Labor Day. You should bring her."

"Will if I can," I promised.

As he stood to slip into his shirt, he turned serious. Eyeing me in the mirror, he said, "What about Ahern? Did he do it?"

"No, he didn't," I said. "But I may have a hell of a time proving it."

He glanced at the paperwork on the desk. "And you think there may be something in there that could help."

"Could be. Peg thinks his death had something to do with an investment."

"What kind of an investment?"

"Don't know. That's what I'm hoping you can tell us."

"Do what I can," he promised.

So, I left it with him and went out to dinner.

When I got back to the hotel, there was a message waiting for me to call Peg.

"The police have closed the case," she told me.

"Where'd you hear that?"

"On television."

"What'd they say?"

"That their investigation is now completed, and they're satisfied that it was a probable case of murder-suicide."

"Probable," I repeated. "That means they're still not sure, but they have too many other unsolved cases on the board to spend any more man-hours on this one right now."

"Then it's up to us," she said.

"Yeah."

I told her what I'd been up to, and it seemed to cheer her that something was being done. After we said good night, I checked in with Molly. Then I took another try at the two numbers from Joe's address book that I'd still failed to reach. I finally managed to catch one of them at home. A man named Dick Odom told me in a gravelly voice that he'd worked his whole life in the oil patch, that he didn't believe in credit, and that he'd never expected any charity from the world. But he said he would always be beholden to Joe for helping to get his son off cocaine and for finding the boy work when he got out of treatment.

In the name of thoroughness, I again tried the Spanish-speaking number, and this time, I talked to the woman's husband. Paul Vasquez was his name. His wife's name was Elisha, and Paco was their son. Joe had tried to get Paco into drug treatment, he said, but the boy wouldn't listen. After explaining that Paco had been killed while trying to stick up a Stop-n-Go on Valentine's Day, he thanked me for calling and added that he was very sorry to hear that Mr. Ahern was dead. "He was good to my son," he said. "I will not forget that."

15

Much of Houston is carpeted with virtually identical brown or beige apartment complexes that were thrown up during the housing Boom of the seventies. They can be seen from the elevated highways, stretching for miles in all directions. But Bayou View Apartments was a throwback to an earlier era, a neat little red-brick complex surrounded by well-kept single-family homes.

The complex was built around a grassy courtyard, with a swimming pool in the middle, and parking spaces running around the outside of the square. The "bayou" apparently referred to the rusty trickle in the gulley at the back.

A black plastic plaque on the door of 1A said, MANAGER, so I knocked. I was about to try it again when the door flew open, and an enormous cowboy stood there grinning out at me. "Howdy, friend!" he said in the oddly high-pitched voice I'd heard on the phone. "What can I do you for?"

"Homer Lusby?" I asked.

"That's me," he agreed. "But my friends call me Bubba."

"I'm Bill Cochran."

"Well, hell, sure you are," he said and stood back to clear the way. "C'mawn in!"

Bubba was bigger than Puckett, with a vast belly stretching his tee shirt and overhanging his jeans, massive hands and feet, and a

77

ridiculously oversized head. With blonde hair and eyebrows so pale they were almost invisible, his head looked like a full moon. But with all that space, his tiny eyes, snub nose, and prim little mouth had been shoved together in the middle.

Stepping past him, I said, "We spoke yesterday on the phone."

"Sure we did," he agreed and shut the door. "Want a beer?"

"Bit early for me."

"Yeah, me, too," he said. "Think I'll have one anyway."

The living room was cool and neat. The furniture was decent enough—Early American maple, bought as a set—but the real money had gone into his entertainment system. His big-screen TV, VCR, laser disc player, turntable, CD player, plus his giant speakers and a vast collection of tapes and discs and LPs and CDs covered most of the front wall.

Garth Brooks was singing, "I Got Friends in Low Places" as Bubba strode behind the counter and hanging shelves that separated the kitchen from the living room. Opening the refrigerator, he said, "You said you wanted to see where they was killed?"

"Yeah."

"Should be all right now," he said. "I aired it out some and cleaned up after the police was through takin' their pitchers and all. Blood soaked through the carpet into the paddin', and I had to cut out a big piece of it. Course you can't really replace a chunk of carpet like that without it showin', so I'll end up havin' to tear the whole damn thing up 'fore it's over." He came back with two beers, finished one on his way, and settled the other on his belly after he was seated.

"Tell me about the shots," I said.

"They was three of 'em," he said, "and they come about a minute apart."

"Did they wake you up?"

He shook his head. "I was in the toilet. Caught with my pants down, so to speak." We laughed at that.

"What time was it?"

"Don't know exactly—wasn't wearin' no watch—but I figured it was a little before one."

"Did they sound close?"

"Close enough."

"How close?"

He scrunched up his tiny features in thought and decided, "That's hard to say."

"Did you think they'd come from inside the complex?"

"No, I wouldn't say that. Like I tole the police, I couldn't tell where they come from."

"What did you think when you heard them?"

"Hell," he said with a chuckle, "I thought some asshole was gettin' hisself shot!"

"Did you check it out?"

The grin broadened. "You mean, did I go walkin' around outside lookin' for a man with a gun?"

When he put it that way, it did sound pretty dumb. "Did you call the police?"

"You know," he said, "I thought about given' 'em a ring. But, as I say, I was occupied at the time, and I figured—what the hell—somebody else was bound to call."

"So, you heard about the deaths from Ms. Gonzalez?"

"Hell, no," he said sourly. "She told the cops, and *they* tole me. Come poundin' on my door Saturday mornin', wantin' to know about the two stiffs they said I had upstairs."

"How'd the room look to you?"

"Except for the bodies, about the same."

I pounced on that. "Then you'd been up there before?"

" 'Course I have," he said. "I'm the manager. When anything goes wrong, they call *me.*"

"How well did you know the dead woman?"

"Not near as well as I'd like to've," he said with a bloated leer.

"Ever ask her out?"

"Nope. She never took no notice a me."

"Did you talk to her?"

"Said hello when I saw her. Tole her thank you when she paid the rent."

"And what'd *she* say?"

"Not much. She was a tad on the cool side."

"Stone cold now," I said, just to see how he'd take it.

He thought it was a hoot. "That's the God's truth." He wheezed and chuckled. "Damn' if it ain't."

"Did you notice any steady boyfriends?"

He shook his head. "I read in the paper what she done for a livin', but she never brung none a her customers 'round here."

"Did you ever see her with Joe Ahern?"

"Not before that mornin', no."

"You sure?" I asked.

"Yeah."

"You would've known Joe by sight?"

"Hell, yes," he said. "You're talkin' about the only pitcher who can ever compare to Nolan Ryan."

"How long did Ms. Oliver live here?"

"About two years. Ever since she come to Houston."

"Were there ever any fights up there?"

"Nope. She was a quiet one."

"Know any of her boyfriends?"

"Not to speak to. Only remember seein' her with two or three men the whole time she was here. And never the same one twice. Choosy, I guess."

"Do you know if she owned a gun?"

"Like a nine-millimeter automatic?" he asked with a grin, letting me know he wasn't as dumb as he looked.

"Yeah," I said.

"If she had one, I never saw it."

Running out of questions, I asked, "Do you have the key to 2-G?"

"Yep." He wrestled his bulk off the couch and walked over to a small white cabinet at the entrance to the kitchen. The inside of the door was covered with keys, labeled in Magic Marker with apartment numbers.

When he handed me the key, I said, "You don't happen to know if Ms. Gonzalez is at home, do you?"

"See a blue Chevy Blazer out there?"

"Parked beside it."

"Then she's here."

16

The apartments faced into the courtyard, connected by concrete exterior walkways, with decorative balustrades of white-painted wrought iron. Dee-Dee's and Ms. Gonzalez' apartments were both on the second floor, across the courtyard from each other.

I caught Ms. Gonzalez backing out of her door. She was small, barely five feet tall, but perfectly in proportion. A pocket Venus. Short curly black hair, skimpy red two-piece swimsuit, white beach towel tossed over a shoulder.

"Ms. Gonzalez?"

She jerked around, eyes wide. "Christ! You scared me to death!"

"Didn't mean to, sorry."

"Well, you *did.*"

"I'm sorry," I repeated.

"What do you want?" she asked, narrowing eyes so dark I couldn't tell if they were brown or black.

"Just want to ask you a few questions."

"Great," she sighed. "Another cop."

"No, I—"

"Reporter, then."

"Well, no, actually."

"Then *what?*"

"I'm a friend of Joe Ahern's?"

She tucked her chin and gave me an up-from-under look. "You're not one of those sports nuts, are you, making a pilgrimage to the spot where your hero died?"

"No, no, I really am, or *was,* a friend of Joe Ahern's. And his wife has asked me to look into his death."

"Look into it," she repeated.

"That's right."

"Are you a private detective?"

"No, I'm a writer, actually, just doing a favor for a friend."

She sighed and glanced away, wondering if there was any way out of this. Deciding there wasn't, she said, "What did you want to ask?"

"Did you know Ms. Oliver?"

"You know the answer to that," she said impatiently, "or you wouldn't be talking to me." Lifting her face to me, she suddenly looked very regal. The *café con leche* complexion went with the Hispanic surname, but there was an Asian delicacy to her features.

"True enough." I said. "Were you friends?"

"We hung out together some."

"Were you and she in the, uh . . ."

Her mouth tightened. "Were we what? In the same business? Is that what you're asking?"

"I suppose—"

"You think I'm a *whore?*"

"No, I—"

"Yes, you do!" she declared.

"Look," I said mildly, "we're getting off on the wrong foot here. This isn't about you or me, and I didn't come here to insult you. The dead man's wife has some questions. That's all. And since you knew Ms. Oliver, I thought you might be able to help us answer them."

After examining me for a moment, she asked abruptly, "You want a cup of coffee?"

· · · · · · · · · · · · ·

"You're a painter," I said.

"Good guess." She smiled back at me on her way to the kitchen. "Be a few minutes on that coffee."

Canvases filled the living room, crowding her furniture into the center of the room. They leaned ten and twelve deep against the walls, all turned away, only their backs showing. A huge blank canvas covered most of the wall to my right, waiting for paint, and six completed works hung on the other walls.

After putting on the water to boil and grinding the coffee beans, she came back. "What's the matter? You look confused."

I waved at the nude of a skinny, brown-skinned old woman lying back in a bed of brilliant flowers. She had a look of rapturous anticipation on her face and was beckoning to someone unseen with grossly twisted arthritic hands. The lush greens, the boldly colored flowers, the warm brown skin, and those hands. I kept coming back to them.

"This's good," I said. "So are the others."

"Why shouldn't they be?" she asked.

"Good enough to *sell,* I mean."

"They do. Or they *did,"* she qualified, "when they were being shown. I sold four at the Naked Eye on Bissonet last year." The kettle whistled, and she went to take it off the flame. She poured a little of the boiling water over the grounds and gave them a moment to expand. "Right now," she added, "I'm talking to a place in the Galleria about showing my stuff."

"Where'd you study?"

"Got my masters from NYU."

"So, you lived in New York."

"Three years," she said. "Sometimes I don't know why I left."

She poured the rest of the water into the filter. "It'll take a moment to finish dripping. How do you like it?"

"Black." I nodded at the huge blank canvas. "What's that going to be?"

She made a face. "I don't know. Thought I did when I had it stretched. Now it looks so big it makes my idea look small."

"So, you rethink it."

Surprised. "Right."

"I know about rethinking," I explained. "I'm on the final slope of a novel that's nothing like the story it started out to be."

"For better or worse?"

"Better, I think. I *hope.*"

She came back with two cups of coffee, handed me one, and waved at the couch.

I sat down and took a sip. "Very good."

"Hawaiian Kona," she said. "At ten dollars a pound, it ought to be good."

She took a chair across the coffee table from me, a little more relaxed now but still keeping her distance. Finding dead bodies would probably make you cautious. Still, in spite of the circumstances, there was something consciously sensual in her every movement. In the way she caressed her coffee cup and peered at me over the rim as she drank, in the way she crossed and scissored her shapely brown legs, or the way she arched her back, thrusting her breasts against the thin red fabric of her bikini top. Small, firmly rounded breasts, with disproportionately large erect nipples.

"Mind if I ask you a question?" I said.

"Thought that's why you came," she replied with a grin, noticing my point of focus.

I smiled. "I just—"

"You want to know why I live in a place like this, is that it? With no light and no room to work?"

"That's my question?" I admitted.

"You could say I'm in transition."

"From what to what?"

"You're a nosy one, aren't you?"

"I'm a writer."

"Likely excuse." She ran a fingernail from the corner of her mouth to her chin. "Your scar. Was it curiosity that got you that?"

"I suppose you could say it was."

"Thought so." She smiled. When she tilted her head down and gave me that up-from-under look again—dark curls dancing around her face—she looked Middle Eastern. Like Cleopatra or Nefertiti or Mary Magdelene. She wasn't really coming on to me, just keeping me off-balance.

84

Pulling out my pad, I asked, "Mind if I take notes? My memory's like a sieve."

"Does that mean we're starting the interview now?"

I grinned. "It's not really an interview. I just want to ask a few questions."

She waved assent.

"Tell me about Dee-Dee."

"Smart," she said. "I kept after her to do something with her mind. Something creative. She said she'd tried dancing and singing and playing the piano, all of which she could do, but just not well enough to make a living at them. I suggested writing, because she was so verbal. She could talk rings around most people. But she told me she'd tried that, too, and the words just wouldn't work for her on paper."

"Did she entertain lots of men?"

"Clients, you mean?"

"Yeah."

"Not here," she said. "Dee-Dee was a real stickler about keeping her private and professional lives separate."

"Do you know if she was ever afraid of any of her clients?"

"She was never afraid of anybody."

"Maybe she *should've* been."

She nodded. "Maybe so."

"Did you ever see her with Joe Ahern before that morning?"

"Once, I think," she said. "Last Tuesday, I believe it was. I didn't get a good look at him, only saw him from behind as he knocked on her door, but he was the right size and build and hair color."

"How long did he stay?"

"I don't know. Didn't see him go in and didn't see him leave. I don't even know if she answered the door."

"Did she have any boyfriends?"

"Nothing steady, not since I've known her."

"How long has that been?"

"About three months."

"Could you identify any of the men she went out with?"

"There was a Navy pilot who came through here on leave about a month ago, but he was on his way to the Mediterranean the last I heard."

"Any others?"

She considered it. "Can't think of any. It might sound strange, but outside of business hours, Dee-Dee was mostly celibate the last couple of months."

I thought that over, then moved on. "Tell me about the gun-shots."

"I was in bed, but not asleep, when I heard the first one," she recited, having been over it too many times already. "The second one came about a minute later, and I sat up, not sure what it was. They didn't sound like gunshots on TV, more like twigs snapping sounds. Another minute or so passed, and I was about to lay down again when I heard the third one. It still didn't sound like a gunshot, but I decided that's what it had to be."

"Did it sound close?" I asked.

"I couldn't tell," she said. "You have to remember that the shots came from across the courtyard, through two doors and two walls. I thought they might've come from out on the street."

"Did you look out the window to see what had happened?"

She took a sip of coffee and shook her head. "No."

"What did you do?"

She settled back in her chair, moving her shoulders to make herself comfortable. A catlike gesture that did wonderful things with her breasts and made it difficult for me to remember my question. "I called nine-one-one to report the shots, and I guess they came by. After that, I listened for a few minutes, then went back to bed."

"Did you think Dee-Dee might be involved?"

"No," she said.

"How'd you happen to find her body?"

"We were going shopping Saturday morning, and she was sup-posed to come by for me at nine, so we could go out for breakfast. When she didn't show up, I went over to see what was keeping her."

"How'd you get in?"

"The door was unlocked, so I opened it."

86

"You didn't knock?"

"Of course I knocked," she snapped back. "But she didn't answer."

"Sorry," I said. "I'm just trying to get it straight."

She nodded and took another sip of coffee.

"What did you think when you saw the bodies?"

"I didn't know what to think," she said. "I could hardly breathe. And the smell . . ."

I nodded, knowing about the smell. "What did you think had happened?"

"I wasn't even sure they were dead, not at first. Even with all the blood around your friend, he didn't really look dead, just like he was resting. Dee-Dee was turned away, and most of her blood was hidden, but she was laying in an odd way, with her arm tucked underneath her, all twisted around. She looked awfully uncomfortable, and I think that's what convinced me she was dead."

"Who did you think had done the shooting?"

"I didn't think about it at first. Then I saw the gun laying near his hand, and I figured he'd done it. Shot her, then himself."

"Did you recognize him?"

"No," she said. "And neither did the cops. Not till they found his wallet. You don't expect to see somebody like that dead on the floor."

"How did the apartment look to you?"

"Like Cordelia Mae had just cleaned up."

"Did she usually keep it clean?"

She stared at me. "You think somebody killed her, then tidied up?"

"I don't know. I'm just curious."

She nodded. "Dee-Dee cleaned in binges, like most of us. She'd let it pile up, then do a kamikaze." She swallowed and looked away. "I'll tell you one thing."

"What's that?"

"I could have done without seeing her dead like that."

"Yeah, I know."

"You *do?*"

I nodded. "Once you've seen it, you don't forget it."

"No," she agreed.

As I got up to go, I told her, "I may need to speak to you again."

She gave me her up-from-under with a sly grin attached and said, "Anytime."

17

Apartment 2-G had been shut up with the air-conditioning off, and the heat met me at the door. I knew the smell Nivia had mentioned—the combination of blood, gunpowder, urine, and evacuated bowels—but I couldn't detect any of it now. The odor of disinfectant overpowered the rest. A jagged six-foot square had been cut out of the carpet and padding, and there were faint rusty stains on the wood floor beneath.

Except for the heat and the stench of disinfectant, it was a pleasant room. Dee-Dee had given her cheap furniture an exotic look with swaths of colorful Eastern fabrics and had used plants to give the room life. They hung from chains and sat on shelves, with a large shefilera and a tall rubber plant standing like small trees in two of the corners.

Then there were the books, shelves of them, covering two of the walls from floor to ceiling. Not just novels, of which there were many, but thick scholarly tomes, with serious covers and titles longer than a good sentence. She had the philosophers: Plato and Aristotle, Marcus Aurelius and Descartes, Heidegger and Marx. The poets: Keats and Shelly, Browning and Blake, Thomas and Frost. Even the scientists: Darwin and Einstein, Freud and Oppenheimer, Hawking and Sagan. She had history and Eastern mysticism, tribal poetry and Lee Iacocca, Shakespeare and Sherlock Holmes. She even had *my* book on a shelf of contemporary nonfiction.

There were candles all around, fresh ones and the stubs of used ones, with overlapping layers of multicolored wax puddled on saucers and plates and dribbling down the sides of wine bottles. That, combined with the macrame hangings, the batik fabrics, the faint but unmistakable scent of sandalwood incense, and the first beanbag chair I'd seen in a decade, took me back to college—late sixties, early seventies—back to pot parties, to us and them, and the War That Wasn't. Who was this Cordelia Mae Oliver, anyway?

Both Cleo Speaks and Nivia Gonzalez had said she was smart, and I could see that she was well read. Why would such a woman settle for escort work? And why would anybody want to murder her? A jealous boyfriend had seemed a likely culprit, but the only suspect so far had apparently flown to the Mediterranean a month before the crime.

For Joe to get involved with a prostitute, she'd have to be somebody special, so discovering that Cordelia Mae had unexpected depths wasn't entirely good news.

Her bathroom was comfortably messy. The tail of a blue nightgown stuck out of the clothes hamper, and a towel lay over the side of the tub. One of a pair of hose hung from a towel rod, while the other lay on the floor below. The shelf over the sink was crowded with oils, lotions, creams, gels, and treatments, while the medicine cabinet was nearly empty and contained nothing more exotic than a bottle of Midol and a half-used packet of birth control pills.

The kitchen was spic-and-span except for a skillet left to soak in the sink. Neither the cabinets nor the refrigerator contained anything noteworthy.

The bedroom was just a room where Dee-Dee had slept. The walls were bare, but there were three photos on the dresser. One was of a skinny young Dee-Dee of eleven or twelve sitting on the porch steps of a white woodframe house. One was of a ripe teenage Dee-Dee in a halter top and hiphugging bellbottom jeans standing in the dust in front of a low-roofed shack covered with road signs.

Beside her, was an earnest-looking young man with long dark hair, rimless glasses, a fringed leather vest, and more bellbottoms. Taken at the Arizona commune, I assumed, and wondered if the young man was the teacher-husband who'd committed suicide. The third photo was of a slightly older Dee-Dee standing in a swimsuit next to a pool, with another slender young man. This one wore the uniform of an Army private and a recruit's burr haircut.

On the bedside table was a reading lamp, two hardback books—*A History of Private Life* and *The Oxford Illustrated History of Britain*—a black satin sleeping mask, and a paperback copy of Sue Grafton's *H Is for Homicide*.

I looked for Dee-Dee's address book, wanting to compare it to Joe's to see if any of the names matched. When I didn't find it in the bedroom, I went back to the living room. Not finding it there, either, I called Minnie Parkhill and asked if the police had taken it. She put me on hold for five minutes and came back with the news from Puckett that they had looked for an address book or datebook or Rolodex or appointment calendar but hadn't found any of those things.

"Isn't that unusual?" I asked.

"Yeah, it is."

"You'd think she'd have a datebook."

"You'd think so."

"Maybe somebody took it," I suggested.

"Maybe so," she agreed.

. . . .

I found a pay phone at a gas station and called the downtown impound lot to see if I could take a look at Joe's pickup, but they told me it had been released and that someone had picked it up. When I called Peg, she said the Dorseys had driven in to get it. I told her I was coming out.

Joe drove a sky-blue 1991 Ford pickup. No stretch cab or four-wheel drive, no roll bar or fog lights, just a basic pickup, with AC and a radio. I'd asked Joe once if he was making a statement with his choice of transportation, but he said he just felt comfortable in it. If you ride around in a limo, he explained, people stare at you, wanting to see who's inside, see if it's a face they recognize. But if you tool around in a pickup, people either don't notice you at all, or they nod or wave or give you the finger. It's a friendly vehicle, he said, and it'll take you just about any place you want to go. I wished he was still around to tell me why, on Friday evening, it had taken him to the Bayou View Apartments.

Peg had some friends over, but she gave me the keys to the pickup so I could start it up. Assuming that Joe had been listening to a news station, I expected to find the radio tuned to AM, but it wasn't. It was on FM, and I heard a string quartet when I switched it on. The numbers on the digital readout were those of the University of Houston's classical music station.

I assumed the police had searched the pickup, but I figured that a good detective would take a look for himself. I looked in the glove compartment, over the sun visors, behind the seats, in the crack of the seats, under the seats, even under the floor mats. The glove compartment contained some gas receipts stuffed into a plastic envelope, a flashlight, a King James Bible with the cover torn off, some napkins, a straw in a plain white paper wrapper, and a couple of pencils. A pair of sunglasses was hanging from the driver's-side sun visor. Under the driver's seat, there was a Houston Key Map, just like mine. He'd made notes to himself on some of the pages, and he'd circled the part of the Braeswood area in which Bayou View Apartments was located. There was only an unopened case of 30-weight oil in the bed, while the lockbox contained a tool kit, a lug wrench, a small empty ice chest, a couple of baseball bats, and a burlap sack of scuffed baseballs. The thought that Joe would never throw one of those again suddenly made me feel old and very sad.

I phoned the University of Houston radio station and spoke to the program director, knowing that even classical stations usually had news programming. But she explained that, on Friday night, they had been in the midst of a marathon broadcast of Wagner's "Ring Cycle," which had preempted their usual news breaks.

So much for that idea.

. . . .

Molly had brought up a suit for me along with my other clothes on Sunday, so I wore it to the funeral home Tuesday evening.

Seeing how jammed the place was, with the press getting shots and quotes from the notables on their way in and out, I thought of Dee-Dee. That morning, I'd read that her uncle had flown in from Oklahoma to claim the body and to take her back home for burial, and I wondered what kind of attention she would receive in her hometown.

When I finally got my chance to speak to Peg, she took my hand and pulled me down beside her, asking, "You'll be there with me tomorrow, won't you?"

"Of course."

She told me that the service had been switched from Calvary Baptist to Victory Baptist, and I said, "That's appropriate." But when she asked, "Why?" I had to admit, "I don't know."

On further consideration, it really didn't sound appropriate at all. Joe and Reverend George Lamp, the minister of Victory Baptist, had had a falling out a year before, which had resulted in Joe and Peg moving their memberships to the smaller, poorer Calvary Baptist, on Richmond. As I understood it, the source of trouble was the use to which Lamp was putting the generous contributions that poured into his church's coffers. Joe felt that too much of it was being spent supporting and lobbying for the Reverend's right-wing causes and too little on the charitable programs Joe had championed. Lamp was, in fact, trickle-down all the way, while Joe preferred a more hands-on approach to the problem of poverty. Given his liberal inclinations, I was surprised Joe had joined Lamp's church at all, but he'd told me once that he'd been attracted by the man's mind and his knowledge of the Bible and that he'd actually enjoyed their political arguments at first. But in those days, the Reverend had also contributed church income to Joe's food drives, scholarship programs, and drug-treatment center.

When I asked Peg why the service had been switched, she explained that Calvary's sanctuary simply wasn't big enough for the expected crowd and that Reverend Lamp had kindly volunteered his for the service. That made it practical to hold the service there, but it still didn't make it appropriate.

I got back to the hotel about eight-thirty and called Molly. After that, I spent a couple of hours reading letters and printouts, then switched on the TV for some mindless entertainment.

I tuned in on a vintage black-and-white thriller as a sweaty young hood was being grilled under the hot lights. Watching him eagerly spill everything he knew, I thought that that was just what we needed right now. If an associate of the killer happened to come forward and confess all, it would certainly save the rest of us a heap of time and trouble.

18

Victory Baptist Church, like Goodtimes Executive Escorts, was located on the edge of River Oaks, and it was there for the same reason—because the well-to-do inhabitants were a good source of income for both.

The church covered half a city block, with the rest of the block paved to provide parking for the congregation. It was an ugly T-shaped building in beige brick, topped by a puny little steeple with an oversized cross.

The invited guests had been asked to arrive before ten-thirty to make way for the general public at eleven. By ten o'clock, there was already a line of cars trying to get into the church lot. IDs were being checked, and I saw them turn away a young couple whose names, apparently, weren't on the list.

It had been a long time since I'd had anything to do with churches and a couple of years since I'd been inside one. My last visit was also for a funeral—Juice Hanzlik's.

The subject of churches suddenly took me back to Saturday morning, at the start of this. Just before hearing the radio newsman confirm that Joe was dead, I'd caught the tail end of a report on a robbery at a local church. I hadn't registered the name of the church at the time, but I realized now that it was Victory Baptist. It was because my unconscious had put the death and the robbery together that I'd thought it was appropriate that Joe's funeral was being held there. A curious thing, the mind.

Spectators lined the sidewalks all around the church, but they were concentrated around the main entrance. Police held them back to allow us VIPs to reach our seats, but the press had claimed the grass in front for its own. I had to run the gauntlet to reach the front door, dodging cameras and microphones, while being asked by half a dozen people who I was and did I have a comment.

When I made it to the doorway, my name had to be checked off another list before I was allowed to enter. The air-conditioning felt icy after the heat, and I sneezed at the sudden drop in temperature.

There was a wall rack in the entry hall containing pamphlets, with a sign above advertising "Free Bible Study Cassettes!" The pamphlet explaining the offer was entitled "Time is Running Out!" Not on the offer, it appeared, but on our lives. We were all living under a death sentence, the pamphlet said, which only God's Holy Son was capable of commuting. Lamp Ministries operated entirely on voluntary contributions, it went on to say. No price had ever, or *would* ever, appear on any of his materials, and anyone desiring Bible teaching could receive his tapes or books "completely without financial obligation." However, if gratitude for the Word of God moved a reader or listener to give, they were naturally free to contribute whatever they saw fit. Judging from the size and the prosperous look of the place, his followers were moved to contribute handsomely.

I had read articles about Colonel Lamp and a few interviews and thought I knew basically what he stood for. I knew he was a retired Army officer, a Korean War hero, a rabid anticommunist, and a staunch believer in the righteous use of American military might. I knew he'd received his calling in the late fifties, that he'd started his ministry in a small church in Deer Park, and had ridden the conservative backlash at the end of the '60s into stardom. Like Saddam Hussein, he'd seen the Kuwaiti War as a holy war, interpreting it in accordance with the signs and portents described in the

Book of Revelations. He believed in the literal truth of the Bible, capital gains, and the cruise missile.

. . . .

When I sat down beside Peg, she took my hand.

I gave it a reassuring squeeze and whispered, "You okay?"

She shook her head, staring straight ahead at Joe's flower-draped coffin.

I gave her hand another squeeze, then leaned forward to ask her father about the robbery.

He couldn't believe my ignorance. "Where've you been?" he wanted to know. "It's not every day that five million dollars gets stolen from a church?"

"Five million?"

"That's right. It's been all over the papers, even up in Austin."

I was embarrassed. "Sorry. Guess I've been preoccupied. If it isn't directly related to the case, I just haven't paid any attention to it."

He nodded, understanding preoccupation.

It was awkward whispering across Peg, but she didn't seem to notice. "Why would a church have five million dollars just sitting around?" I asked. "Surely donations aren't *that* good."

"It was the El Salvadoran Relief Fund, collected by churches all over the country. It was supposed to be presented to an El Salvadoran official at a ceremony to be held here on Friday, but it was stolen earlier that morning."

"Why wasn't it in a bank?"

"Lamp doesn't trust banks," he said. "He's downright paranoid on the subject. He believes that bankers tattle on their depositors, and to him, the church's money is strictly the church's business. He has a counting room and a vault downstairs for his money, and there were security guards on duty the night it was stolen."

"So, how was it taken?"

"The guards were knocked out and tied up."

"How'd the robbers get into the church without setting off the alarms?"

"That I don't know."

"Any arrests?"

"Not to my knowledge."

Five million dollars stolen the day Joe died, stolen from a church Joe had once attended. Was it coincidence, or was there a relationship? I recalled Juice Hanzlik's theory about coincidence: one's a possibility; two's a conspiracy.

Eight of Joe's teammates flew in from the coast to serve as pallbearers, but they'd have to fly back right afterward, since they were playing tonight in San Diego. They trooped down the center aisle and came over to speak to Peg.

Dwight Samson took his turn with her, then shook my hand and pulled me aside. He wanted to know how I was coming with the investigation and was clearly disappointed in my lack of progress.

"You gotta *do* something, Bull," he said. "Everybody's sayin' Joe did it. Even the team's startin' to believe it."

"People believe what they hear," I said, as the public started filing into the balcony.

"I was hopin' this might pull us together," he continued, "that some good might come of it. But it's just tearin' us apart. We're at each other's throats half the time, and we're playin' like dog shit because of it."

I clapped him on the shoulder. "Maybe we can all turn it around," I said. "But I'm just getting started, and I'm going to need help. So, if you think of *anything* I should know, call me at the Warwick."

"That reminds me," he said. "Mussleman sent you a letter."

"Kurt Mussleman?"

"Yeah, you believe that? I think it's the first time he ever spoke to me directly." He pulled an envelope out of his jacket pocket.

I took it, asking, "He say what was in it?"

"No. He told me I didn't need to *know,* that it was none of my damn business anyway. Said it was purely between him and you, and that all he wanted me to do was deliver the damn thing."

I had to smile. "A charmer, isn't he?"

"A reg'lar Cary Grant," he agreed.

When Dwight was called over to meet somebody, I tore open the envelope. The letter was written on a sheet ripped from a long yellow legal pad, but the penmanship was surprisingly elegant, like my mother's.

It said:

Cochran,

You wanted to know about Ahern and the Oliver girl. Well I saw them together about three weeks ago just before we left on that road trip to Atlanta. I saw her after the game one night standing off to the side near the top of the ramp like she didn't want to be noticed. She was a little older than I usually like them, but she still looked good. So I walked over and introduced myself and offered to buy her a drink someplace quiet. She let me down nice and easy with a smile and said she was waiting for somebody, so I walked on. As I was driving off I remembered I'd left my new gamer in the club-house and I wanted to do some work on it, so I went back.

As I pulled in I saw Ahern and the girl standing by his pickup. I went in to get the bat and when I got back outside the pickup was gone. I figured Holy Joe had finally fallen to temptation, but as I was leaving I saw the girl walking along all by herself. So for what it's worth they didn't leave together that night.

That was the only time I ever saw her and I don't know what good any of this will do you, but there it is. It's no secret that I never liked the son of a bitch, but I still can't picture him killing anybody. Unless he did it like you did with a baseball.

Mussleman

Talk about an unlikely source. Maybe the man had a heart after all. Peg had told me that Joe had been worried since before that short road trip, and I wondered if the meeting in the parking lot was Joe's first with Cordelia Mae.

I would have told Peg about the letter, but she was talking to the mayor, and the service started a few minutes later.

The eulogy was given by Reverend Nathaniel Slocumb, the

minister of Calvary Baptist. Other speakers included the mayor, Dwight Samson, and Reverend George Lamp. Peg had agreed to let Lamp say a few words because he had been kind enough to volunteer his sanctuary.

When his turn came, the Reverend strode up to the lectern, firmly gripped the sides with his hands, and said in the voice of a man who enjoys hearing himself talk, "Joe Ahern was a great American. He loved his God, his wife, his sport, and his country—not necessarily in that order." He paused for polite chuckles. "We didn't always agree on politics, but I have no doubt that he loved America as much as I do. As much as we *all do!*" His voice rang out proudly in the hall. "Of President Bush's thousand points of light, Joe's work in the name of the poor people of this state has to be considered among the brightest."

An ironic comment, I thought, given the source of their conflict.

"Such a man is irreplaceable," he went on, "and we're all poorer for his passing. But the manner of that passing should be a caution to us all." Peg went rigid beside me. "We are born in sin," continued the Reverend. "We live and die in it. And none of us stands immune to the weaknesses of the flesh. Only the holy grace of the Redeemer lies between us and perdition."

Peg's father muttered something under his breath.

"Joe represented all that is great about this nation," the Reverend went on. "Born into a humble household, he climbed by grit and determination to the absolute pinnacle of his profession, winning the love of a beautiful woman along the way and reaping all the rewards that a free marketplace can offer. If he didn't find that sufficient for his happiness, then perhaps the fault lies as much with us as it did with him. Perhaps it's the price we pay for no longer valuing excellence in this country."

Justice Sanders whispered, "Sonofabitch."

The Reverend took a dramatic pause, as he slowly scanned the sanctuary, then quietly concluded, "I believe that Joe was among the chosen on this Earth, one of those tapped by the Almighty to serve as his vessels among us. Like all who are selected for such duty, he was an impure vessel. It's the only way we come. But in Joe's short stay on this planet, he surely did his best to live the life of a Christian. And if, in the end, he faltered, you can be likewise assured that he now stands forgiven at the feet of his Gracious Savior!"

The Reverend stood there for a moment afterward, listening to the murmur of response sweeping over the congregation, then turned and walked to a highbacked throne chair to the right of the lectern and sat down.

He'd spoken in a reasonable tone, and there was something in what he said, particularly in that bit about our not valuing excellence anymore. But his cruelty was obvious. Every word he'd spoken implied acceptance of Joe's guilt, and it struck me that only a particularly low kind of character would use a funeral service as a forum for vengeance.

. . . .

While organ music accompanied the exit from the sanctuary, many of the dignitaries stopped by to express their personal condolences. Near the end of the line was Reverend Lamp.

He was smaller up close than he'd appeared at the lectern—nearly a head shorter than me—and I figured he must have stood on some sort of fold-down platform when he'd spoken.

Peg told him coldly, "I should never have let you speak. I see that now, and I won't make the mistake of trusting you again."

He seemed honestly shocked. "You misunderstood me," he said. "The last thing I wanted was to offend you or Joe's memory. I was only trying to say that we are *all* imperfect—it's the human condition—and that Joe should not be judged too harshly for his humanity." Seeing that she wasn't buying it, he gave up and turned to her father. "Justice Sanders, I assure you that—"

The Justice cut him off, saying in a tone as frigid as his daughter's, "I have nothing to say to you. The law says you can't slander the dead, so what you said here can't be considered actionable. But I assure you it *won't* be forgotten."

The Reverend drew himself up, nodded at the Justice, then at Peg and me, and walked away. He looked every inch the injured party and seemed unaware that he'd done anything objectionable.

The man behind him just smiled at us nervously, glanced at his watch, and walked on, but I recognized him as Lamp's son, Jerry. As the developer of Shady Lane Estates, he was Joe and Peg's landlord, and they'd mentioned to me once that he was a famous architect. Since then, I'd often noticed his name and picture in the paper—in both the business pages and the art sections.

If you'd put his father in a lineup with any other ten men present, he'd have been my first pick for the retired Army officer and fundamentalist minister, but I would never have pegged Jerry as the high-powered real-estate tycoon.

He was glossy enough, better looking and taller than his dad. Dressed by Giorgio Armani, shod by Gucci, consulting a gold Rolex for his time of day. He took a good picture, but in person, he seemed much less substantial than his father, with the sun-dazzled look of a surfer.

He didn't fit, and that interested me.

19

Joe joined Howard Hughes and other Houston notables in the Glenwood Cemetery, on the northwestern edge of downtown.

I caught sight of Bubba Lusby, the manager of Bayou View Apartments, as we were leaving the graveside service, but I almost didn't recognize him. No tee shirt or sloppy jeans today. In honor of the occasion, he was dressed as a cattle baron, in a tan, western-cut suit, a string tie over a white ruffled shirt, and a brown ten-gallon Stetson. I saw him speak to Reverend Lamp, but after a few words, Lamp hurried him into the back of his limo.

After a long and mostly silent lunch with Peg, her father, and Aunt Florence, I drove to the downtown library and went through back copies of the *Post* and *Chronicle,* reading everything I could find on the robbery at Victory Baptist.

While the five million had been at the church, the drill had been three security guards on duty at all times. One outside, walking patrol, one inside the counting room, and one shuttling between the other two. All connected by radio. The first shift came on at three o'clock on Thursday afternoon to take delivery of the money, which arrived by Brinks at around three thirty-five. With the Brinks people and two of the guards present, Reverend Lamp supervised the counting of the money, and it was all there. It was returned to the bags in which it had arrived and placed in the vault, then the Reverend personally spun the wheel to lock it. After the shift changed at ten that evening, Lamp and the three new guards confirmed that the loot was still there.

At around two-thirty in the morning, the guard in the hall radioed that he was going to the crapper. A couple of minutes later, the one outside was knocked unconscious with two blows to the head. At about the same time, the guard in the restroom and the one in the counting room fell asleep, victims of a knockout gas that was fed under the doors.

The one outside woke up about forty-five minutes later, gagged and tied up behind an oleander bush at the side of the church. He was now in the hospital recovering from a concussion. The one tied to the john got an overdose of the gas and slept until the paramedics were prying him off the toilet seat. He was having trouble with his vision.

When the one in the counting room came to, he saw the door to the vault standing open and yelled for help. When that didn't work, he headed for the phone. He was still tied to the chair at the time, but he somehow made it to his feet and started hopping. He had to move very slowly, knowing that, if he fell down, he'd never get back up again. But he finally reached the phone and managed to knock the receiver off the cradle, then used a handy ballpoint pen clamped between his teeth to dial 911. The call was logged in at five-twelve A.M. and patrolmen were on the scene in five minutes. But by that time, the robbers and the money were long gone.

A slick operation all around.

. . . .

From the library, I went back to the hotel.

After a couple of more hours of hitting the files and printouts, I stopped and tried to make sense of what I'd learned so far. Some of the letters were angry. Several were written to people with whom Joe had had unpleasant business dealings—a landscaper and a plumber whom he believed had failed to live up to their contracts. One to a woman who'd refused to honor a pledged charitable contribution that was to be used for sending kids to summer camp. One to the sponsor of a commercial on which Joe had backed out—Joe's letter explaining that he'd found the spot insulting, sexist, juvenile, and not at all of the quality he'd been led to expect. And there was a whole sheaf of letters to Jason Grimes, the man who was writing his authorized biography. Joe had rejected the first draft, feeling that it was unfairly weighted to emphasize the dark period in his late teens. Grimes had stood his ground, insisting that the period was emphasized only because it was pivotal to an understanding of Joe's life. I knew Joe had dropped out of college in his freshman year and had almost died of a cocaine overdose. I knew it was a fundamentalist minister who had helped him get back into college and had even talked the school into reinstating his athletic scholarship. The biographer believed it was gratitude for his salvation from cocaine that lay at the root of Joe's religious fervor. Joe agreed that gratitude might have pushed him in the right direction, but he wanted to make it clear that God was real to him, not just a symbol of his gratitude. Until Grimes understood that, Joe said, he'd never understand the man he was writing about.

Anger was there, in some of his letters, as it was in some of those he'd received, but none of it seemed worth killing over. As for the story Joe had mentioned on the phone, I'd seen no sign of it. I'd read through about a third of the printouts and maybe a quarter of the letters in the box files, and I wasn't sure I was accomplishing anything. So, I decided to put the reading on hold for a while and concentrate on legwork. I'd been to Joe's and Dee-Dee's places of business. I'd read the police reports and a large chunk of Joe's correspondence. Now, all I had to do was figure out where to go from there.

. . . .

In Thursday morning's *Chronicle,* there was an interview by Floyd Malcovitch with Nivia Gonzalez, in which she said she'd seen Joe with Cordelia Mae Oliver off and on for months, whenever the team was in town. In answer to a direct question, she said that, yes, she believed they were having an affair.

It was so far from what she'd told me that I called her right away.

105

After ten rings, I slammed the receiver down, swept my keys off the table, and headed for the elevator. If she wasn't taking calls, then we'd just have to discuss it in person.

I was angry at myself as well as at her. I'd felt good after our talk and thought I'd done a fair job for a novice investigator. Now I found out she'd lied to me, or to Floyd Malcovitch. I didn't know why she would lie to either of us, but for Peg's sake, I hoped it was Floyd who got it wrong.

I caught Nivia leaving her apartment again, this time with a basket of laundry. She stopped when she saw me, then got a stubborn look on her face and started past.

When I stepped into her path, she butted me with her laundry basket and said, "Let me by."

"As soon as you tell me the truth."

She stepped back and started around me the other way, but again I blocked her.

"Move!" she said and butted me again.

"No."

"Damn you!" She turned and went back into her apartment, slamming the door behind her.

I knocked.

"Go away!" she called through the door.

"I'm not going anywhere," I called back, "until you tell me why you changed your story."

She pulled the door open the length of the chain and said coldly, "I don't have to tell you *anything.*"

"You didn't have to lie to me, either." I expected her to slam the door in my face again, but she didn't. "What happened?" I asked her. "Why did you tell me one story and tell Malcovitch another? What did *that* get you?"

"Please go away," she said quietly.

"At least tell me which story is true? I need to know that much."

"I can't tell you anything."

"Why not? What're you scared of?"

She sighed, said, "Just leave me alone," then closed the door again.

106

That was all I got out of her. I pounded on the door and told her I wasn't leaving until she answered my questions. But she wouldn't open up. I thought seriously about breaking it down, but in the end, I *did* leave without my answers.

20

I stopped at a pay phone and checked in with Pete Shirmer.

"Been trying to call you," he said. "Finished going over the Ahern stuff, and I talked to some people."

"And?"

"There's too much to go over on the phone. You had lunch yet?"

I hadn't, so we agreed to meet at a family-run Mexican place on Buffalo Speedway, almost in sight of the Dome. Over bottles of Dos Equis and plates of *huevos rancheros* he told me what he'd learned.

"Your friend had some good investment counseling from Bobby Rich and Max Abrams. They gave him a solid foundation—the usual mix of blue chips, treasury bonds, annuities, and some choice chunks of undeveloped real estate—but he demonstrated his real talent, or luck, in the area of high-tech, high-risk investments. That's odd because Rich and Abrams are extremely conservative and usually steer their clients toward sure things and steady, modest yields, so they must have been following his instructions on this. If so, he had even better aim here than he did on the mound. Only threw strikes—and he was painting the corners at that. He started in the late 'seventies by putting fifty thousand into a minor media company. After two mergers, that company is now one of the largest licensers of cellular technology in the nation. He also made sizeable investments in two bioengineering firms, both of which have registered major patents within the last two years. What can I tell you?" he concluded. "The guy had amazing control. His only iffy pitch was that research thing he was into with Jerry Lamp."

I sat up straight. "What's that?"

"You know, that center they were building for studying alternate energy sources."

It rang a faint bell. "I remember something. I think Joe showed me some literature on it one time. What's wrong with it?"

"Just that there've been some delays in starting construction."

"Why?"

"The site includes two lots in what used to be a middle-class white neighborhood, now mostly black and Hispanic. Lamp was only trying to square off his property boundaries, but the tenants say they should have been given first option to buy and that their homes were illegally sold out from under them."

"How does it look?"

"Well," he said judiciously, "the first-option clauses weren't written into the leases, but both insist that they were given verbal assurances from the owner. And depending on the discretion of the court, a verbal ammendment to a contract can be considered binding."

"Then it could mean a serious delay?"

"Depends on what you mean by serious. Delays are common in projects like this. The financial backing appears to be solid, and the building fund's in escrow, just waiting for construction to start. More than anything else it's a matter of bad PR."

"How's that?"

"Picture it." He pushed his plate aside. "Here you have this important research institute, a prestige project all the way, with a nationally known athlete putting his face and reputation on the line for a worthy cause. And it has to be damn embarrassing to have all this important work brought to a standstill by these people claiming that their homes have been snatched away from them."

"What part does Jerry Lamp play in this?" I asked.

"The center was his idea from the start, and he donated the land."

"What do you know about him?"

He sipped his beer. "I know he's a talented architect, and I wouldn't mind owning one of his houses."

"Ever spoken to him?"

"Once or twice."

"How'd he strike you?"

"Not a sparkling conversationalist."

"I met him yesterday, and he didn't impress me much."

"He may not be a whiz kid outside his specialty," Pete concurred. "But then not everyone can be as well rounded as you or I."

"Touché," I said. "I just meant he didn't strike me as the hotshot developer type."

He shrugged. "It was Alex Leiter who made him a star."

"Who?"

"Alexander Leiter. Lamp's former partner. The business end of Lamp and Leiter."

"You're kidding."

"No. I remember some people laughing at the name at first, but not for long. They made money from the start."

"Leiter," I repeated to myself.

"A good man," he said.

"You know him?"

"All my life."

Another coincidence, this time a lucky one. The generic variety were getting to be as common as Republican Presidents.

"We played tennis every week," he said, "from the time I was twelve until he got too sick a couple of years back."

"Did he ever say why the partnership broke up?"

"He claimed he was tired of the business and wanted to get out while he was still on top. Said he wanted to do some traveling and maybe work on a few smaller projects of his own, both of which he did. But his secretary told me he and Jerry had the worst fight

110

of their partnership the day before he announced his intention to leave."

"Know what it was about?"

He shook his head. "Alex didn't want to talk about it, and I finally gave up asking."

"No theories?"

He shrugged. "It was 'eighty-three, so the Bust may have been a factor. If so, it didn't slow Jerry down much."

"Know if Jerry was ever involved in anything shady?"

"Shady?" He laughed. "The man's a developer, for Christsake!"

"I'm serious."

"So am *I*."

"What about your friend, Leiter?" I asked. "He was a developer, too, wasn't he?"

"Sure, but he never found it necessary to discuss how he financed his projects."

"How'd Jerry manage to keep building when others couldn't?"

"Good question," he said. "But remember, they built the Empire State Building during the Depression. If you have the right project and know where to look, you can find the money."

"Yeah, but who had money *then?*"

"Well," he conceded, "you hear rumors about everybody."

"What do they say about Jerry?"

"I heard once that the feds were looking into his finances, suspecting him of laundering drug money."

"How does a developer launder money?" I asked.

"Oh, the opportunities are there," he assured me. "Big construction projects are money-rich environments. The weekly payrolls alone are often astronomical, not to mention the expense of materials. With a little creative bookkeeping, such a project could be made to conceal a lot of loose cash."

"Who was investigating him?"

"I heard it was the F.B.I."

"How long ago was this?"

"Three, four years."

"What happened?"

"Guess it was just a rumor, because I never heard any more about it."

"Any other rumors about Jerry?"

"He's always on the griddle. The doomsayers have been predicting his downfall ever since he split with Alex. But he keeps hanging on."

"What do they say about him now?"

"He's supposed to be in trouble again. They say he's overextended and has cash flow problems. It seems to me I also heard something about a big loan of his coming due, but I'd have to check on that."

"You don't happen to know where I might find Alex Leiter?"

"At home, I imagine. He just got out of the hospital."

"Where does he live?"

"The Rice area, not far from the Warwick."

"You have his address and phone number?"

"Of course," he said, and gave me both.

"Thanks," I told him. "I'm impressed. Didn't expect you to come up with all of this."

"Don't worry. I'll bill you for the time."

"I, uh—"

He laughed. "Just joking. Financial humor."

"Well, "—I waved for the check—"thanks again, and let me know if you think of anything else."

"You bet," he said. "I'm having a *ball.*"

Back at the hotel, I found the phone book and turned to the blue pages for the government agencies. There was a number for the Houston Headquarters of the F.B.I., so I gave it a try.

The phone was answered by a sexy female voice. "Federal Bureau of Investigation."

"Could I speak to the agent in charge, please?"

"He's out of the office at the moment, but I could let you speak to another agent."

"Yes, that would be fine, thank you."

After a moment, a youthful-sounding male voice said, "Special Agent Satterfield. Can I help you?"

"I'm calling about an investigation your office may have conducted."

"I'm sorry, sir, but all of our files are confidential."

"The information I'm seeking could have relevance to a current murder investigation."

"Are you a police officer?"

"No, I'm not. But I've been engaged by the wife of the murder victim to investigate the crime. If you have any questions regarding my authenticity, you can speak to Sergeant Puckett in Homicide. My name is Bill Cochran. He'll vouch for me."

"Yes, sir, but I'm afraid our files are *still* confidential."

"I understand that," I said. "But could I at least talk to the man who handled the investigation? Maybe he could answer some of my questions without having to reveal any confidential information."

He was silent for a moment. "That might be possible. When did this alleged investigation occur?"

"Around 'eighty-seven, I believe."

"Then it might have been handled by Agent-in-Charge Summers. I could make an appointment for you to speak with him."

"That would be perfect," I said. "What about this afternoon?"

"I'll check his schedule," he said. After putting me on hold for a moment, he asked, "How does three o'clock sound?"

"I'll be there. Thank you."

After that, I phoned the number of Lamp's ex-partner.

It was answered by an abrupt female voice. "Mister Leiter's residence."

"May I speak to Mister Leiter?"

"I'm sorry," she said, not sounding sorry at all, "but Mister Leiter is resting and can't be disturbed."

"Could I make an appointment to speak with him later this afternoon?"

"Mister Leiter is not receiving visitors."

"I only need a few minutes of his time."

"I'm afraid that's not possible," she said firmly and hung up.

I didn't have anything else to do at the moment, so I decided to drive by the place and at least take a look.

The house was only a few blocks off Main and five minutes from the hotel, in the section of the Rice University area where Shirley MacLaine lived in the movie *Terms of Endearment*. Her house was supposed to be in River Oaks, but this was where it was actually filmed. An upper middle-class neighborhood of grassy, tree-shaded lawns and two story, brick or frame homes, not quite big enough to be called mansions. But close.

Leiter's came closest of all. It was the biggest house on the block, two and a half stories, in white-painted brick, occupying an oversized corner lot. His lawn was impeccable, a rich carpet of freshly trimmed green. Bougainvillea blazed bright-red, yellow, and orange along the front of the house. A brick walk led from the front door to the sidewalk, splitting to form a circle around the base of a majestic live oak, which was also encircled by a wooden bench.

I took a right at a large magnolia and drove down the side of the house. Seeing that the back yard was hidden behind a tall redwood fence, I pulled over to the curb. The gate was in the side yard, across a stretch of grass, at the end of another brick walkway that ran around the corner from the front of the house. When I lifted the wrought iron handle, the gate swung open.

A tall man was sleeping in a wooden lounge chair, long skinny legs stretched out before him, chin on his chest, wearing only red plaid swimming trunks. He was bald on top, with a thin salt-and-pepper fringe, and had the gray pallor, loose skin, and flaccid muscles of the bedridden.

"Mister Leiter?" I said.

He didn't stir.

"Alex Leiter?"

The sun beat in at an angle over the trees behind me. Although it was only ten A.M., the temperature was already in the nineties. Sweat dripped from my armpits, running down my sides under my shirt, and a sheen of it covered the man from scalp to toes.

As I stepped in, my shadow moved to cover his face, and his eyes blinked open. He blinked some more, then lifted a long-fingered hand to shade his eyes.

"Mister Leiter?" I repeated.

The face was hardly lined at all, except for deep grooves arcing from the wings of his nostrils, around the corners of his mouth, to his chin, and two vertical lines between his eyebrows. When he squinted up at me, they lengthened up onto his forehead. It was a good face, with a broad brow, a square chin, high cheekbones, and eyes the same turquoise-blue as the water in his pool.

His free hand snaked out to the table beside him and found his sunglasses. He settled them on his nose and took a look, asking in a weak, but resonant voice, "Who are you?"

"My name is Bill Cochran," I said. "I'm a friend of Pete Shirmer's. He told me I might find you at home."

115

The storm door at the back of the house screeched open, and a woman cried, "What're you doing out here?"

"I represent Joe Ahern's widow," I told him.

"You get away from there," the woman said, coming down the steps.

Searching for his eyes behind the glasses, I said, "I'd like to talk about Jerry."

Slapping closer in her house slippers, the woman continued sternly, "Mister Leiter isn't seeing visitors."

He held up a hand to the woman and said, "It's okay, Bess."

She slap-slapped to a halt. A heavy young woman in a white nurse's uniform, with an angry red face.

He told her, "You can go back in, Bess. I'm all right now."

"Are you sure?"

"Absolutely."

"You don't have to talk to this man if you don't want to."

"I know that."

"I could throw him out," she added hopefully.

"I know," he said soothingly, "but I really don't mind a little company right now."

She turned a glare on me, then softened as she looked back at her patient. "Well, is there anything I can get for you?"

"Some lemonade would be nice."

"Good," she said, "I'll go make some."

"Thank you, dear," he said. As she turned and slap-slapped away, he added to me, "Won't you have a seat, Mister Cochran?"

I did.

11

As I pulled up another wooden lawn chair, Leiter clasped the arms of his chair with his hands and forced himself into a more upright posture, his muscles quivering desperately under the strain.

After Bess had closed the storm door behind her, he said in his precise, old-school, almost British manner of speech, "Bess is an excellent nurse and takes her responsibilities very seriously."

"I can see that."

"Is Jerry in trouble, Mister Cochran?"

"I don't know," I admitted. "Why do you ask?"

He smiled. "When a man sneaks past my nurse, a man I don't know, to speak to me about my ex-partner, it's logical to assume that the ex-partner might be in some sort of difficulty."

I grinned back. "Elementary?"

"In other words," he agreed.

"I'm investigating Joe Ahern's murder," I explained. "I was planning to see Jerry Lamp today. But, when I found out you lived nearby, I thought it might be interesting to hear what his ex-partner had to say first."

Leiter nodded. "Jerry was the best I ever worked with, Mister Cochran, and the projects we developed together were the highlights of my career." He looked off for a moment. "He was my discovery, you know? I was a judge in a university design competition, which Jerry won hands down with a marvelous modular design for subdivision housing. The modules could be arranged in many different configurations, so that no two of the houses would look exactly alike. A big improvement over the usual rows of clones.

"To shorten a long story," he said, "I hired him as an architect. After six months, I sold him a piece of the business. A year later, I made him my partner."

"Were you friends?"

"Not really," he said. "We shared few interests outside of the business. And when you take Jerry away from his models, he doesn't really have much to say."

"Models?"

"Have you been to his office?"

"Not yet."

"Then I won't spoil it for you," he said. "But, you see, Mister Cochran, some architects work on slant boards, some on PCs, but Jerry often skipped the plans altogether and went straight to the model. He worked easily in three dimensions. But when he went to blueprint, it was always precisely rendered. And when he said you needed ten thousand feet of lumber, you never had to buy an extra foot."

"You admired him," I said.

"I admired his abilities very much."

"What *didn't* you admire?"

His jaw tightened. "If it's gossip you're after, Mister Cochran, you've come to the wrong man."

"No, sir," I assured him. "I'm trying to find out why two people are dead. To do that, I need to know the people *they* knew. Jerry's one of them. I've only met him once, and to be candid, he didn't strike me as very bright."

"Intelligence wears many guises," he said. "Geniuses are often incompetent at the basic duties of existence simply because such duties are of no concern to them. Although the word is bandied about much too freely these days, I'd have to say that Jerry is possessed of a true genius for design. Yes, I admire him," he said. "But such a man, a man who lives in a world of waking dreams, of holographic images in the mind, is not easy to work with. At his model table, Jerry was precise, tireless, and unstinting, but trying to talk business with him was one of the more challenging aspects of our professional relationship. No, Mister Cochran, it's not intelligence Jerry lacks; it's attention. And if he appears absent at times, it's only because he *is*."

I nodded. "Why did you break up the partnership?"

"We had a difference of opinion."

"About what?"

He lifted his chin. "It was a business matter."

"When you asked me if Jerry was in trouble, what sort of trouble did you have in mind?"

He pursed his lips. "It was an idle question."

"I've heard a rumor that he was involved in money laundering."

"Rumors!" he scoffed. "More people have been ruined by them than disease or poverty."

I wasn't sure about that. "So, the substance of that rumor had nothing to do with your breakup?"

He considered me for a moment. "How long have you lived here?"

"Since 'seventy-nine."

"Then you were here during the Bust."

"I was running a moving-and-storage business at the time."

"You felt it, too, then. As for me, I wasn't up to coping with the added stress, and I thought it was time to cut our losses. But Jerry wasn't ready to mark time."

"So, he bought you out?"

"Had to mortgage everything he owned to do it, but he managed. Had to slow down a bit, even abort a few projects, but he kept going."

"How'd he do it?"

He mulled that over for a moment. "I've spoken with him half a dozen times since I left the firm, none within the last few years. I don't know what he's made of himself, and all I could offer would be speculation. Suffice it to say that I have no firsthand knowledge of any wrongdoing on his part."

I nodded. "Did Joe Ahern ever come to see you?"

He opened his mouth, then closed it, and I could feel him looking at me through the tinted glasses. "No," he finally said, "but we spoke on the phone one day last week. Tuesday, I think it was."

"I'm surprised Bess let him talk to you."

"Bess," he explained with a tinge of humor, "is an Astros fan. And when Mister Ahern introduced himself, I believe she may have temporarily forgotten her professional responsibilities."

I smiled. "If you don't mind my asking, what did you and Joe talk about?"

"He, too, wanted to talk about Jerry, and we had virtually the same conversation I've had with you."

"Did you tell the police about his call?"

"No, I didn't. I had a relapse on Friday morning and only got out of the hospital yesterday. In between, I've been mostly occupied by the task of breathing regularly."

"I didn't mean to sound critical."

He shrugged. "I had no reason to think that the matters Mister Ahern and I discussed had anything to do with his suicide."

"I don't believe it *was* suicide."

"Of course you don't, or you wouldn't be here." The last word was hardly out of his mouth when his hands went white-knuckled on the chair arms. His jaw clamped down with a *click,* and his eyes rolled up into his head.

"Sir?" I said. "Are you all right?"

The storm door screeched open, and Bess cried anxiously, "What is it?"

"He's in pain, I think."

She was across the terrace and on me in a blink, shoving the tray of lemonade and glasses into my hands. As I juggled them, she turned to Leiter and pulled out a plastic-wrapped syringe and a sealed packet of cotton balls. She deftly tore them open and swabbed a place on his thigh, soothing him with, "You just hang on, sir. We'll chase that pain in no time."

He was rigid as a board as she slipped the needle into what was

120

left of his thigh muscle. She slowly depressed the plunger, then slipped the needle out as smoothly as she'd inserted it. After swabbing the point of injection with another ball of alcohol-dampened cotton, she turned on me with the syringe extended like a weapon. "I think you should leave now," she said tightly.

I waited to see Leiter relax slightly as the drug began to take hold, then nodded at her grimly professional face and left the way I'd come.

23

The Houston Headquarters of the F.B.I. is on East T.C. Jester, where it winds along White Oak Bayou, just above the North Loop. It's housed in a twelve-story, glass and cement building called Park on the Bayou, which is connected by a covered walkway to a five-story gray concrete parking building.

The building was pleasantly cool inside and smelled new. The lobby was two stories tall, floored in marble tiles, and decorated with long green-leaf plants. The F.B.I. offices were on the second floor, behind glass doors.

The sexy voice I'd heard on the phone belonged to a woman of retirement age, with overly hennaed hair a peculiar shade of mauve and semaphors of rouge on her cheeks. Her name plaque said MS. COOK.

"Can I help you?" she asked.

"Bill Cochran to see the Agent-in-Charge."

"Ah, yes, sir. You're a bit early, I'm afraid. Won't you please sit down? He'll be with you in a few minutes."

"Thank you."

I watched the government-issue wall clock count off the final three minutes and twelve seconds before the hour. As the long, skinny second hand ticked forward on the last second, Ms. Cook said quietly, "All right, Mister Cochran, you may go in now."

The man was younger than expected, younger than me by five years at least, in his middle thirties. He was five-ten or so, had a slender build, a bouncy walk, and wore round, wire-rimmed glasses.

"Bob Summers," he said and extended his hand.

"Bill Cochran." I took it.

He gave me a firm grip, said, "Have a seat," and crossed back behind his desk.

It was uncluttered, with both his IN and OUT baskets empty. The screen on his computer terminal was turned away from me, but I could see green lines of data reflected in his glasses.

His manner was easy, his voice a pleasant baritone. "Special Agent Satterfield said you were interested in one of our investigations."

"From around 'eighty-seven," I said. "I'm not sure of the exact dates."

"The agent told you that our files are confidential."

"Yes, he did. But after I explained that I was investigating a murder, he agreed to let me speak to you."

He nodded. "You're not a policeman, I understand."

"No, I'm not. But Joe Ahern's widow has asked me to look into his death."

"Are you a private investigator?" he asked.

"No, I'm just helping out a friend."

He nodded. "And what is this case of ours that you're interested in?"

"One concerning a developer named Jerry Lamp."

His eyebrows went up a centimeter. "How," he asked, "could this alleged case of ours have any bearing on a murder investigation?"

"I'm not sure," I admitted. "It's just a hunch."

"You have some basis for your hunch?"

"Jerry Lamp had a business relationship with Joe Ahern, and there was some trouble in the business. Joe called Lamp's ex-partner a few days before he died to ask him some questions about

Jerry. And the manager of the apartment building where Joe died knows Jerry's father. When I heard a rumor that Jerry was once investigated by your office for laundering drug money, I thought I might be onto something."

"You think there might be a motive in it for murder?"

"Possibly," I said.

"Any evidence?" he asked.

"No," I conceded.

"And you're hoping I can provide you with a lead?"

"That would be nice."

"Well,"—he settled back—"I'm sorry, Mister Cochran, but I would need a court order to reveal the subject or substance of any of our files or investigations."

That certainly sounded like a dismissal, but he didn't get up to show me out, so I stayed where I was. I said, "You recognized Jerry's name, didn't you?"

"Of course, I did," he said mildly. "Mister Lamp is a prominent member of this community."

"I think it was something more personal than that."

"Do you?" he asked with amusement.

"I do," I said. "I think something about Jerry Lamp bothers you, and I think that's why you agreed to see me."

"You didn't mention the subject's name when you made the appointment," he pointed out.

"No, but I said the case was in 'eighty-seven, and I mentioned a current murder investigation. You would remember a major money laundering case, even four years later, and there's no recent murder that's received more press than Joe Ahern's. It's public knowledge that Joe and Jerry are connected, so you could have added it up."

"Interesting theory," he said. "I could argue that I was merely performing my civic duty in assisting with a murder investigation."

"And even if you *knew* something, you couldn't tell me about it, could you?"

"Probably not," he conceded.

"If you *could* tell me," I went on, "I wonder what you would say."

"I *could* say anything," he said. "I could tell you a bald-faced lie, and you'd never know the difference."

"You could," I agreed.

He stared at me for a beat, then deliberately turned his chair away to look out the window. For a long moment, he said nothing, and when he finally spoke, he did so quietly, as though talking to himself. "I could tell you that the F.B.I. listens to rumors, too, that we follow up leads from other local and federal agencies and wade through reams of printout. Sometimes, we receive a helpful call from a nosy neighbor or disgruntled relative or anxious competitor. But even with that kind of help, putting a case together is never easy. And sometimes, after an agent goes to all the trouble of putting one together, just when he has the bad guy in his sights, the bastard slips away. The subject's father, for example, might be a powerful man, with friends in high places, and he might use his influence to block the investigation. Hypothetically speaking, something like that might stick in a person's craw."

"Would this person be likely to share what he knew with the police?"

"Not if he wanted to keep his job," Summers said, "hypothetically speaking, of course."

"And I don't suppose it would be kosher to quote such hypothetical speculation."

"Wouldn't do much good, would it? As speculation, it certainly wouldn't be accepted as evidence."

"No, of course not."

He turned back and put his hands palms-down on the blotter. "Sorry I couldn't be of more help."

"Thank you anyway," I said and stood up.

He shoved back in his chair, got up, and strode around the desk. "Thank you for coming," he said. Showing me to the door, he added, "I hope you find what you're looking for."

. . . .

When I got back to the hotel, I went through the printouts and box files until I found all the letters between Joe and Jerry. There were thirty-two of them, written over the last eight years. The first in order of date was Joe's declaration of his intention to purchase the property in Shady Lane Estates. Next, came a series of letters discussing the terms of the transaction, then one from Jerry officially welcoming Joe to Shady Lane. This was followed by several about the design of the house Joe proposed to build there. Only a handful of letters were exchanged over the next few years, all having something to do with the Estates, though I'm sure there were also Christmas and birthday cards, invitations to housewarmings and other parties, that wouldn't appear in these files. In '88, they began to discuss a notion Jerry had for an energy research center in Houston. Joe took to the idea immediately. It seemed appropriate to him that the former capital of the oil patch should be in the forefront of the search for new energy sources. Renewable sources. Ecologically safe sources. So, he'd gladly given his name and some of his money to the project. He'd loved Jerry's architectural design for the building, and the fundraising had gone well. The money had come in, and they'd met their goal without much difficulty. They'd bought the last two parcels of land, and the date for the groundbreaking had been set. Then the trouble had started. The *Chronicle* had published an interview with the two tenants, in which they'd publicly aired their grievances. Then the tenants had gotten legal help and had filed for a restraining order against the Center. Joe had sympathized with the tenants from the start and had wanted to know if the two parcels were really necessary to the project. Jerry had insisted that they were. Joe had wanted to stop the trouble by finding homes for the people, but Jerry had said it wasn't their problem and that to behave otherwise would only encourage further lawsuits. The land, he'd said, was now property of the Research Center, and any legal problems were between the original owner and his former tenants. The last letter was dated about two weeks before Joe died. If there was any further discussion of the matter, it wasn't in writing.

24

I went to see Jerry the next morning. He had a suite of offices on the twentieth floor of the Pennzoil Tower, one of twin trapezoidal monoliths in dark glass that filled a block of downtown on Milam, just south of Jones Hall. The office decor was Navaho Modern, with brilliantly colored rugs hanging on earthtone walls, fragments of pottery in glass cases on sandstone pedestals, and potted cacti strategically placed about the room.

The receptionist's plaque said her name was Cynthia Simms. She was cute, birdlike, and costumed as a schoolmarm, in a prim white blouse, pinned-up hair, and bookish hornrims. "Can I help you?" she asked with a bright bucktoothed smile.

"Hope so," I grinned back. "I'd like to have a word with Mister Lamp."

Ms. Simms nodded and asked politely, "Do you have an appointment, Mister, uh—"

"Cochran," I said. "No, I'm afraid I didn't make an appointment."

She emitted a regretful "Oh."

"Is that a problem?"

"Well—" she began.

"Couldn't you work me in?" I begged. "I only need a few minutes of his time. Fifteen minutes at the most."

"I don't know," she said hesitantly. "Mister Lamp is awfully busy this morning."

"Won't you please try?" I batted my lashes at her.

She emitted an unprim laugh. "Don't suppose it would hurt to try. I'll have a word with him as soon as his conference is over. Could you give me some idea of your business?"

"Just say that I'm here to represent Joe Ahern's widow."

"Oh," she said, with sudden sympathy, "I feel so sorry for that poor woman."

"Me, too."

"You know, Mister Ahern was in here only last week."

"He was?" I asked as conversationally as possible.

"On Monday, a few days before he died." She shook her head. "It's so sad."

"That it is," I agreed. "How did he seem to you?"

"A little distracted, maybe," she said. "When I told him good-bye, he didn't seem to hear me. And he was usually so friendly."

Joe saw Jerry on Monday. On Tuesday, he spoke to Alex Leiter and was seen at Cordelia Mae's. There seemed to be a pattern here.

"I'll see what I can do," Ms. Simms promised.

"Thanks."

There was a large display table off to the right. As I strolled over, I could see what Leiter had meant about not wanting to spoil it for me. Architectural models are always dressed up with trees, even if the actual site will be bare of vegetation. Because nature is hard to fake, these "natural touches" are usually the weakest part of the illusion, but the stand of pine trees that surrounded this model looked remarkably like the real thing. Even up close. The key, I realized, was that no two of the trees were exactly the same height or shape or had the same pattern of branches.

The building wasn't bad either, and not just in the quality of its model work. It looked natural and appropriate to its environment. Its scientific purpose was revealed in solar panels and satellite dishes, but the panels were decorously confined to the rooftops and the satellite dishes to the inner courtyard. The building was two stories tall, but the wide, sheltering eaves made it appear to hug the ground. The first level was walled in rounded river stone and the second in carved wooden panels. The mossy earth mounded up to the sides made the structure look half-buried, giving the impression of an iceberg, as though nine-tenths of it was hidden from view.

That was no exaggeration, judging from the architectural plan displayed in three-dimensional cross section on the TV monitor hanging over the model. The graphic depicted a ten-story building, with all but one and a half of its levels under ground.

"I like it," I said.

The receptionist looked up from her computer terminal with a proud smile. "That's the Energy Research Center."

"Great model work."

"Isn't it?" she agreed. "Mister Lamp always executes them himself."

Wondering how a busy executive found time for something like this, I said, "He's very good, isn't he?"

"The best," she concurred.

I was thumbing my way through an *Architectural Digest* when the conference finally broke up. A chubby young man in red suspenders charged out of the double doors leading back to the executive offices, shedding loose sheets from an enormous armload of paper. He was trailed at a more seemly pace by a man of about my age, who stooped to gather the pages on his way out. They exited through a door behind the model table, which apparently led to more offices.

After a word with Jerry on the phone, the receptionist told me, "Mister Lamp will try to work you in after lunch. Perhaps you could come back then."

"Thanks," I said. "But if you don't mind, I'll just sit here awhile. I don't feel like going out in the heat right now."

"Another scorcher," she cheerfully agreed.

Truthfully, I didn't have anywhere to go and thought I might learn something just by sitting in Jerry's outer office.

"Care for a cup of coffee?" she asked.

"If it's no trouble."

"None at all. How do you like it?"

"Black, no sugar."

"Della," she said into the phone, "would you bring out a cup of coffee, please. Black, no sugar. Thanks."

A moment later, a pretty young black woman in a bronze business suit came out of the doors to the executive offices. She brought me coffee in a delicate bone china cup, with the Lamp Enterprises logo embossed in gold. The coffee wasn't Kona, but it wasn't bad. I sipped it, watching people go in and out of the double doors.

Mixed in with the guys in suits, there were several construction types in work boots, jeans, and plaid shirts. Two of the visitors were women, one in a severely cut business suit, carrying an artist's portfolio, and one in tennis togs, carrying her rackets.

After an hour of this, a visitor of a different sort appeared. He was a skinny young man in a black tee shirt and black jeans, with white pipe-cleaner arms, a thin sickly face, and the twitchy, strung-out look of a speed freak. He had enough earrings and studs on his left ear to give his head a permanent tilt. He had a tattoo of a snake on his upper arm and a hairdo of blonde spikes with pink tips.

Ms. Simms made a face when she saw him. He didn't give her his name, and I couldn't hear what she said when she spoke on the phone to Jerry. "One moment," she told the young man.

He nodded, then wedged his fingers into the back pocket of his skintight jeans and pulled out a flattened pack of Tiparillos. I glanced at his feet, but his black cowboy boots were scuffed and down at the heel, with no fancy red designs on the toes.

The first two cigars were broken, but he finally found a whole one that was only a little bent. He got it going and managed a puff or two before a secretary came out to fetch him.

Five minutes after the kid vanished through the double doors, he reappeared, minus his cigar, his face twitching even worse than before.

After he left, I got up and thanked the receptionist for the coffee, saying, "Think I'll try Mister Lamp another day."

"I could put you down for two o'clock."

"I'll give you a call," I promised and hurried out.

130

15

I caught the elevator doors as they were closing and squeezed aboard. The car was crowded, and I was jammed in against the kid, close enough to smell him. Under the sticky sweet odor of his styling mousse, was a resinous hint of marijuana and Mennen Speed Stick. My brands, both of them.

The kid took no notice of me, so I surreptitiously looked him over. He kept his head down and tucked between his shoulders, as though expecting a blow, his lips moving as he talked to himself. No doubt about it: he was worried about something. Or very stoned. Or both.

As I was carried out with the flow at the lobby, I looked back to see that the kid hadn't moved. Not wanting to call attention to myself, I didn't get back on, but I stuck around to see the doors close. Assuming he was headed for the parking garage, I made my way out of the building at a fast walk, then broke into a trot on the sidewalk. I'd parked in front of the new Federal Building two blocks down Rusk, so I'd have to hurry to get back in time to catch him.

I'd left the windows down to keep the heat from building up, but the seat sizzled on the backs of my thighs, and the steering wheel was almost too hot to touch. It amazed me that, with all the tall buildings downtown, there never seemed to be any shade.

I started the pickup, saw an opening in traffic, and pulled out. Because the streets were mostly one-way, I had to go up three blocks, a block past the Pennzoil Towers, then take a left on Travis, another left on Capitol, and backtrack two blocks to the Towers. I drove past the exit from the parking garage, crossed Louisiana, then pulled to the curb, got out, and lifted the hood. Anybody leaving the Towers' garage would have to drive my way, and if I hadn't taken too long getting back, I might be able to spot him.

A snazzy red Mazda Miata came out of the garage and went past, driven by a dark-haired woman. A Mercedes with a balding male driver followed. Then a Volvo appeared and cut right onto Louisiana before it reached me. I didn't get a look at the driver, but I didn't picture the kid in a Volvo. Too sensible a vehicle, not to mention expensive. There was nothing after that for maybe thirty seconds, and I was starting to think I'd missed him. I was sure of it when the driver of a slightly seedy ten-year-old Toyota turned out to be a gray-haired woman. I'd taken too long getting back; that's all there was to it.

Then I saw the gray van. It was older and more battered than the Toyota, dappled with primer like a pinto's spots. When I caught a flash of pink spikes on the driver, I slammed the hood.

By the time I pulled out, he'd vanished around the corner onto Smith. But I spotted the van as I made the turn—stopped at the red light ahead.

When the light changed, he kept going south, past Tranquility Park—dedicated to the space program—past Hermann Square in front of City Hall, and past the main library. In the next block, he flicked on his blinker and drifted into the left lane.

I was behind him as he made the turn onto Dallas. I trailed him straight across downtown, past Foleys and Sakowitz, past the Four Seasons Hotel, beyond which I could see the George R. Brown Convention Center off to the left.

The building seemed to stretch forever and appeared to be constructed of white Lego blocks. Decorated with a framework of

132

oversized red and blue pipes running up the sides, over and around the top, it looked like a titanic set for *Anything Goes.*

The Center was coming up on the left when the kid made a right. I stayed one car back as he turned left and then right again onto Hamilton, which runs alongside and sometimes under Highway 59. I caught a light and lost sight of the van for a moment, but I picked it up again before he took the upramp to 59, which at that point is called the Southwest Freeway.

Once on the freeway, I eased back and let him show the way. It wasn't eleven o'clock yet, and traffic was light. As light as it ever got.

I was a little too casual about it and when he took the Shepherd-Greenbriar offramp, I was in the wrong lane and couldn't get over to catch it. I had to drive on to Kirby and circle back, then spend the next hour cruising around, trying to spot him.

In keeping with its Wild West heritage, Houston has always preferred to do without zoning laws, leaving commercial and residential development to shoulder each other for space. This area was typical, with its chaos of strip centers, apartment complexes, and single family homes. Along Shepherd, the strip centers were winning.

The Houston Key Map lists ninety-six shopping centers, a category that includes malls, squares, villages, commons, and plazas, plus combinations of the above, such as the Easton Commons Plaza Shopping Center. But I suspect that many of the smaller strip centers weren't on the list, as there appeared to be far more than ninety-six of them. It was in a strip center that I finally caught sight of the gray van.

The strip included a gardening supply store, a video arcade, a "homemade" ice cream shop, and as a reminder of the recession, two empty store fronts with FOR LEASE signs prominently displayed. There was also a large wholesale electrical supply outlet at one end, set at a right angle to the strip, the front facing across the length of the parking lot to the Hardees that sat off to itself at the other end.

There was a line of trees beyond the Hardees, separating the center from the house next door, and I found a parking place in a skimpy patch of shade. Unfortunately, the sun kept moving, taking my shade with it, and the pickup was an oven by the time I saw the kid again.

He came out of the electrical supply outlet and went to his van. After he got out what looked like an leather tool belt and took it back inside with him, I decided he must have a job to do. I figured it should be all right to leave for a while, but to be on the safe side, I stopped at a phone on my way out of the strip and called Jerry Lamp's office.

"Mister Cochran," Ms. Simms said eagerly. "Would you like to make your appointment now?"

"Not this time, sorry," I said. "But I wanted to ask you for a favor."

"Of course," she said. "How can I help you?"

"Could you tell me the name of the young man I saw in your office this morning, the one dressed in black, with the pink hairdo. I know him from somewhere, but I can't place him."

She said with undisguised disapproval, "That would be Jimmy McBride."

"Doesn't he do restoration work or something like that?"

"Not to my knowledge," she said. "He works for an electrical supply place."

"Right. That's it. Thanks a lot."

"You're welcome," she said. "Sure you don't want to make that appointment now?"

"I'll call you, I promise. Bye, now."

26

I took the Southwest Freeway back through downtown. Beyond the Convention Center, it swung to the north and became the Eastex Freeway. I got off onto I-10, called the East Freeway, took it over to 610, called the North Loop East, and got off onto East 90, also called Liberty Road or the Beaumont Highway. It's a two-way truck route, with two narrow lanes running in each direction, and I had to battle semis for the pavement.

I passed a huge trucking center with battalions of shiny new tractorcabs standing at attention in ordered rows of green and red and blue and white, their trailer hitches sticking out like long black tails behind them. I drove on for several miles, passing a truck stop and several gas stations shouting DIESEL, an office and warehouse park, and a large recycling center. Then I made a right onto Oates Road at a container storage terminal, with its stacks of silver boxcars that could be towed by truck, or carried on container ships, or loaded onto railroad flatcars.

The first stretch of Oates Road was sparsely populated, except by the dead. Harris County Cemetery lay green and thick with headstones off to the left. The number of houses picked up after that. Then a sizeable older development appeared to the left, and what

135

looked like pastureland to the right. Gently rolling grassland with a few clumps of trees. The fences had been torn down; the grass had been mowed, and a billboard had been erected about thirty feet back from the road, announcing the soon-to-be-constructed Energy Research Center.

Pete Shirmer had said the contested lots were on the south side, so I kept going in that direction. A brand new house with yellow aluminum siding stood at the edge of the field, new grass sprouting through a layer of straw in the yard. After a stretch of woods, I took a right. The street led back into another older development, with solid brick homes built in the fifties. Some were a little rundown, and several stood empty, with FOR SALE signs in the yards. Conager was the third street to the right. The houses and yards were well cared-for here, most with glassed-in porches or carports. Kids ran about or raced along the sidewalks on tricycles and bikes with training wheels. It was easy to see why somebody might not want to leave such a place.

The street ended at a line of trees, beyond which I could see open pasture. The last two houses had signs in front announcing that they were to be torn down to make way for the new Energy Research Center, and the house on the left had been gutted by fire.

I pulled to the curb and got out. The front of the house was mostly intact, with boarded-up windows and soot-stained brick above the windows and the door, but one of the side walls had collapsed and had brought most of the roof down with it.

The smell of damp ashes dueled with the scent of honeysuckle as I walked over for a closer look. As I stepped onto the sidewalk, the next-door neighbor stopped clipping his hedge and walked over to see what I was up to.

He was a handsome black man, probably in his seventies, wearing bermuda shorts, a short-sleeve shirt, and a straw hat. "Can I help you?" he asked.

"I saw this,"—I nodded at the gutted house—"and had to stop."

"Yes," he said, rocking on his heels, "a real shame, isn't it?"

"Sure is. When did it happen?"

"Friday night," he said. "Went up like a bomb." He gestured with the clippers at his house. "Blew out two of my windows in

136

the back there, and it's lucky my place didn't catch on fire, too."

"Friday night, you say?"

"That's right."

"Were you around when it happened?"

"Always around," he said. "I'm retired now. Don't travel much anymore."

"Notice anything suspicious?"

"Other than a house blowing up, you mean?"

I smiled. "Yeah, other than that." Thinking he might clam up if I told him I was investigating a murder, I said, "I was a volunteer fireman for a few years, and it just naturally makes me suspicious to hear you say it went up like a bomb."

He seemed to buy it. "Well, I don't know about you, but *I* think it's suspicious when a car drives by and cases a house. I was sitting on the porch that evening right at dark, when this vehicle turned around and parked in front of Mister Grace's house. It sat here a minute or two and pulled away as soon as I stepped off the porch."

"Could the driver have gone into the house without your seeing him?"

"No, sir," he said, "he couldn't. From my rocker, I had a clear view the whole time."

I nodded. "Get a look at the driver?"

He shook his head. "He threw his lights on bright to blind me as he pulled out."

"You only saw it that once?"

"That's right."

"When was that?"

"About an hour before the house went up."

"You didn't get a license number, did you?"

"No, I didn't."

"Do you know if any of your neighbors saw it?"

"I talked to Miz Hayes, the Williamses, and most of the others, but none of them saw a thing."

"What kind of car was it?"

"Wasn't a car at all. It was one of those vans."

"A gray one?"

He considered it. *"Could* have been. But, as I say, it was dark, and I couldn't rightly tell you what color it was."

I looked back at the house. "What about the people who lived here?"

"There's only Mister Grace now, and he was off visiting his sick sister."

"What'd he do when he saw what had happened?"

"Stood and looked at it awhile," he said, "then he walked around in the ashes some. I could see him through where the wall fell in, picking things up, looking them over, and putting them back down. He went away with a couple of things, though. Looked like a picture in one of those gilted frames and some kind of metal box with a handle on it, probably for his papers."

"Not much," I said.

"No, sir," he concurred, "not much at all."

. . . .

I drove back to town thinking about an explosion on property belonging to Jerry Lamp and a robbery at his father's church, both on the same day, the day Joe died.

An overturned tractor-trailer on I-10 stalled traffic and held me up for about fifteen minutes, so it was three o'clock by the time I made it back to the strip center. I half expected Jimmy to be gone, but the gray van was still parked in the same spot.

I was hungry and thirsty, so I bought three large cups of ice water, a burger, and some fries from Hardees, then settled down to wait.

A couple of hours later, a few minutes after five, Jimmy came out, climbed into his van, and pulled away. He headed north to Westheimer, then took it east to a gourmet sandwich shop in the Montrose area. I tailed him into a small gravel lot, big enough for twenty or so cars. He pulled in up front, so I drove on to the back. I watched him go inside, then waited a few minutes to make sure he wasn't just making a phone call before following him in.

It was a small restaurant with only as many tables as it had parking spaces. You didn't get much walk-in business in Houston. The decor was Spartan, with cheap yellow pine furniture and amateurish paintings on the walls, all with overly optimistic price tags. The hostess seated me across the room from Jimmy, who had his forehead pressed to that of an overweight, but pretty young woman, with tightly curled brown hair.

She appeared to be giving him a pep talk, and sometimes I could read her lips. Twice I saw her tell him, "It's gonna be all right."

Jimmy wasn't sure about that. And I had a notion that, if I knew what was worrying him, I'd be a whole lot closer to finding out what had happened to Joe.

As I was taking my first bite of lemon meringue pie, they got up to leave. I tossed money on the table, overtipping because I didn't have any small bills, then wrapped my pie in a paper napkin, and took it with me.

Jimmy was helping the girl into the van when I came out, and I had the pickup started by the time they pulled away.

He led me further east on Westheimer, which turned into Elgin as it ran southwest of downtown. He took a left at a small park, headed straight back to the Convention Center, and made a right on Dallas. I followed him under 59, past the brightly painted, pagoda-fronted home of the Chinese Merchants' Association. Behind it, were a few rows of two-story buildings that served as home to a number of small manufacturing concerns. When the van slowed and turned into an alley, I drove on by. Taking a quick look down the alley as I passed, I saw the van's brake lights go on. We'd run out of traffic, and there was nobody behind me, so I made a U-turn and parked at the curb, then got out and ran over to see what was up.

The van was parked about a hundred feet down the alley, half-hidden in a little niche on the right. Across from it, Jimmy was pulling down a fire-escape ladder with a hooked stick, like a cane. He and the girl climbed the ladder to the first landing, slid a window open, and slipped inside.

I thought at first they were there to burgle the place, but after half an hour, I began to wonder. I fetched the remains of my lemon pie from the pickup, and by the time I finished licking melted meringue off my fingers, I was sure that at least one of them lived there. Either that, or they were ridiculously slow burglars.

139

About 7:30, I walked up close enough to see that there were lights on inside. I figured they were settling in for the night and decided I wasn't going to learn any more standing in the alley, and there was something I wanted to check on at Peg's house.

Peg's father was visiting a sick friend at Hermann Hospital, so she was alone with Aunt Florence and eager as always for any scrap of news.

"What is it?" she asked, sensing my excitement.

I headed for the stairs, promising, "I'll tell you about it. But there's something I have to check on first."

"What?"

"C'mon. I'll show you."

She followed me up the wide staircase and down the second-floor corridor into the master bedroom. The windbreaker was still hanging where I'd left it, with the crushed pack of Tiparillos still in the pocket. I held the pack by a corner until I could get a tissue from the dresser, being careful not to smudge any fingerprints. Inspecting it more carefully than I had the first time, I used another tissue to pull out the book of paper matches from under the cellophane on the back. There was an advertising logo on the front and back of the book. Nothing was printed inside, but two telephone numbers had been scribbled there in pencil. No names, just numbers.

I held it out to her. "Is this Joe's writing?"

She examined it carefully. "No. Whose numbers are they?"

"I don't know yet," I said as I walked to a bedside table and picked up the phone. I let the first number ring a dozen times before hanging up. The second was answered almost immediately by the unmistakable high-pitched voice of Bubba Lusby. "Bayou View Apartments. C'n I help you?"

When I put down the receiver, Peg said, "Bull?"

"One second." I pulled out my notepad. The first number looked familiar. After a brief search, I found out why. It was the number I'd copied down from the phone in Dee-Dee's apartment.

By that time, Peg couldn't stand it anymore. "Will you *please* tell me what is going on?"

I smiled at her. "I just made a breakthrough, I think."

"Tell me," she pleaded.

"This"—I held up the box of Tiparillos—"belonged to a young man named Jimmy McBride. At least, I think it did. This"—I showed her the matchbook—"was slipped under the cellophane on the back."

"Whose numbers are they?"

"They belonged to Cordelia Mae Oliver and the manager of Bayou View Apartments."

"What does it mean?" she asked. "Do you think this Jimmy McBride killed Joe?"

"I'm not sure what it means, exactly, but there's more. Quite a bit more, in fact." Feeling uncomfortable standing in her bedroom, I said, "Why don't we go down to the study, and I'll tell you all about it?"

When we were settled on the Chesterfield, I told her what Pete Shirmer had said about Jerry and explained how it had led me to Alex Leiter and the F.B.I. I told her about spotting Jimmy at Jerry's office and tailing him to his place of business. I described my visit to the Research Center building site, told her about the gutted house and the neighbor who'd seen a van like Jimmy's there shortly before the blaze. I told her about following Jimmy home.

"So, you think Jerry had something to do with Joe's death?" she asked.

"I can't be sure of that. But I know there's a connection between

Jerry and Jimmy. And if this pack of Tiparillos *was* Jimmy's, then he had the numbers of both the manager of the apartment building and one of the victims."

"How did Joe get it?"

"That's another thing I don't know. But I *do* know that he was talking to people. He was seen with Cordelia Mae three weeks ago in the parking lot at the Dome."

Her eyes widened. "Just before that short road trip?"

"Right." I gave her the letter to read.

She finished it, shook her head, and asked, "Kurt Mussleman?"

"People can surprise you."

"Isn't that the truth?"

"I know Joe spoke to Jerry last Monday and that he talked to Leiter on Tuesday. And he may have spoken to Cordelia Mae the same day."

She swallowed hard. "So, you think Joe found out about the arson, and Jerry had him killed for it?"

"I think somebody had him killed," I said. "But since the house burned down the night he died, I don't see how Joe could have already known about it. Maybe it was the plan to rob Victory Baptist that he was on to. Maybe he knew Jerry was involved in that."

"A lot of maybes," she said.

I nodded. "Maybes and ifs. *If* Jerry was involved in the robbery, then I would guess that somebody else did the planning. Designing buildings is one thing; planning an armed robbery is another. All I have to do is figure out who planned it."

"Any suspects?"

"What about Reverend Lamp?"

She was surprised, then thoughtful. Finally, she shook her head. "I have only contempt for the man right now, but I can't see him stealing from himself like that. Why would he need to? There's plenty more where that five million came from."

"Not for his personal fortune," I said. "He has to be considered a suspect. The robbery sounds like an inside job, and who'd make a better insider than the Reverend?"

"How does Jerry fit in?"

"That's a problem," I admitted. "I don't have anything yet that ties him to the robbery, except the coincidence that it was his daddy's church."

"So, what will you do now?"

"I'll keep an eye on Jimmy McBride and see where he leads me."

She nodded and slumped back into herself, clearly at a low ebb this evening.

"You okay?" I asked.

"No," she said. After a moment, she said quietly, "Would you stay here till Daddy gets back?"

"Of course."

Aunt Florence brought us hot chocolate with tiny marshmallows on top, and Peg and I sat together on the Chesterfield, blowing on our drinks until they were cool enough to sip.

After tasting hers, Peg said, "You know what I'd really like right now?"

"What?"

"A drink."

That surprised me. "As in alcoholic beverage?"

"As in a frozen daquiri," she said. "But the only alcohol in this house is for external use only. Joe wouldn't have liquor around. His mother was an alcoholic, you know?"

"No, I didn't."

"I went along with it because I knew what it meant to him. But tonight, I wouldn't mind getting plastered." She looked at me. "Does that sound awful?"

I shook my head. "You want me to go out and pick up something? I could even take a shot at daquiris, if you have a blender."

"No." She shook her head. "It was just an idea, and I don't want you to leave."

After a moment, I said hesitantly, "I have a joint."

"You do?"

"Uh huh."

"With you?"

"Yep."

"I haven't smoked marijuana since I was at UT," she said.

144

It felt strange offering pot to Peg, but she seemed to want to get high. And if anyone could use it right now, she could.

"Where is it?" she asked.

My boots were custom-made by a man up in Conroe, each with a zippered pocket inside the top, each pocket now containing a fat joint of Maui. Molly didn't like it when I smoked—her being a law enforcement officer and all—so I wasn't doing much weed these days. But I still carried a stash for emergencies.

After a week in my boot, the joint was more flat than fat, but I rolled it between my fingers and thumb until it took on something of the appropriate shape. Then I offered it to Peg.

She took the joint and held it awkwardly as I lit it for her. She took a small experimental hit, then lost it in a hacking cough, made a face, and handed it back to me. She passed on the second round but joined me again on the third. She took a longer pull this time and held it down. After the fourth round, she sighed on the exhale and laid her head on the back of the couch. "Good stuff."

I didn't argue.

We talked about everything and nothing, staggering from random thought to thought, as you sometimes do on grass. When we happened to stumble over the subject of children, Peg remarked that she wished they'd had some.

"But we couldn't," she explained. Anticipating my question, she added, "Nothing wrong with Joe. It was me." She got up to get a tissue from the desk, blew her nose, wiped her eyes, and sat back down. "We talked about adopting kids, and we did take a foster child for a year back in 'eighty-six, until his mother got out of prison. Jason Patrick Hickman was his name. He had his twelfth birthday while he was with us, and we had to be careful not to give him too much, since his mother would never be able to compete. He was a quiet boy, and this place scared him at first. It's so big. He hardly spoke at all for a couple of weeks, and it wasn't until we went on a fishing trip up to Big Bend that he finally opened up to us. He was confused about his mother being in prison and had somehow gotten it into his head that it was his fault. He and Joe spent hours sitting down by the river, talking about it and other things. Man and boy things, I suppose. The two of them sitting so close they looked like one animal with two heads." She sighed. "I loved having Jason with us, but . . ." Her hands tightened into fists. "When the time was up, it was just too hard letting him go."

She got up and brought the whole box of tissues back with her this time. When she'd tended to her eyes and nose, she said, "After that, we kept putting off filing for adoption. I don't know why, but we did. Of course, I had the kids I work with at church, and Joe had the ones at his sports center. The fact that they weren't *ours* bothered me, but Joe . . ." She shook her head. "He said once, not long ago, that maybe it was meant to be this way." She pulled out another tissue. "But then, he always did have a stronger belief in God's plan than I do."

28

I was back in the alley the next morning when Jimmy McBride and the unidentified girlfriend appeared on the fire escape. At this point, my plan had me running back to get the pickup so I could follow them. But I didn't. I stayed where I was, behind a jog in the wall, and watched them climb down the ladder. I let them get into the van and drive away, and still I didn't move. I gave them a few more minutes, time for them to realize they'd forgotten something and to come back for it. Only then did I finally come out of hiding.

The buildings to either side had few windows at ground level, but lots of them above. In case anybody happened to be looking down from one of them, I shoved my hands into my back pockets and casually strolled down the alley, just taking in the sights and stopping for a casual look behind a certain trash can. Oh, what's this?

The "cane" turned out to be a straight length of three-quarter-inch steel pipe about four feet long, with a curved piece of pipe screwed onto the end. I used it to catch the bottom rung of the fire escape ladder, and when I put my weight on it, the ladder slid down to me.

If anybody *was* watching, I'd just blown my cover, and they were already calling 911. It was time either to finish the bit or head for the truck, so I went up the ladder. The window was unlatched and slid silently upward. I climbed through, stood up, and looked around.

It was a loft, a big one, maybe sixty feet deep and twice that in length, mostly empty. Dead ahead, between me and the front door, two sprung sofas and several sagging armchairs circled a wagon wheel coffee table. To my right, there was a workout area with a tumbling mat, a Soloflex machine, and beside it, a setup for portrait photography—a blue sheet tacked to the wall, facing a grove of standing lights. To my left, rooms had been built out from the wall, with the new wall stopping a few feet short of the fourteen-foot ceiling. This wall had four doors in it. The first opened into a toilet, the second into a bedroom, and the last two were locked. At the far end of the new wall was a kitchen alcove, with a counter on the left and a refrigerator and stove on the right. A table and three chairs sat outside the alcove.

The Mr. Coffee was still turned on, and the pot was half full. I thought about turning it off or pouring myself a cup, but did neither. The fridge contained a festering slice of anchovy pizza, a lidless jar of Smucker's grape jelly, and a bottle of Rolling Rock beer. The garbage can was overflowing onto the floor, and the sink was mounded with dirty dishes. The open shelves above the counter held canned goods, foil, and plastic wrap. The cabinets below were mostly empty, except for a mop bucket, a can of Comet, and a family-sized box of laundry detergent under the sink. The cabinets had no backs to them, and the builders of the new addition had skimped on Sheetrock by omitting the panels that would have finished the wall behind the counter, so I could see into the darkness of one of the locked rooms beyond.

Grabbing the flashlight clamped to the wall next to the Mr. Coffee, I climbed into the cabinet, then slithered between two studs and climbed to my feet.

The flashlight showed me a workshop, with counters running the length of the room on both sides, divided into various work spaces. There was an area devoted to general repair, with several disassembled electronic components, an area for darkroom equipment, and a space with, among other things, two large plastic jars of unidentified powders, rolls of insulated wire, and a box of flattened red paper tubes like the one I'd found in Joe's safe.

I slipped one of them into my shirt pocket and looked around for something to take samples of the powders in. In a shoe box, I found a half-dozen small plastic containers that would have been perfect for the job, but I was afraid Jimmy might notice if two of the six were missing. Remembering the roll of aluminum foil on the rack over the sink, I put down the flashlight and crawled back through the cabinet to get it.

I straightened up and said, "How ya doin'?"

A short, hairy guy in jockey shorts and black socks sat at the table, looking up at me blearily from a mug of coffee.

"What the fuck?" he said in a gruff voice.

As he started to get up, I headed straight toward him, drawlin' in my best East Texas, "Dang pipes're leakin' agin."

That sat him back down. "Pipes?"

"Sprung a leak," I said, edging past.

"How'd you know to—"

"Reg'lar inspection," I explained, heading for the windows.

"Where ya goin'?"

"Need a wrench," I said and kept walking. "Gotta git it outta my truck."

I lost him somewhere in there, and when I looked back, he was up and moving toward one of the formerly locked rooms. As I dove for the window, he vanished through the door. To call the cops, I thought. But that wasn't it.

I made it down the ladder and was loping up the alley when I heard a flat crack behind me, and a slug slapped into the brickwork to my left. As the second shot went singing past my ear, I threw up my arms to cover my head and ran for my life. If he got off a third shot, I didn't notice.

149

29

When I got back to my room, I called Homicide. Puckett wasn't in, but they said they'd beep him for me.

Five minutes later, the phone rang, and Puckett said, "What can I do for you, Mister Cochran?"

"You got a pad handy, Sergeant?"

"Yeah, why?"

"I want you to take down a name and an address for me."

He was silent for a moment. "Okay, I'll bite. Let me have it."

I read him the address and gave him the name Jimmy McBride.

"Okay," he said. "Now, what am I supposed to do with it?"

"This young man might be able to tell you who killed Joe Ahern and Cordelia Mae Oliver."

Puckett sighed impatiently. "I know Ahern was your friend, but the case is closed now, and unless you care to tell me who the sonofabitch is who blew away two citizens at point-blank range, I've got other work to do."

"Are you satisfied that your investigation was as thorough as it should have been?"

"Satisfaction's got nothin' to do with it," he said. "When the Captain says it's closed, that's all she wrote. You show me new evidence, and we'll see what we can do."

150

"What if I told you I *had* new evidence."

Beat. "Do you?"

"You remember that red paper tube I found in Joe's safe?"

"You mean the one you lost before we got a chance to look at it?"

"I didn't *lose* it; it was stolen. But that's beside the point. If you search that loft, you'll find more of them, along with whatever they were being filled with."

The line was silent. "How do you know that?"

"I know," I said, "that's all."

"You haven't broken into somebody's home, have you?"

"I've told you all you need to know. The question is what're you going to *do* with it?"

"Let me try to explain something to you," he said. "To make a search, I need a warrant. For that we need evidence. And even if you gave me some, no judge'd even look at it if it was illegally obtained. Without it, we got no probable cause. Without probable cause, we got no search warrant. And," he added, "I hate to remind you, but it's thanks to you that we don't even know what the cylinder was for."

"It was an incendiary device," I informed him, "like the one Jimmy used to burn down a house the day Joe died."

"Where's your evidence?"

"In that loft."

"No, it isn't," he said with another sigh. "Even if it was there, it's not there *now*. If you did break in, and if these people were involved in something, then you've given them time to cover their tracks."

He was right. I could see that. I'd pulled a real boner. But it was embarrassing, and I hated being embarrassed more than just about anything. I knew all about it. I'd pulled real boners in Fenway Park in front of twenty-five thousand people. I knew it was time to back off and take my well-deserved licks, but I just didn't feel up to it. Instead, I told him, "At least I was doing *something.*"

He didn't yell at me. He was silent for a beat or two, then said quietly, "That may be so, Mister Cochran. But doesn't it seem

151

peculiar to you, that wherever you go, evidence just up and disappears?"

He had me there.

"You think that's helping Ms. Ahern?"

He knew I didn't, so he left it at that.

. . . .

After an early lunch, I sat in my room and thought about the case. Puckett was right. I wasn't helping Peg like this, not by losing every lead I stumbled over. I was proving to be just as incompetent as I'd feared, and I was tempted to say to hell with it. Especially after being shot at.

The trouble was, I'd made a promise to Peg. Plus, I'd long since proven I was good at quitting, and I was trying to cut back. In that spirit, I decided that what I needed was a visual aid, something to help me focus my thoughts. So, I got up, found pencil and paper, and sat down at the desk.

I printed in large capitals the name JERRY LAMP. Beneath it, I printed JIMMY MCBRIDE. Beneath that, BUBBA LUSBY. And beneath that, REV LAMP. I looked at it for a moment, then added three short vertical lines, one connecting Jerry to Jimmy, one connecting Jimmy to Bubba, and one connecting Bubba to the Reverend. Out to the right, I printed JOE and, under that, DEE-DEE, then I connected their names with another short vertical line. From JOE, I drew lines to Jerry, Jimmy, and the Reverend. From DEE-DEE, I drew lines to Jimmy (because he had her phone number) and Bubba (because he managed her apartment building). Then I sat back and admired my work.

After staring at it for another minute or two, I wadded the sheet up, slammed it into the trashcan, and decided that what I really needed was a nap. I hadn't had much sleep, and I thought I might think better after a little shut-eye.

I pulled the drapes, took off my clothes, slipped under the covers, and closed my eyes. But I didn't sleep. I couldn't get comfortable. I tried it on my back, on both sides, and on my belly. None of it helped.

It wasn't that my mind was hot on the trail of a solution to the puzzle, or anything like that. The best my tired brain could offer was a high-speed scan of snapshots from the past week. They whizzed past, often too fast to follow, meaningless and worse than useless, disruptive of both sleep and thought.

After an hour of that, I got up and found my boots and got out the other joint. Then I chased down my lighter and sprawled on the bed. I stoked her up, took a long drag, and held it down for the count.

After a couple of more tokes just like that one, the montage began to slow down. Within minutes—or what passed for minutes in that condition—I discovered that I could linger over a scene if I wanted. I could slow it down, or bring it to a stop, even speed it back up, if I took a notion. Once or twice, I actually made it run backward for a brief stretch. All that was very entertaining, but whatever the speed or direction, it made no more sense to me stoned than it had straight.

Cannabis dries up the mucous membranes, including those of the stomach lining. This leads to contractions of the stomach walls that mimic those of hunger. Hence, the munchies.

I had a taste for something spicy, so I ordered a Bloody Mary and a shrimp cocktail from room service. After my snack, I felt sleepy, so I gave the bed another try. And this time, I slept.

. . . .

I was caught in a giant's fist, massive fingers closing in. I tried with all my strength to hold them off, but finally gave it up and curled into a protective ball. That was useless, too, of course. The strength of the fingers was too great to resist. As they clamped down, tightening into a fist, I could feel my ribs snapping under the pressure as air was forced from my collapsing lungs.

I awoke in a sweat, gasping for breath, heart pounding, remembering the pain. The clock radio on the bedside table said 7:33, and I decided it was time to get out of here. I needed to go home and wash clothes anyway.

I gave Peg a call, told her about my day, and explained that I was driving to Galveston for the weekend.

"You're coming back, aren't you?" she asked anxiously.

"Of course. I just need to get away from it for a couple of days."

"But you seemed to be making such progress," she said.

"You think so?"

"Sure you are," she said. "You found out about Jerry, didn't you? And you know now that Jimmy McBride is an arsonist."

"*I'm* convinced, but the cops aren't."

"What do they know?" she said. "They've been wrong about this from the start."

"Maybe so," I said. But in spite of any progress she thought I was making, it seemed to me that I was blowing it.

After a week, I could still see only isolated pieces of the puzzle, and I couldn't even be sure it was the right puzzle. My bungling had cost us the original red tube and had probably given the villains time to dismantle the workshop where it was made. My hunch said it was an incendiary device, but thanks to me, we had no proof of that. I suspected that Jimmy McBride had torched the house for Jerry Lamp, that Jerry and Bubba were both involved in the church robbery, and that the Reverend was the brains behind it. But I didn't have a thimbleful of evidence for all my suspicions, and I still didn't know what any of it had to do with Joe. If he had uncovered evidence of a crime, he might have been killed for it. But even if I could prove that, I'd still have to give him a good reason for being in Cordelia Mae's apartment. Just clearing him of the murder was no longer good enough. I'd come too far for that.

30

I stopped at a Wendy's for a burger and fries on my way out of town, so it was nearly dark by the time I left Houston. Tired and still a little stoned, I paid minimal attention on the drive down. Not the recommended condition in which to take on fifty miles of interstate highway. The best I can say was I survived.

I lived a few blocks south of Broadway, a wide shaded boulevard with a tree-lined median that cut the eastern half of Galveston Island in two, east to west.

My house was a three-story Victorian gingerbread with long dark-green shutters and a widow's walk. Like most of the island homes built in the nineteenth century, the first floor was elevated—in this case about eight feet—to protect against flood damage, with white latticework covering the open space between floor level and the ground.

The house didn't look bad at all on the outside—the new white paint job glowed in the street light—but on the inside it still needed plenty of work. I was doing most of the renovations myself, and the task seemed endless.

Car doors slammed as I headed up the walk, and a friendly voice called out, "Mister Cochran?"

"Yeah?"

Two pairs of hands grabbed me as I turned and gave me the bum's rush up the stairs. They slammed me facedown on the porch, then one put a boot on the back of my head and started grinding my face into the hardwood.

"You gotta give this thing up," the voice drawled.

Forcing my face to the left, I blurted, "Give *what* up?"

He ground harder, working on my left ear now. "C'mon now. You know what I'm talkin' about. You just gotta stop it, you hear?"

They jerked me up and turned me around. I caught a glimpse of the one holding me—a well-filled muscle shirt, pug face, buzz haircut—but I didn't recognize him. The other was only a large manshape against the streetlight, with a silhouette of long stringy hair.

"Who are you?" I asked.

Instead of answering, he stepped in to deliver a punch, and I kicked him in the kneecap. He grunted, and I took a slap across the back of the head that brought out the stars.

Hobbling in on his injured knee, the speaker gave me two quick, hard punches to the belly. The first exploded most of my breath, and the second took what was left.

"Don't forget we know where to find you," he added and concluded with a stiff knee to the testicles.

His helper let me go, and I collapsed to the porch, heaving up my Wendy burger and fries. A little of it splashed onto the speaker's boots, earning me a kick to the ribs as a bonus.

I continued to lie there after they drove away. At first, I couldn't move, then I just didn't *want* to.

It was obvious, even to me, that somebody believed I was on to something. But the beating wouldn't have hurt nearly as much if I knew what the hell I was supposed to be *on to*.

. . . .

Molly almost stepped on me.

"What the—?" She squatted beside me and said anxiously, "Bull?"

156

"Hiya, Babe."

"Who did this?"

"You called me Bull," I said.

"I asked you who *did* this."

"Would you believe I don't know?"

"Yes," she said with sigh. "I'd believe that."

She half-carried me inside, then called the police and a doctor friend of hers, who agreed to come over and check me out.

A patrolman was on the scene in minutes. By the time he'd finished taking my statement, the doctor was there to look me over. As far as he could tell, I had no broken bones or other serious injuries, but he recommended that I have X rays as soon as possible.

When he left, Molly helped me wash up. After putting me to bed, she brought me some Tylenol and a glass of water, then climbed in with me. Another problem with getting beat up is that you can't take full advantage of such opportunities. But I did what I could.

. . . .

Molly was gone when I woke up, but she was back before I finished my shower. She made breakfast, then drove me to *my* doctor's office for a complete checkup.

Doctor Riggins had sourly agreed to meet me there on Sunday morning, but he made me pay for it when he examined me.

"That hurts," I said.

"Does it?" Riggins asked. "How about *that?*"

"That, too."

He confirmed what Molly's doctor friend had said and suggested in his wry way, "I don't mean to sound critical, but perhaps you should consider an alternate occupation."

"Ouch!"

"Did that hurt?"

Molly spent the day with me, tossing a huge chef's salad for lunch and grilling shrimp for dinner. I did my laundry, and we talked a little about the case, but mostly we just enjoyed each other's company. During the afternoon, she made a few phone calls, but she wouldn't tell me who she talked to or what was discussed.

Monday morning, I was sore and moving at half-speed, and I didn't make it out of the house until nearly noon. I was lugging a full suitcase and a garment bag this time because I wasn't sure how long I would be staying in Houston.

A small but extremely muscular man in a gaudy flowered shirt and khaki pants was leaning on the door of my pickup. I thought at first he might be one of my attackers from Saturday night, hanging around to make sure I was following orders, but this one was shorter, and his expression didn't look very threatening. More amused than anything.

When I asked, "Can I help you?" he handed me an envelope. Inside, was a note written in Molly's small, precise hand.

> This is Roy Rodgers. That's Rodgers with a "d," not like the one who rode Trigger. And I wouldn't recommend that you make fun of his name. He used to be real sensitive about it. He was a Houston cop when I was there, but he's on a disability now. As a state-licensed private investigator, he's authorized to carry a handgun, so he'll serve as your backup.

So far, you've been knocked out and beat up, and it seems likely that sooner or later you're going to be shot at.

I hadn't told her it had already happened.

And I would personally feel better if you had somebody with you who could shoot back. If Peg doesn't want to pay for it, you can send me the bill.

Love,
Molly

"You know what this says, Roy?"

He nodded. "She read it to me over the phone. It says I'm gonna be your backup."

"You think so?"

He lifted his thick shoulders and let them down nice and easy. "She said you might resist, but I told her we'd get along."

"Will we?"

"Sure, we will," he said. No threat in it, just the fact. "I can help you. I know Houston. I know the cops. And I know how to put a case together." He had me beat, three out of three. "So," he said, "I think we'll get along fine."

I surrendered with a shrug. "Do I go with you? Or do you go with me?"

"You're the boss," he said. "But if you don't wanna walk, we should probably take your pickup. I left my car in Houston and caught a ride down."

"Then, let's go."

. . . .

We were on the causeway, arcing over Galveston Bay, when I decided to test the water. "Molly says you're sensitive about your name. That so?"

Roy turned with a cold cop squint and said, "That stuff 'bout Dale and Trigger does get kinda old sometimes."

"Bet it does," I said. "But you're not still *sensitive* about it, are you?"

He thought about it, then shook his head. "You know, I just don't know about that. Ain't been tested in a long while. You feel like givin' it a try, you go ahead."

I didn't have to think about it long. "No," I said, "just checking."

"Suit yourself," he said.

I grinned. "Molly said you were disabled."

"Cop doc said I had a bad ticker."

"Do you?"

"Still around, ain't I?"

"What's wrong with your ticker?"

"Doc called it atrial fibrillation. Just means irregular heartbeat. 'Course they'll never use a small word when a big one'll do."

"Is it serious?"

"Enough for me to flunk a stress test. Doc says, I can't pass the test, I can't go on the street. I tell him my heart never gives me any trouble on the street. He says, maybe not, but what if I have to chase down a suspect? I ask him why would I want to do that? Tell him that's why I drive a car. 'Sides, I ask him, who walks in Houston? Let alone runs?"

"Didn't help?" I asked.

"Nope. Cop doc is God."

"You take medication?"

"Yeah, plus they put me on this diet." He made a face, sighed, and shook his head. After a stretch of silence, he asked, "So, where we goin'?"

"To talk to Jerry Lamp."

"Name's familiar."

"He's a big-time developer."

"Ain't they all?"

I laughed.

"I seem to recall a preacher name of Lamp," he said.

"That's his daddy, Reverend George Lamp."

"Wasn't it his church that was robbed of that five million?"

"That's the one."

160

"You think the kid had something to do with the robbery?"

"Maybe. But that's not all." I told him about the Energy Research Center, the delay in construction, the torched house, seeing Jimmy McBride at Jerry's office, the witness who'd spotted what looked like Jimmy's van in front of the burned house, and what I'd found in the loft.

Roy laughed. "I like the part about the guy sittin' there in his shorts. That's good."

"Thanks."

"You think Lamp hired the kid to commit arson?"

"That's my theory."

He nodded. "About that robbery, I've never been clear about what the hell five million dollars was doin' at the church?"

I told him about the El Salvadoran Relief Fund and explained about the Reverend's attitude toward banks.

He stared down the highway. "I just don't know."

"What?"

"If it adds up."

"How do you mean?"

"Five million is a lot of money for somebody like you or me, but not for a shaker like Lamp. As for that Research Center, what's his hurry? So what if he has to wait a coupla months and maybe pay something to resettle those people? Big deal. What's another coupla hundred thousand dollars on a hundred million dollar project? Why take the risk of burnin' a house down?"

"Maybe he's running out of time."

"*Is* he?"

"Word is he's heavily mortgaged. I'm still not sure why he had the house torched, but I see the five million as getaway money."

"From his debts, you mean?"

"It may be more serious than that. Jerry was investigated by the feds for money laundering a few years back, and if they're after him again, that might explain his rush. I know somebody who might be able to tell us if they are."

"A *fed?*" He made it sound like something you didn't want to step in.

"F.B.I."

161

"Boneheads," he said in disgust, "ever' last one of 'em."

"This one's not so bad," I said, "and he thinks he got robbed the last time he was on to Jerry. He says Jerry's father arranged to have pressure put on his bosses, and they called off the investigation."

"It listens," he agreed. "So, you went to the cops with it?"

"I took it to a homicide detective named Puckett."

"Good cop," Roy said. "Haven't seen him since his wife's funeral."

"Seems okay, but I don't think he believes my theories, either."

"Puckett's not a believer," he said, "but he'll stay the course."

"Nobody stayed on this one," I said. "They had it wrapped up before Joe was cold."

"It's all about time," he explained. "This town's averaging almost two murders a day, and if most of them weren't open-and-shut—complete with eyewitnesses and signed confessions—none of them would ever get solved."

"Sounds pretty cynical."

He shook his head. "Voice of experience. And I got no complaints. It's the cops' caseload that leaves room for private operators like me."

"You know anybody we could ask about the red tube?"

"Would the chief arson investigator for the fire department do?"

"You're kidding."

He shook his head. "Know him through my father, who was a fireman, too. I'll give him a call soon as we get to a phone. When's the appointment with Jerry?"

"One-thirty." I glanced at my watch. "We should make it."

32

Ms. Cynthia Simms, the schoolmarm receptionist, greeted me as a regular customer and was pleased to meet Roy. I had an appointment this time, and we were right on time, so she called out an attractive blond secretary or administrative assistant, who led us through the double doors and down a corridor to her boss's office.

Jerry was waiting for us in the doorway, hand extended. "Good to see you again, Mister Cochran."

We shook, and I introduced Roy.

Jerry didn't even blink at the name, and I figured he was either seriously distracted, had no sense of humor, or was simply polite. Maybe all three.

I liked his office. Hi-tech, but not stark or cold. Furnished in undyed leather, blond wood, and sandstone. There were couches on either side of a low table, and two chairs in front of the desk. The window wall looked across Louisiana to the Republic Bank Center. The other walls were painted a pale shade of tan, broken up by architectural drawings and floorplans. Along both of the long walls, miniature models sat in glass cases on sandstone pedestals.

I nodded at one. "Mind if we take a look?"

"Please," he said with a smile.

Roy and I walked to the nearest model.

"It's a terrarium," said Roy.

"A vivarium, actually," Jerry politely corrected him. "Like a terrarium, but with standing water."

The water not only stood but ran, with several of the models featuring fountains or waterfalls. All contained a combination of artificial and living plants that looked like tiny trees and bushes and flowers.

Roy liked them, too, even got down on one knee a couple of times to view one from ground level. He finally asked Jerry, "You do these yourself?"

Jerry lit up. "Yes, I did."

"They're somethin' else," Roy said. "Never seen the like."

"Thanks."

"Don't know about vivariums," he said, "but the trouble I always had with terrariums was having them fog up on me, so you couldn't see inside no more. And what good's a terrarium you can't see into?"

"That's a problem," Jerry agreed. "The keys, of course, are temperature and humidity."

"Of course," said Roy, getting into it.

"To control them, I set my 'varium on a hollow pedestal with a heating-cooling unit inside."

Roy tugged at his lip and asked, "Where does it vent?"

"Intakes around the base of each pedestal," Jerry explained. "Outputs around the top."

"Ingenious," I said.

"I just wish my kid was here," said Roy. "She'd go nuts over these."

Jerry was pleased. "Kids *do* love them."

"Are the designs yours?" I asked.

"Oh, yes," he said, "I'm the architect on all my projects."

"Have all of these been constructed?"

"All but that one." He waved at the largest case of all, taller and wider than the others. Inside it, was a mountain, with one sheer rock face and other gentler, treeclad slopes.

He picked up a remote control device from the low table,

pointed it at the window, and the curtains started to close. Then he turned it on the case, and the mountain split in two. As the room darkened, the cliff face parted up the middle, and the two halves swung to the sides like wings, revealing a glowing mountain-within-a-mountain, sculpted in transparent plastic and honey-combed with tunnels. As I stepped forward, he touched a third button, and living spaces sprang into view along the tunnels. As I leaned in closer, I could see tiny people going in and out of tiny rooms, sitting on tiny chairs and couches before tiny television sets, even rocking tiny babies in tiny cradles. The figures were transparent, and if you looked too closely, they slid out of focus, but it was still the most remarkable use of holograms I'd ever seen. The people and familiar objects gave the structure scale, and I could see that the tunnels were wide and lined with greenery. Then they suddenly went dark, as the front half of the mountain-within-the-mountain split open, and light rose on a great interior cavern.

"The sunlight," Jerry explained, "would be brought in by a system of mirrors. And even on overcast days, it could be simulated with proper lighting."

A waterfall fell a hundred feet or more down one wall of the cavern, with the other walls looking like the Hanging Gardens of Babylon. I thought it was splendid. And I could tell from Jerry's expression that, for him, the thing was already built. The model *was* the thing.

"I didn't know holograms had progressed this far," I said.

"Only a handful of people in the world could have done this," he said. "The sculptor lives in Hong Kong. He speaks no English, and I speak no Chinese, so we have to talk through interpreters. But when he heard my idea, I could see he was interested. What I wanted, he said, would be difficult, and he couldn't guarantee success, but he was willing to try. So, I had the plexi mountain molded and installed the plumbing and lighting, then decorated the cavern and shipped it to him."

I said sincerely, "It's remarkable."

He smiled, looking like a kid. "All I'm waiting for now is the right mountain." He waved us to chairs. As I lowered my aching body into one, he asked me, "How's Peggy Ann?"

165

"Surviving."

"It's tragic," he intoned, shaking his head, "tragic."

"That it is," I agreed.

"How can I help you?" he asked, as he crossed behind his desk—a slab of polished wood resting on two upright slabs of sandstone. Taking a seat, he added, "Cynthia said you wanted to talk about the Lyndon Baines Johnson Energy Research Center."

"The name's getting longer."

"Yes," he eagerly agreed. "Just today, we received word of a very large equipment endowment from the LBJ Foundation."

I couldn't resist asking, "Did they stipulate that you had to name it after Lyndon?"

"Of course not," he said, shocked that I could suggest such a thing. "We did mention the possibility in our application, and we were honored that they chose to accept." He slid a glossy, magazine-size brochure across the desk. "It's all there," he said proudly, "from architectural drawings to an analysis of the various avenues of research that will be explored."

Paging through the brochure, I said, "Joe must have been very proud to be part of something like this."

"Yes, he was," Jerry agreed.

"Is that what you talked about that Monday before he died?" I watched Jerry's mouth open and close, then asked casually, "He *was* here that Monday, wasn't he?"

Finding his voice, he said, "Yes, he was."

"Did you talk about the Center?"

"That's right."

"Was he worried about it?"

"Not really worried," he said. "Concerned, I suppose you'd say, about the delay in the groundbreaking."

"Delay?" I prompted.

His eyes briefly touched mine in passing. "We purchased several small parcels of land to square the project boundaries. They included two developed lots in a residential neighborhood, and the former tenants are protesting the sales."

"On what grounds?"

"They say they should have been given first option to buy."

166

"Should they?"

"Well," he said with a nervous laugh, "that's not for me to say. But I can assure you that we have clear title to the properties, and if there's any fault, it lies with the original owner."

"Where do the cases stand at present?"

"They've filed for a restraining order."

"Then the delay could be a long one."

"Oh, no, no," he quickly assured me. "A matter of months at most."

"How do your investors feel about it?"

He spread his hands. "They understand that these things happen and have to be dealt with."

"How?"

"I beg your pardon?"

"How do you deal with it?"

"Well, you obviously begin by obtaining the best possible legal representation. Beyond that . . ." He trailed off with a shrug.

"Beyond that?" I repeated.

"You just have to be patient," he said, "and let the matter run its course."

I stared at him for a moment, trying to decide if he was capable of having a man killed. "Did you know there was a fire on one of those properties?"

He suddenly became interesting in his manicure. "Yes, I did. Fortunately, no one was injured. And the house *was* going to be torn down in any case."

"Do they suspect arson?"

He looked up in surprise. Whether by the idea itself or by my bringing it up, I couldn't say. "Not to my knowledge," he said. "I understand the fire was caused by a gas leak."

"How well do you know Jimmy McBride?"

His eyes darted to mine, then away. "Not very well. The outlet he works for is providing some fixtures for a project of ours." He glanced back. "Why do you ask?"

"Just that a van like his was seen in front of the burned house the day it went up."

"It was?"

167

"Do you think Jimmy would be capable of torching a house?"

After brief consideration, he shook his head. "As I say, I don't know him very well, but I really can't see him doing anything like that."

"Maybe not," I said. "But you have to admit it's an interesting coincidence that his van was seen in front of the house."

He nodded, chin rising and falling, getting into a rhythmical thing now. "Yes, I see what you mean."

"What about Bubba Lusby?"

The nodding stopped. "Who?"

"You don't know him?" I asked.

"I don't believe I do," he said, head now moving from side to side.

"He's a friend of Jimmy's."

"Lusby, you say?"

"Uh huh."

"No, I don't think I know him. Why?"

"Just curious."

He nodded some more and checked his watch. "Well, I'm sorry, gentlemen. But you asked for fifteen minutes, and I'm afraid I'll have to hold you to it. I'm flying out to San Antonio this afternoon."

When he got to his feet, I realized the interview was over.

33

Waiting for the elevator, I said, "Didn't get much, did I?"

Roy said, "Don't worry about it. Nothin' else, I got a look at Jerry. Those models of his are really somethin'. He should work for Disney, he's so good. But he seems a little dim for a tycoon."

"Did you notice it bothered him to talk about Joe?"

"Maybe he just has a thing about dead people."

"He was a little cottonmouthed about Jimmy, too."

"Yeah, I wouldn't mind havin' a tap on his phone right now. See who he calls."

"In lieu of that, we could follow him."

He thought about it. "Worth a try."

As we stepped into an empty elevator, he said, "You didn't tell me Bubba Lusby was in on this."

"Guess it slipped my mind. You need a score card to keep track of the players in this thing." I told him about the phone numbers I'd found on the book of matches. "You know Bubba?"

"Some."

"What's he do?"

"He's a licensed private detective, among other things."

"What other things?"

"Used to run a sports book," he said. "And last I heard, he bought into a restaurant on South Main."

"He also manages the apartments where the killings took place."

"That so? Probably owns that, too."

"I didn't know detectives made that kind of money."

"One man operations usually don't," he said. "Not honest ones."

The elevator stopped to take on a man and a woman. Since they were talking, too, we continued in a whisper.

"You're saying Bubba's dishonest?" I asked.

"Dirty as they come."

"What's his scam?"

"Extortion's one of his favorites."

"How does he do it?"

"Say he runs across a piece of information that somebody doesn't want made public. He might go to them and ask, just out of curiosity, how much it would be worth to them to keep it a secret."

"You *know* he's done this?"

"I believe it."

"Then why isn't he in jail?"

"Because the people he takes money from still don't want their secrets to get out, and they're not eager to talk to the cops about it."

"So, he keeps on doing it?"

"See any reason for him to stop?"

I'd parked in the underground lot this time, so we took the elevator down to the parking level. We exited from the garage onto Capitol, crossed Louisiana, and pulled over at the same place as before. Then I opened the hood again and pretended to tinker, while Roy watched for Jerry.

"Maybe I should drive," he said.

"Why don't *I* drive," I suggested, "and you coach me?"

He thought about it. "Will you do what I tell you?"

"All right."

"Why not, then?" he said. "Give it a try."

We didn't have long to wait. Jerry drove a flashy red European sports car—low and fast-looking, a Lamberghini or Maserati, one of those—but he didn't look comfortable in it. He came out of the exit tunnel hunched over the wheel, having trouble with the gears, and he never once exceeded the speed limit, even on 45. There was a woman in the passenger's seat, but she was turned toward Jerry when they drove past, so all we saw was blond hair.

Jerry and the moderate traffic offered less challenge than they might have, but Roy's coaching was still damned impressive. He sat sideways, so he could see forward and backward, telling me when to speed up, when to ease off, when to shift lanes. He'd say cut, and I'd cut. Sometimes, I had to shut my eyes to do it, sure that we were going to end up smeared across the highway like jam. But we hung right in there, never more than six cars back, usually closer, but never too close. Roy taught me to memorize the rear of the car, the plate, the silhouette, every detail, which in this case was easy, as Jerry's car was so distinctive. But it was also built so low to the ground that it sometimes disappeared in front of another car. Because of that, Roy usually kept us a lane to the left or right, so we could see around the car behind Jerry.

At Hobby airport, we followed the car up to the front of the terminal, where Jerry and his passenger got out. It was the same secretary or administrative assistant who'd escorted us back to his office. She handed him a carry-on bag, and he said something that made him smile. As he headed inside, Roy got out to follow him, and I went to park.

After we watched Jerry board a Southwest Airlines flight to San Antonio, I had to concede that he'd probably told us the truth. I was disappointed, but Roy said sagely, "You never know till you check it out."

We stopped on the way out of the terminal so Roy could find out who was handling the robbery at Victory Baptist. It turned out to be a cop he knew, who told us to come on over.

. . . .

The church was in the jurisdiction of the Central Patrol Station, downtown on Reisner. Robbery was on the third floor, just down the hall from Homicide, and the investigating officer was a young black man named Yancy Carpenter.

Sergeant Carpenter was five-ten or so, wiry, and quick. Like the other detectives, he was dressed in dark trousers, white long-sleeved shirt, and tie. But he wore them better than most and looked like he'd just stepped out of a Sakowitz ad.

"What say, Roy, my man?" They shook hands.

"How's it goin', Yance?"

"Not so bad."

Roy introduced me, and Yancy shook my hand.

"Come on back to the lieutenant's office, so we can talk." He led us across a sparcely populated squad room into an office cubicle and shut the door. "While the cat's away," he explained, "the mice get to use his office." He waved at chairs and sat on the edge of the desk. "Sorry, I don't have much time now. Gotta be somewhere in fifteen minutes. But you said you might have something for me."

I told him what I knew.

"Have to talk to the feds," he said. "Summers, you say?"

"Yeah."

Roy asked him, "So, how's the church thing comin'?"

Yancy made a face. "Other than the fact we got more suspects than we know what to do with, it's all *copacetic*. Scope this out: the Reverend usually keeps his heavy cash at an undisclosed location—not a bank 'cause, except for an account used for cashing contributer's checks and one for payroll, the Reverend don't have no shuck with banks—but a safe place nonetheless. The precise whereabouts was revealed to me only with the understanding that it would go no further, so my lips are sealed on that subject."

"Gotcha," said Roy.

Yancy went on, "The decision to present the Relief Fund to the El Salvadoran consul in cash—which sounded pretty screwy to me to begin with. Especially since it was only symbolic, on account of the consul would, of course, be carrying the dough back to his country in the form a bank draft. Anyhow," he said, "the decision was made less than a week before the robbery and was never made public. But in spite of that, we figure that at least twenty-three people knew the cash would be in the vault that Thursday night."

He ticked them off. "The Reverend. His son Jerry. Donald Kent, the head deacon of the church, who says he argued against the cash presentation. At least two other members of the congregation, who are confidants of the Reverend. Deborah Preuss, the church secretary. The custodian and his helper. Nine security guards, their supervisor, and the manager of the security firm. The armored car driver, the guard, their supervisor, the manager, and who know who else at Brinks. Not to mention various unnamed spouses and significant others." He shook his head and dramatically lifted his arms to the heavens as he concluded, "The list goes on and on!"

We laughed. "Anyway, back to the scene. You probably know they hit the place about two-thirty in the morning and took out the three guards almost at the same time, two with gas."

"Have you traced the gas yet?" I asked.

"Military stuff," he said. "Two containers of it were stolen from an Army supply depot in Louisiana back in the spring, and one was found in a raid on a paramilitary group in Arkansas last month."

"What about the son?" I asked.

"Jerry? He was at the church that night. First time in years that he'd dropped in on one of his father's seminars, which struck us as sort of suspicious. But we can't put him there after nine-thirty Thursday night. He had friends over to his house for a late supper, and the last of them left about two A.M. He says—and the servants agree—that he went up to his bedroom shortly after that. And they all swear he didn't leave the house until just before nine o'clock Friday morning."

"How reliable are the servants?"

"Hard to say," he admitted. "And as big as his place is, he could've snuck out and back in without anybody seeing him."

"Do you suspect the Reverend of being involved?" I asked.

"Well, the cash presentation *was* his idea," he said. "But we don't have a good motive for him yet."

"Five million dollars isn't enough?"

He shrugged. "Far as we can tell, he isn't hurting for money. His personal worth is estimated at better than three million. We haven't found any evidence that he's incurred any recent debts, but we're still looking. And he has an alibi for the time of the robbery. He was called to the deathbed of one of his congregation at Presbyterian Hospital, and the nurses tell us he was there from about twelve-thirty that evening until after the woman died at about six-fifteen the next morning."

I was disappointed that the Reverend wasn't a more promising suspect, but I wasn't ready to give up on him yet.

Roy told him, "You might wanna check out the whereabouts of a man named Homer Lusby that night."

"Do I know him?" Yancy asked.

"You mighta seen him," Roy said. "We brought him in back in 'eighty-eight for killin' a man outside a pool hall on Shepherd. Big fat moonfaced shitkicker with a high kiddie voice, known as Bubba. Victim was beat to death with a cue stick. M.E. said he was clubbed at least two dozen times, half of 'em *after* he was dead."

Yancy nodded. "It's coming back to me."

"We couldn't make a case 'cause he had an alibi that put him across town at the time. And the witness who ID'd him changed her mind."

"How is he involved in this?" he asked.

"That's the question," Roy admitted. "But he knows the Reverend and may know his son."

"And he keeps popping up everywhere I look," I added.

"Bubba Lusby," he repeated and glanced at his watch. "Whoa! Gotta go. Have to bust it just to get there late. But what the hey? That's why they give us sirens, right?"

We thanked him, and he left us to find our way out.

Before we left Robbery, Roy called the chief arson investigator's office. He was just leaving for the day, but said he'd see us at ten the next morning.

"While we're here," Roy added, "there's somebody else I wanna talk to."

. . . .

It was an older cop named Rufus Dunn, waiting out his retirement in the evidence room. He looked like your central casting southern

174

cop—complete with thinning flat-top, spreading paunch, and fading Marine Corps tattoo on his forearm—but Roy had informed me that Rufus was something special.

The hangdog face brightened when he saw Roy. "Say, Roy, I been thinking."

"Just don't let 'em catch you at it," said Roy.

"I was just wondering if it's really true about Dale and Trigger."

"Only when your wife isn't available."

"I mean, how could they—you know—*do it.*"

"I'll give you a hint," said Roy.

"What's that?"

"He likes it on top."

Rufus laughed, and they caught up on gossip. When they ran out of people to badmouth, Roy brought up Bubba Lusby.

"What's that asshole up to now?" Dunn asked.

"I thought *you* might know."

"Nah," he said. "I ain't seen him in years. Last time he wanted me to ID a license plate for him, but I tole him to send a request to motor vehicles. You're nice to the sonofabitch once," he explained, "and you're doin' him favors for life."

"How long ago was that?"

"Spring of 'eighty-seven. May."

Roy laughed and told me, "Rufus don't forget nothin'. Do you, Rufus?"

He worked up a halfhearted grin. "Not much."

Roy tapped his skull. "Got a 'photographic memory.' "

Dunn ducked his head and said with some embarrassment, "Truth is, Roy, my memory's not like it was. And I don't talk about it around here much anymore because the young bucks treat me like a freak."

"They're idiots," said Roy. "But you can't tell me you've lost it. I bet if I asked you who Bubba was working for back in May of 'eighty-seven, you could tell me."

"Hell, Roy," he complained, "that was a long time ago."

"Sure it was, Rufus."

"And pee-eyes like to keep their clients to themselves."

175

"I know that, too. But I'll bet the ranch you got the name of his client out of him."

"Prob'ly did at that," he allowed.

"So, it's only a matter of you comin' up with it."

"Yeah." Dunn sat back and stared up at the ceiling, as though he expected to find the name written there.

"Knowin' Bubba," Roy went on, "he probably laid some of that redneck brotherhood horseshit on you, didn't he?"

"Sounds like him," Dunn agreed, then raised a hand, on to something now. "I can hear him plain as day, sayin' that he couldn't lose this time, not with me and *God* on his side." He gave us another look at his stained teeth and said, "I heard later he was workin' for that soldier preacher."

"Reverend Lamp?" I asked.

"That's the one."

I looked at Roy, who looked at Dunn and asked, "Any idea what he was investigating?"

"Nope."

I asked, "Did he mention the preacher's son, Jerry?"

"Not to my recollection."

As we left the building, Roy said, "Think we should have a word with the Reverend?"

"Do we call for an appointment?"

"Why don't we just drop by the church and surprise him?"

34

As we stepped through the front doors of the church, a pretty young woman in a pink summerweight suit appeared quickly out of an office to the right. She smiled politely and asked, "Can I help you?"

"Hope so, ma'am," I said. "We'd like to speak to Reverend Lamp."

"I'm sorry, but the Reverend isn't here right now."

"When do you expect him back?"

She nodded at a chalkboard propped on an easel, announcing a Bible Study Seminar to be held in the Lower Church, one floor down, at 8:00 this evening. "He'll be back for the seminar."

"If we dropped by at seven-thirty, do you think we'd be able to catch him?"

"Certainly," she said. "He'll be in his office then, going over his notes. If you'll give me your names, I'll tell him to expect you."

We went out for an early dinner. When we got back to the church, the young woman came out of her office again to escort us to the Reverend's office. She led us downstairs, through a small auditorium, where two men were setting up chairs for the seminar, then led us out a door to the left of the dais and up another flight of stairs. At the top, I could see the pulpit through an open door to the right. There was light on the lectern, but the rest of the sanctuary was in darkness. The young woman led us down a short corridor straight ahead. The door was open at the end, and the Reverend was at his desk, making notes on three-by-five cards.

Our guide said respectfully, "Reverend Lamp." As he glanced up and took off his reading glasses, she added, "Mister Cochran and Mister Rodgers are here to see you."

Getting to his feet, he said, "Thank you, Deborah."

Deborah smiled at us and left, as the Reverend came around his desk to greet us. "Mister Cochran, I remember seeing you with Peggy Ahern and her father at Joe's funeral."

"Yes, sir, that's right."

After we shook hands, I introduced Roy, and they tested their grips.

I said, "Sorry to bother you, Reverend."

"No bother," he insisted. "Won't you have a seat?"

I sat and glanced around. The office was small but comfortable, with windows behind the desk, two walls of books, and one of photographs. They featured the Colonel, in uniform and out, with famous faces in many of the more recent photos.

"You have a very impressive operation here," I said.

"Thank you," he said. "With God's aid and a little help from our friends, we do our best."

"Peggy Ann has asked me to look into Joe's death for her," I explained. "But, so far, my investigation has produced more questions than answers."

"That can happen," he acknowledged with a smile.

The man's infernal self-assurance made me angry. "I thought you might be able to help us answer a few of them."

He spread his hands. "If I *can,* certainly."

"What is the El Salvadoran Relief Fund?"

He didn't expect that. "Well, it—it's just what it sounds like."

"Why El Salvador?"

"Because it's currently the most strategically significant country in the region."

"To whom?"

"To us."

"Why?"

"It was a close one in Nicaragua. We were almost too late with too little. Now there's trouble again in El Salvador, and we have to put a stop to it before it's too late."

"Why?"

"Because a communist victory there could give new life to the Sandinistas."

"I thought communism was pretty much a dead horse these days?"

"Wounded," he corrected me. "Maybe even dying, at least in the Soviet Union. But as any hunter will tell you, even a seriously wounded animal can be dangerous. Especially if it's armed with thermonuclear weapons."

"Was the five million earmarked for humanitarian aid?" I asked.

"There were no strings attached. How it was used would have been entirely up to the Salvadorans."

"Then it could have been used for buying arms and ammunition?"

"*Could* have," he agreed. "Though it would have gone much further for medical supplies and foodstuffs than for military equipment. But," he added, "I don't quite see what this has to do with Joe Ahern."

"That's what I'm trying to find out," I said. "Do the police have any idea who took the money?"

"Not to my knowledge, no."

"Do you know Jimmy McBride?"

He clasped his hands on the desk. "I don't believe I do."

"He's suspected of torching a house the day Joe died, the same day as the robbery. The fire was on a contested piece of property that your son purchased for his Energy Research Center, and I saw Jimmy McBride at Jerry's office a few days ago."

The knuckles of his clasped hands were white. "Are you suggesting that my son was involved in arson?"

"No, sir. As I said, I don't have answers yet, just questions and a few connections."

"Between what and what?" he asked.

"Between Joe Ahern and Jerry, between Jerry and Jimmy McBride, between Jimmy and Bubba Lusby, and between Bubba and you."

"Me?" he asked, outrage simmering. "How am *I* supposed to be connected?"

"You hired Bubba to watch your son, didn't you?" That was only a guess, but Eddie Dunn had said Bubba was working for the Reverend about the same time that Jerry was being investigated by the feds. So, it seemed logical.

He said, "I don't know what you're talking about."

I shook my head. "I saw him get into your limo after the graveside service."

He nodded abruptly, then said quietly, "I want you out of my office."

I didn't move. "You should know that Jerry's in trouble again, Reverend, and this time, it could be more serious than laundering drug money."

"Out!" he snapped, then snatched up the receiver, punched a key, and said, "Deb, get Big Tom down here now."

I was up, and Roy had me by the arm, pulling me sideways toward the door.

"Just do it!" the Reverend shouted at Deb, then crashed the receiver back into its cradle and charged around his desk.

As Roy tugged me through the doorway, I got out, "I didn't mean to upset you, sir," just before the Reverend slammed the door in my face.

As we reached the end of the corridor, Big Tom came charging through the door to the Sanctuary. I assumed it was Big Tom. He was even larger than Bubba, but he didn't identify himself. He slid to a panting halt on the carpet and waved a hand the size of a fielder's glove at a short corridor leading to a side exit. We took the hint.

• • • • • • • • • • • • •

"You know what your problem is?" Roy asked, as we walked around to the pickup.

"No, Roy, what's my problem?"

180

"You don't understand about questioning, that the idea is for you to *ask* questions, and for the subject to *answer* them."

"I realize that."

"But that's not what you did," he said. "You started out okay, flattering him on his church and all. That's good. But then you got impatient and went for the kill, when you shoulda still been feelin' him out. And in the end, you got to showin' off and tellin' him everything *you* know. So, now he knows everything, and you know zip."

"We know he hired Bubba to watch Jerry."

"How do we *know* that?" he asked.

"From his reaction."

"He'd say he was reactin' to being harassed."

"But we know better."

He shook his head. "There was more there. But you had the man up on his hind legs before we could hardly sit down."

"You said we should surprise him," I said.

"I said surprise him, not abuse him."

"I thought if I hit him with it all at once like that, he might blurt something out."

"That only happens in movies."

"So, how would *you* have gone about it?"

"Like we did with Jerry. I'd've gone on strokin' him awhile longer before *easing* into the serious questions."

"If I remember right, we didn't get much out of Jerry, either."

"With Jerry," he reminded me, "we can go *back*. But Big Tom's never gonna let us through the door again."

"All right. I see your point," I said. "And I'll try to do better next time."

"That's all I ask," he said seriously. But I thought I caught a hint of a smile.

35

Roy joined me for a beer in the Warwick bar, and we found a quiet table in the back room to work on our plan of attack. Talking about it helped me get it straight in my mind. And because Roy actually seemed to know what he was doing, it made me feel more confident that *I* was headed in the right direction.

After seeing me up to my room, he caught a cab home.

I was trying to organize my notes, when a knock came on the door. It was Sergeant Puckett, so I let him in.

He was sniffing as he stepped inside. "Smells like pot."

"Does it?" I asked innocently.

He turned and looked me over. "You're standing kind of crooked," he said. "Like you took a beatin'."

I tried to straighten up, but it hurt too much. I told him, "Two men followed me back to Galveston Saturday night and tried to warn me off the case."

"Hmmm," he said. "Sounds like you're stirrin' up somebody's nest."

"Don't suppose that means you'll be reopening the case?"

"Not my decision," he said. "And whatever you're on to might have nothing to do with the killings."

182

"I was afraid you'd say that." Crossing to one of the armchairs in front of the window, I asked, "How can I help you?"

"Thought you might want to know that I took a look at the loft."

"When?"

"Saturday afternoon."

"Glad to hear somebody's on the job," I said and sat down.

He let that one slide as he walked over. "Talked to a man named Wilmer Ott," he said.

The name sounded familiar.

Puckett lowered himself into the other chair. "Mister Ott says he's a free-lance photographer and computer programmer, and he had all this fancy computer gear in his bedroom. Claims to live there alone."

"What about the people I saw climbing through his window?"

"Said he had a coupla friends over that night, but he doesn't know anybody named McBride."

"So he *says.*"

"That's right."

"Did you look in the workshop?"

"Uh huh," he said. "But I didn't find any red paper tubes or plastic jars of powder."

"Then they were moved."

"Could be," he agreed. "I did find out that McBride pays rent on a garage apartment in the Heights."

"That may be so," I said, "but he spent Friday night at the loft."

He eyed me in his quiet way. "You couldn't have followed the wrong man, could you?"

"No," I said firmly, "I couldn't."

He shrugged. "Just checkin'."

"If I gave you an unlisted phone number, could you give me a name and address to go with it?"

"I probably *could,*" he said.

"Would you?"

He gave it a beat, then said, "Let me see it."

I copied down a phone number from my notebook and gave it to him.

He glanced at it and started to put it away, then changed his mind and pulled out a pocket notebook. After paging through it for a moment, he stopped and nodded. "It's Wilmer Ott's number. The one at the loft."

"Thought so," I said. "I copied it down from Joe's address book. It just had the name Wilmer written beside it."

He nodded. "Guess I'll have to have another talk with Mister Ott."

"What about Jimmy?" I asked. "Does he have a sheet?"

"Yeah."

"Serve time?" When he didn't answer, I said, "You looked up his record, didn't you?" When he still didn't say anything, I added, "If you don't tell me, I'll just have to find out some other way. And look what my curiosity has cost us so far."

He shrugged. "McBride was Army Special Forces."

"You're kidding. That scrawny kid?"

"I hear he had more muscle back when he was in the service. An Army buddy of his told me he stopped eating and hitting the weights after his court-martial."

"Why was he court-martialed?"

"He was accused of blowing up an officers' club at Fort Bragg."

"Then he *is* an arsonist," I said.

"He was accused of blowing something up, not setting anything on fire."

"Close enough," I said. "You know he torched that house."

"Neither of us *knows* anything," Puckett declared. "You don't even know it was arson." Before I could argue, he added, "Besides which, the charges were dropped after the chief witness against him was found to have an undisclosed felony record. But they still gave McBride a dishonorable discharge, because the explosives used in the bombing were taken from a storehouse he was supposed to be guarding."

"So, he was cleared on a technicality," I said. "That doesn't make him innocent. You should pick him up anyway."

"You think so?" he asked.

"I do."

"Then I guess we better *do it,* hadn't we? I mean, seein' as how

184

you think so." He stopped me with a raised hand and said mildly, "As a matter of fact, I've been trying to find him, but he didn't show up for work today. He didn't call in sick, and nobody's seen him since Friday. Could be that somebody gave him too much of a head start."

Ouch!

Choosing not to rub it in any more than he already had, he took out his pad and scribbled something, then tore off the sheet and laid it on the table. "Here's my home number," he said. "I don't give it out to just anybody, but it doesn't mean that we're going steady or anything. I'd just like you to keep me informed."

I agreed to do so, and Puckett left.

Fifteen minutes later, Pete Shirmer called. "Got a couple of things for you," he said. "Talked to some people about Jerry Lamp, and I got lucky. One of my sources is a banker, and another recently had an executive position at Lamp Enterprises. If what they say is true, then he's in more serious trouble than we thought. Apparently, he's way behind schedule and nearly out of money on a big project in San Antonio. And the rumor is that building inspectors are about to shut down construction on the office tower he's putting up in Austin. They're accusing him of using substandard steel. Worst of all, he has a ten million dollar short-term note coming due the first of September, and at this moment, according to the banker, Jerry couldn't borrow a farthing. The consensus is that he isn't going to make the loan payment. And if he doesn't, we're looking at a real possibility of bankruptcy here."

"I'm impressed," I said. "When you go looking for dirt, you don't mess around."

"Thanks," he said. "But the news isn't all bad for Jerry. That appeal for the restraining order against the Energy Research Center was dropped today. Word is it was settled out of court."

"For how much?"

"An undisclosed amount."

"I should've guessed. Does that mean a lot of money?"

"In this case, I'd say not more than a hundred thousand total. You're talking about people who just want a decent place to live."

"Guess arson *does* work," I said.

"Arson?" he asked.

"Tell you about it later."

"You promise?"

"I promise."

36

The next morning, Roy and I dropped in at Fire Station No. 1, which was downtown on Bagby, between the Post Office and the Coliseum. The Chief Investigator's office was on the fourth floor.

A handsome older black woman was on the phone at the desk in the outer office. Seeing us, she spoke a few final words into the receiver, then hung up and said politely, "Can I help you?"

"Yes, ma'am," Roy said with a grin. "You can tell Miles that his ten o'clock appointment is here."

"You must be Roy Rodgers."

"Guilty as charged," he agreed.

She smiled. "I'll tell him."

As she reached for the phone, a voice asked from a doorway to our left, "Is that the singin' cowboy himself?"

"It's me, Miles."

Miles appeared to be in his late forties. He was losing his hair, but keeping fit, and he still looked pretty spiffy in his uniform. He had the kind of heavy beard that required three shaves a day, and his face was shiny from a recent scraping. I imagined he kept a shaving kit in his desk.

Roy introduced us, and we shook hands. Then Miles slapped

Roy on the shoulder and led us through another anteroom with a desk, chairs, and couches into his office. He asked about Roy's mother and daughter. While they caught up, I looked around.

His office was roomy and pleasant. Good carpeting, a couch, comfortable guest chairs, and an executive-size desk, with a computer terminal and laser printer on a table behind the desk. He had more photos than the Reverend, but with fewer famous faces. Most were pictures of fires, or the charred results of fires, or firefighters.

He waved us into chairs, then perched on the edge of his desk. "So, what's this about arson?"

I handed him the red paper tube.

He turned it this way and that, then stuck it on his finger and held it up. "Tell me about it," he said.

I told him about the original, as well as the one on his finger, then explained about the house fire.

He took a closer look at it. "It could be an incendiary."

"How do these things work?"

"That varies," he said. "You want to keep it simple, you douse a place in ninety-eight octane and toss in a match. Trouble is, we'll spot that every time, and the perpetrator has to get foxier if he wants it to look like an accident, so he can collect the insurance and all. Incendiary devices," he concluded, "are usually bigger than this and have metal parts."

"The first one had wires trailing out of one end."

"Electrically ignited," he said.

"According to a witness, the house went up an hour after the alleged arsonist drove away."

He nodded. "Had a timing device. The kitchen stove have a clock on it?"

"Why?"

"If the guy was smart, he could've broken the glass on the stove clock, wired it to the incendiary as a timer and a power source, then switched on the gas. The kitchen fills up with it, and when the accelerant gets the juice, the place goes up like a bomb."

"That's the way the witness described it."

"Could be it, then." He held up the tube. "This is paper, so it

188

burns up and leaves no evidence. And a couple of short wires would be easy to miss."

"Can you think of a powder that could be used as an accelerant?"

"Half a dozen. With gas, the simplest would be flash powder, which you can buy in any good novelty shop. I'm not saying that's the way it happened," he said, "but it *could've* been."

"Did you investigate this fire?" I asked.

"My people did. We were suspicious because the property had been sold, and the former tenant was still living in the house, even though he'd been officially evicted. It was a real soap opera, with the tenant suing the former owner for selling the property without proper notification. We talked to the neighbors, the ex-owner, the new owner, and the tenant. The tenant left the house a few hours before the fire to drive to Beaumont to be with his sick sister, so we got the sister's phone number and contacted him to ask if he'd left the gas on. At first, he said he didn't think so, but he finally had to admit that it was possible. He also said the pilot light on the stove had a tendency to blow out."

"Did your investigators speak to the neighbor who saw the van?"

"Yeah, but he couldn't give them a make, model, or color of the van. He didn't get a plate number, either, or a description of the driver, or see anyone enter or leave the house, so that was pretty much a dead end. The examination of the scene revealed no evidence of arson, just the textbook results of what happens when natural gas is ignited at explosive concentrations. The stuff is lighter than air, which gives you high displacement, with walls usually blown out at ceiling level. That's what we found, so in spite of any suspicions, we wrote it off as an accidental fire resulting from natural gas ignition."

"Would you take another look at it?" I asked him.

"Have to now," he said. "Not tomorrow, though. Gotta be in court. Maybe Thursday."

. . . .

As we walked out into the heat, Roy said, "I wanna see the murder scene. And if we can catch the Gonzalez woman at home, maybe I can get her to talk to me."

"Talk to you alone, you mean?"

"Probably be best, wouldn't it? She won't talk to you, but she doesn't know *me*. Maybe I can catch her off guard."

"And surprise her? Like I did with the Reverend?"

He shrugged. "Long as Big Tom isn't around, I think I can handle her."

"You planning to work some scam on her?"

"If I can think of one."

"She's pretty sharp."

"Then it'll have to be a sharp scam. One with room to walk around in."

"You could tell her you're a cop."

"Impersonatin' an officer could get me arrested," he pointed out. "No, I was thinkin' of sayin' I was a friend of Dee-Dee's from that commune up in Arizona."

"What if she told Nivia all about her life on the commune? Things that only a resident would know."

"That's a risk," he said, "but it might at least get me through the door. The worst that can happen is she throws me out."

It took us half an hour to reach the apartments. As I pulled into a parking space in front of the building, a blue Chevy Blazer backed out of another space at the other end of the building and headed north. Nivia Gonzalez was at the wheel, and a large man was beside her.

"Was that Bubba?" asked Roy.

"Sure looked like him. And Ms. Gonzalez was driving."

I waited a couple of beats after they went past, then pulled out and gave chase. We followed them back to the West Loop and headed north. Traffic was thicker now, but with Roy's coaching, I managed to keep the Blazer in sight.

Skyscrapers rose to the left, then to the right as we approached the Galleria area—a sort of mini-downtown of high-ticket stores like Neiman-Marcus, Lord & Taylor, Sakowitz, and Saks Fifth Avenue. Appropriately, it's also the home of National Republican

Headquarters, which is positioned strategically near the headquarters of such corporate giants as Control Data Corporation and Tenneco. All this development stopped abruptly at the edge of Memorial Park. Then the road climbed over I-10, and I could see downtown in the distance over the oak trees to my right.

As the West Loop became the North Loop, a flock of precision-flying starlings swooped across the highway, sketching dark patterns against the sky.

It was green out here in suburbia. There were occasional commercial strips, scattered office parks, and isolated industrial developments—often shielded behind decorative rows of trees—but it was mostly residential. No tacky apartment complexes, just handsome, if overwhelmingly similar, single-family homes.

I caught a last glimpse of downtown off to the right before we set off north on 45. A billboard blared EARTHMAN FUNERALS. As opposed to what, I wondered? Venusian funerals? But it turned out that Earthman was the name of a funeral home.

Beyond the Northline Mall, we ran into the stretch of used-car dealerships, filling stations, convenience stores, and carpet outlets that rings the city. Around Little York, we encountered heavy new-car sales, boat sales, car phone outlets, and day-care centers.

Traffic thinned out considerably beyond the Greenspoint Mall. By the time we passed the Goodyear Blimp hangar and launching field, the highway was mostly lined on both sides by pine forest. With a long straight run of Interstate ahead, Roy instructed me to hang well back and try to stick with other cars as much as possible, except when we approached an exit.

We drove past long rows of shiny new tractors in a green field, past an antique-car museum called Vida's Vintage Vehicles (as in Vida Blue?), past a couple of strip centers, then we were back in the woods again. Houses were half-hidden in the trees to left and right, a sort of suburbia-in-the-pines.

We were a few miles past the exclusive Woodlands development when Nivia took an exit. She got onto the access road, drove past a new strip center under construction, and turned right onto a brand new four-lane road that led arrow-straight back into the forest.

The freshly laid pavement was black and the lane stripes vivid yellow and white. Other new roads led off this one, and I caught glimpses of a few model homes under construction, but the place was still pretty quiet, just getting started.

The new pavement ran out after a couple of miles, then the road immediately narrowed to two lanes and started to wind. The blacktop was gray, cracked, and washed out in places. It eventually gave way to gravel, and the gravel to a rutted dirt trail. As the ruts deepened, our progress slowed, until we were creeping along. We'd lost sight of the Blazer, but I kept going until Roy told me to stop.

He got out and carefully pushed the door closed without latching it, then ran ahead to scout the scene. He was back a few minutes later to say that the Blazer was parked behind a cabin a hundred yards ahead. We stashed the pickup on a fire trail we'd passed about fifty yards back, then I followed him to the cabin.

. . . .

It occupied most of a small clearing. A frame house with a rusty tin roof, a green glaze of mildew over gray shingles, and a porch running across the front. I didn't see anybody at first, then a screen door slammed, and Bubba appeared on the porch. He stood there for a moment, looking our way, and he appeared to be staring straight at me.

I was starting to pull back when Roy laid a hand on my arm and whispered, "Don't move."

Bubba hawked and spat, then turned and walked off the porch. He disappeared around the corner, and a few seconds later, an engine started.

Nivia's blue Blazer pulled into view and went up the trail. I figured Bubba was driving, but I couldn't actually see who was at the wheel.

I watched the Blazer disappear, then turned to Roy. He'd dropped into a squat and looked perfectly comfortable sitting there on his haunches, but it made my knees hurt just to watch.

"What now?" I whispered. "Do we go up and knock on the door?"

192

"Why don't we just watch for a while?"

I saw the wisdom of his caution when a man of about Bubba's size came strolling around the side of the cabin with a shotgun in the crook of his arm.

"If we're gonna try anything," Roy whispered, "we should wait till dark."

I glanced at my watch. It was 12:10. "That's eight or nine hours away."

"Yep."

"So, we just wait?"

"Yep."

"If we're going to be here all day, we're going to need something to eat and drink."

"Uh huh," he agreed.

"Which one of us goes?"

He looked back at the man with the shotgun, who was on the porch. "Guess it better be you."

I drove back to the access road and found a convenience store, where I bought some sandwiches, a few candy bars, a couple of apples, a quart of juice, and a gallon of water. I should've bought two gallons.

37

It was hot and still under the pines, and the tangy sweet odor of pinesap made the humid air feel sticky. Sweat didn't evaporate; it rolled off in sheets. We ran through half a gallon of water in the first hour and had to ration ourselves to occasional sips after that. Flying bugs, ranging in size from microscopic gnats to huge bluebottle flies, were a constant harassment.

"You didn't pick up any insect spray, did you?" Roy asked.

"No, but I could go back for it and pick up another bottle of water while I'm at it."

He shook his head. "Bubba could come back at any time, and I don't want you runnin' into him."

Roy reconnoitered, making a big circle around the house. I wanted to go with him, but he said it'd be too noisy with two of us. What he meant was that *I* was too noisy, but he was too polite to say so.

He started off across the pine needles, making no more than a faint rushing sound as he went. At twenty feet, I could no longer hear him, and I lost sight of him within a hundred.

Fifteen minutes later, he whispered my name, and I jumped halfway up a tree. He said there was a well in back, along with an outhouse, and a rotting shed. "I could see straight through a row of windows all the way to the front door," he added. "Looked like it's mostly one big room."

The mosquitos began to send in scouts around five o'clock, and by six-thirty, they'd arrived in force. I swatted at them until Roy said flatly, "Do that again, and I put you down."

. . . .

By nine, it was pitch-black under the trees. There was no moon yet, but there was a shimmer of starlight on the clearing and a yellow incandescent glimmer from the back of the cabin.

The guard was on the porch again, and I watched the glowing tip of his cigarette as Roy worked his way toward the cabin. When I couldn't hear him anymore, I started circling around to the right, feeling my way from tree to tree. I tried to move like Roy, but I knew I was making too much noise. I stopped after a hundred feet or so and looked back toward the porch.

The plan was simple. When Roy reached the edge of the clearing, he would rustle some bushes to attract the guard's attention and try to draw him away, and I would use the diversion to approach the house.

When I'd asked Roy what would happen if the guard just opened fire on the bushes, he'd showed me a ball of twine he'd found in the lockbox of my pickup and said he intended to be behind a thick tree at the time. I'd worried that the guard would find the twine and realize he'd been tricked, but Roy had promised to take it with him if he could. Though the guard hadn't shown a flashlight yet, that didn't mean he didn't have one. If the man pulled one, Roy said, he'd just have to try to stay out of the light.

Roy's ploy seemed to work. The guard left the porch to investigate, still without a flashlight, and I headed for the cabin.

There were three windows in the side wall, but only the small one near the back showed a light. When I reached the edge of the clearing, I stopped to listen for any sound of the guard's return. Hearing nothing, I jogged toward the house.

The window was too high to see into, but there was a rusty wheelbarrow leaning against the wall, so I pulled it up to stand on.

I got my hands on the sill and pulled myself up until I could see inside. I made it just in time to see Nivia leave a small room, one hardly bigger than a cell, furnished with a cot, a chair, and a lamp.

I got down from the wheelbarrow and moved around to the back of the cabin. The door was open, and yellow light spilled through the screen door and the row of windows beside it. The nearest window overlooked the sink, and I could see Nivia standing there pouring herself a glass of water from the tap.

She was bringing the glass to her lips when she caught sight of me, and the glass slipped from her fingers.

As it shattered in the sink, I rushed the screen door, shushing and pleading with her, "Don't scream, please. It's only me, Bill Cochran." When I pulled the screen open, she stumbled back and almost fell. "There's nothing to be scared of," I told her.

Finding her voice, she demanded, "How'd you get here?"

"We followed you."

"You *did?*"

"Yes. Are you being held here?"

"What does it look like?"

"We can get you out."

She laughed weakly. "Can you?"

"Yes."

"You'll protect me?"

"Yes, we will."

She turned to the front door as the guard stepped inside. "Good work so far," she said.

As the man raised his shotgun, Nivia sensibly stepped out of the way. I was worried until I saw Roy slip through the door behind him. As the shotgun came level with my belly, Roy laid the barrel of his revolver against the side of the guard's head and said quietly, "I wouldn't." The man froze, and Roy told him, "Move real slow now, and lean your weapon against the wall."

The guy didn't move, just stood there looking at me, his shotgun pointing at my midsection and a disagreeable look on his hairy face. I thought he might shoot me anyway, just out of spite, but in the end, he muttered "Shit!" and regretfully parked his shotgun against the wall.

He was a big fellow, only slightly smaller than Bubba, but softer and more unkempt. Long stringy brown hair, a scruffy beard, and a sweat-stained tee shirt, with Andrew Dice Clay on it, puffing a cigarette and saying, "Suck my fumes, momma!"

"Step away from the gun," said Roy. "Over there to the post."

The interior of the cabin was rustic, with an open beam ceiling and a row of support posts cutting the main room in half.

"Put your arms around it," Roy told the guard. When the man complied, Roy cuffed his wrists around the post. "Now, step back two steps, lean on it, and spread 'em." Roy waited for the guard to do as he was told, then pressed the revolver to the back of his head and patted him down with the other hand.

One of the back pockets yielded a small .22 pistol, the other a blackjack.

I said, "You're the one who followed me back to Galveston, aren't you?"

He turned and spat a gob of white sputum onto the floor. As it hit, Roy's hand came up smoothly and brought the blackjack down on his shoulder. The man slumped and hissed, but he didn't resist any further, and Roy continued his search.

The front pockets contained a longhorn money clip and a couple of hundred in cash, plus some loose change and a ring of keys. Roy also pulled a switchblade from a sheath in the man's right boot.

"No wallet," Roy said, then asked him, "What's your name, chubby?"

"Fuck you," the man said.

Roy gave him a short, hard punch to the kidneys.

He groaned as he slid to the floor, and Roy said, "Yeah, that's it. Why don't you sit down?" Turning to me, he added, "If you don't mind a suggestion, boss, I think we should get out of here."

"What about him?"

"We can't get more'n three of us into the cab of your pickup, and it's be chancy puttin' him in the back."

"Yeah." I asked Nivia, "Is there a phone?"

"Not that I've seen."

Roy asked the guard, "Hey, chubby, this place got a phone?"

"Fuck you."

"Was that a no?" Roy asked me.

We searched the cabin, but we didn't find a telephone.

We left the guard his clip, his money, and his loose change, but we kept his pistol, blackjack, switchblade, and shotgun. Roy told him to sit tight, that somebody would be along for him shortly.

I let Roy drive and put Nivia between us. As soon as we were in motion, I said, "Now, I want you to start by telling us how many times you saw Joe Ahern with Dee-Dee."

"Like I told you," she said, "I never actually saw them together. I only saw what might have been him knocking on her door."

"Then you lied to Malcovitch."

"Yes."

"Why?"

"Because I was told to."

"By Bubba?"

Her mouth tightened. "I'm not talking about that now. Not here."

"Where, then?"

"Not anywhere near Houston."

"What about Dee-Dee? Will you talk about her?"

She thought about it. "What do you want to know?"

"Everything. How she was involved in this. How she knew Joe. Why she was killed. Why Jimmy McBride would have her phone number."

"Jimmy?" She laughed. "Why *wouldn't* he have her number?"

"Why *would* he?"

"Because he's her *brother*."

Roy snorted.

"Her brother?" I asked.

"Half-brother," she said and turned to me. "You don't know anything, do you?"

"Less than I thought," I admitted.

She nodded and came to a decision. "I don't think I should tell you any more until we're away from here."

"Is that really necessary? I mean, the police should be able to protect you."

"Not a chance!" she said. "I've heard of too many *protected*

198

witnesses getting killed. You get me out of here—out of Houston—then we'll talk. Not before."

I looked over at Roy, who was concentrating on the road. We were back on gravel now, but the way was still dark and narrow.

"So, where do you want to go?" I asked her.

She said without hesitation, "Dallas."

"If I take you there, will you tell me everything?"

"Yes."

"What do you think, Roy?"

"I don't care much for the idea."

"Why not?"

"You think Cobb'll like it?"

"What choice do we have?"

"We could try beatin' it out of her."

"You feel up to that?"

He glanced at her. "Guess not."

38

We stopped at a phone, so I could make a couple of calls. The first was to the Sheriff's Department. I gave the officer my name, told him about the man in the cabin, and explained how to get there. When he asked me how I was involved, I referred him to Sergeant Puckett. Then I called Puckett at the home phone number he'd given me, thinking he wouldn't be at the station at ten-thirty at night. He wasn't at home, either, so I left a message on his device.

Roy drove us to Houston Intercontinental, where I used my credit card to purchase three tickets to Dallas.

I left the waiting area to call Peg. The closest bank of phones were all in use, in spite of the hour, so I had to find another one down the corridor. I woke Peg up, but she was glad to hear from me and excited that I might be on the verge of another breakthrough. She wanted to know all about it, but I held her off, promising to tell her everything as soon as I really *knew* something.

When I got back to the waiting area, Roy was leaning against the wall of the corridor.

"What's up?" I asked.

"She's in the ladies' room."

After a couple of minutes, I asked, "What's she doing in there?"

"Beats me."

Sixty seconds later, I was starting to get antsy. "Maybe you should go in and see if she's all right."

"Me?" he said. "This was *your* idea."

I thought about it. "We could find a woman to do it for us."

"Sure," he said, "give 'em a try."

After several especially tough-looking Texas women strode past, I told him, "Gotta find the right one."

"I'll buy that," he said.

Spotting a studious-looking student-type, who (1) didn't look too intimidating and (2) appeared composed enough not to go to pieces over an unusual request, I said, "Excuse me, miss."

She stopped a few feet away, eyes narrowing suspiciously. "Yes?"

"A friend of ours went into the restroom about ten minutes ago, and we're worried about her. Would you mind checking on her for us?"

The woman glanced from me to Roy and back. "Cops?"

Roy chuckled.

"No," I assured her, "we're not cops. We're not out to arrest her or hurt her in any way. We just need you to help us with this."

"Why are you chasing her?" she wanted to know.

"We're not chasing her," I said. "We're traveling with her, and we just want to make sure she's okay."

She examined me for a moment and, in spite of my size and the scars on my face, apparently decided I looked harmless enough. "All right," she said. "What does she look like?"

"Small, Hispanic, about five feet tall, and very pretty, wearing a red blouse."

She said brightly, "Should be easy enough to spot," and headed for the restroom. But she was back a couple of minutes later to say, "She's not there."

"Not *there?*"

"Not a red blouse in the place."

I asked Roy, "She had a bag, didn't she? Maybe she changed her blouse."

201

Our helper shook her head. "There's nobody in there who looks anything like the person you described."

After she left, I asked Roy, "Nivia couldn't have gotten past you, could she?"

"*Could* have, I guess," he conceded, "if she wore any kind of disguise. I didn't expect her to try to give us the slip here. I thought she really wanted to get out of town, so I might not have noticed if she snuck out the other exit."

Not wanting to admit I'd blown it again, I said, "Maybe it's a trick. Maybe she paid the girl to tell us she wasn't in there, hoping we'd go away."

Roy frowned. "I don't think so."

I didn't think so, either, but I had to know. We finally found an airport cop, who agreed to check it out for us, but she only confirmed what the young woman had said: nobody of Nivia's description was in there.

After getting refunds for our tickets, I tried Puckett at home again and caught him as he was coming in. After hearing what had happened, he let out a long sigh and said, "I'll see you downtown in one hour."

"What about the man we left in the cabin?" I asked. "Maybe he can tell us something."

"Don't worry about him," he said. "I'll call the Sheriff and find out if they've picked him up. I'll also call Cobb and get him to meet us at the station."

"Don't want to forget Cobb," I said.

"Downtown," he repeated. "One hour."

. . . .

When Cobb saw us enter the squad room, he spun on his heel and vanished into an office, slamming the door behind him.

Puckett ambled over. "He was ready to toss both a you in the hoosegow till I talked him out of it."

"Thanks," I said.

His face hardened. "The way you can thank me is by telling me everything. And I mean *everything*."

When he put it that way, I had little choice in the matter. After he was satisfied with my story, I asked about the man we'd left handcuffed in the cabin.

"He got away, too," Puckett said.

"How?"

"When the County car got there, he was gone, handcuffs and all."

"I'll be damned," I said.

Cobb was waiting for us in the hallway when we left the interrogation room. "You just had your last chance," he snarled at me, pale face darkening. "You hear me?"

Roy inserted, "It was my fault as much as it was his."

"You shut up!" Cobb snapped, sticking his chin in Roy's face. "One more fuckup, and I'll see that they pull your license. You get me?"

Roy stood his ground. "Yeah, I get you."

"At least Cochran's got an excuse, being a civilian. You were a cop once."

Roy set his jaw and didn't speak again until we were in the pickup. Then he had some foul things to say about Cobb.

When he was finished, I asked, "This doesn't mean you're off the case, does it?"

"Not on your life," he said. "We're gonna crack this thing now, just to spite the sonofabitch."

39

We had a late night, so I didn't get up until about ten. I ordered a pot of coffee and French toast from room service, then gave Agent-in-Charge Summers a buzz. He was in, and the elderly receptionist with the sexy voice put me through.

"Mister Cochran," Summers said pleasantly, "how are you today?"

"Still plagued by questions."

"Ummm," he said with some reserve. "Sorry to hear that."

"Do you remember the case we discussed?"

"I recall discussing a hypothetical case with you."

"I wondered if the subject of that hypothetical case might again be under investigation. Would you care to speculate on that?"

There was a brief silence, then Summers said, "I'm not at liberty to comment on that subject, not even on a hypothetical level. Sorry I can't be of more help. Thank you for calling." And he hung up.

I figured he'd answered my question, but it was nothing I could take to the police.

Roy called and said he was going to meet Miles Paysee at the torched house. I offered to drive him out or meet him there, but he told me not to bother. He said he was only fifteen minutes away from the house and that Paysee was already on his way. He told me to stick tight and said he'd drop by as soon as they were finished.

It was understood that I would wait for him, but I felt that I should be doing something. Running as fast I could, I always seemed to be a step or two behind, and I decided I couldn't afford to waste a day.

Thinking that it was time I had another chat with Jerry Lamp, I called his office. When Ms. Simms told me he'd called in sick, I phoned the home number listed in Joe's address book.

I got an Asian-sounding man on the line. "Lamp residence," he said very carefully. "May I help you?"

"Could I speak to Jerry Lamp, please?"

"Mister Lamp is not here now."

"Do you know where I could find him?"

"I am afraid I could not tell you that, sir. May I accept a message?"

I thought about it for a moment, then said, "No, thanks," and hung up.

. . . .

Traffic was light going west on I-10, and I made it from the Warwick to Shady Lane Estates in about forty-five minutes. The guard on the gate recognized me and waved me through, assuming I was going to Peg's.

Jerry's twenty-five–acre estate was at the end of the lane, two houses past the Aherns'. Oak trees towered over the high stone fence in front. Through the ornate iron gate, I could see the continuation of the oak-shaded lane climbing a gentle rise to a gleaming white Mediterranean villa.

The intercom stood just below window-level on a shiny steel post. A tiny video camera on top swiveled to focus on my face, and the Asian-sounding voice said, "May I help you?"

"I'm here to speak to Jerry."

"Mister Lamp is not at home."

I shook my head. "I think he is, and I'm guessing that he just wants a little privacy. But I think he'll see me. Just say that Bill

Cochran wants to speak to him. Tell him I have something I want to discuss before I take it to the police."

It was a hollow threat, since the police already knew virtually everything I knew, but Jerry wouldn't know that.

"Please wait," he said, and I didn't hear anything for several minutes. Then he said, "You may come in now," and the gates swung inward.

The villa was built on the scale of a castle, reaching fifty yards to right and left, a fanciful creation in whitewashed stucco, with towers and domes and minarets and projecting balconies. It looked more like a walled city than a home.

I drove through an open gate into a cobblestone courtyard. The air was heavy and sweet with the scent of roses and jasmine, and the towering walls dripped with scarlet trumpet vines.

I walked around a gushing fountain up to the main doors, one of which opened gravely at my approach.

The Asian servant emerged, greeted me, and instructed me to follow him. I asked his name, and he said it was Kim Suk Soo. Mister Kim led me from the bright, fragrant heat into the sudden cool of the darkened interior.

We clicked across a vast entry hall, where green marble staircases swept upward on either side to a balconied second story. Overhead, naked men and women gazed down at us from a painted dome, and I imagined that I could hear them whispering about me. I followed Mister Kim across the hall, through another set of doors, and down a corridor into a large conservatory, with three walls of glass and a domed skylight. The room had probably once been filled with growing plants, but now served as Jerry's workshop.

The windows showed a formal garden, but I hardly spared it a glance. My attention was held in the room. One corner was occupied by what looked like a miniature city of the future. Bullet trains whizzed through transparent tubes around and through glittering translucent towers. The back wall of the room was covered with shelves containing models or pieces of models, one section devoted entirely to miniature artificial plants, arranged in precisely ordered rows, ready for use.

Jerry's long work table was crowded with unfinished projects.

The one he was working on was in a fifty gallon aquarium filled with water. It was a model for an undersea city—a system of domes and spheres standing on stilts, connected by more transparent tubes. As I drew closer, I could see tiny fish swimming in the tank, apparently chosen for their similarities to larger fish, appropriate to the scale of the model.

Jerry held a remote control unit with an extended antennae in his hands, trying to control the direction of a tiny submarine.

"Turn, turn, turn," he muttered, twisting a joy stick, but the little sub didn't respond and kept heading straight for the largest of the translucent spheres.

When it struck with a *tonk,* Jerry said, "Doggonnit!" then switched off and turned to me. "I built the sub to scale," he explained, "and the mass is too great for the area of the control surfaces. To make them workable, I'll have to go out of scale, and I hate to do that. It'll spoil the effect."

"Nice model, though," I said.

He nodded absently.

I said, "I spoke to your father and tried to tell him you were in trouble again, but he didn't want to listen to me."

He snorted. "Don't you know by now that daddy doesn't listen? Daddy talks. And when he talks, even the Almighty is supposed to drop whatever he's doing."

"You sound bitter," I said.

"I'm forty years old. You'd think that would make me an adult."

"Maybe he's just trying to help."

"Help *me?*" he asked in disbelief. "It's *him* he's worried about. He's afraid I'll make him look like a fool in the eyes of all the important people, and they'll stop coming to see him. He doesn't care any more about me than he did about my mother. He was in D.C. for some conference when she died. I called him and told him she was asking for him. I begged him to come back, but he wouldn't. Said he couldn't. Said he had to speak that night. And by the time he made it home, it was too late."

He looked down, staring at the remote control in his hand as though seeing it for the first time. He reached out to collapse the antennae, then turned it around and swung the heavy metal case with all his might into the side of the aquarium.

Glass exploded. Water gushed out, spewing across the work table. As he pulled his hand away, I saw a wedge of glass sticking out of his arm just above the wrist.

I sprinted around the table and grabbed his arm. Not seeing anything that would serve as a bandage, I tore off my shirt, then quickly pulled out the glass and wrapped the shirt around his forearm. I raised his arm straight up to slow the bleeding, while applying direct pressure through the material, and yelled, "Mister Kim!" Seeing him standing in the doorway, I snapped, "Bring the first aid kit!"

He nodded once and was gone in a blink.

Still holding the arm raised, I helped Jerry across the room, then lowered him into a chair and squatted beside him. He seemed stunned, maybe in shock, breathing rapidly and staring at nothing.

"Just hold on," I said and looked up as Kim appeared silently at my shoulder, holding out a blue cotton pullover.

I took it, and he said, "I will care for him."

As I slipped into the pullover, he took my place, unwound my shirt, and handed it back to me. I rolled it up and watched as he staunched the bleeding, cleaned the wound, and applied a bandage. Then he gave Jerry a shot of something—I didn't ask what—and stood up.

"Thank you," I said.

He said dryly, "It is my job," then picked up his bag and left us alone again.

I pulled up a chair and watched Jerry recover.

It was an interesting process. After a minute or two, all of his tension seemed to ease out with a sigh. His eyes flickered shut for moment, then opened, blinked a few times, looked around to see where he was, and finally focused on me.

"I'm sorry," he said dreamily.

"My fault," I said.

He shook his head. "My father . . ." He trailed off.

"You *are* in trouble, aren't you?"

He nodded.

"I don't really care what you've done," I said. "All I want to know is who killed Joe."

He rocked his head from side to side. "He would kill me."

"Who would?"

The head kept rocking.

"Tell me," I said. "Your father?"

Nothing.

"Whoever it is, we can stop him."

But he was off on his own track now. "You know," he said, sounding drunk, "it's crazy. How one thing leads to another."

"That's the way it happens," I agreed.

"One little step," he said.

"That's all it takes."

He yawned broadly. "My daddy thinks he's in control—him and God—but they're not."

"No."

"I mean, you do something, and . . ." He stared off, blinking as if to clear his eyes. Then the lids began to droop, his mouth lolled open, and his head wobbled on his neck.

"Talk to me," I said.

His chin dropped to his chest, and he was snoring.

"Jerry," I said.

As I reached out to shake him, Kim said from behind me, "He is sleeping now."

"What did you give him?"

"He needs rest now," he explained, "or he will injure himself."

"What did you give him?" I repeated.

"You must go now," he said.

There was a small chrome-plated automatic in his hand.

"Guess so," I said.

"Yes."

"I only wanted to talk to him," I said. "I think he could use somebody to talk to right now."

"He needs rest," he repeated. Gesturing politely with the gun, he added, "I will show you out."

40

I made it back to the Warwick about 2:30 and found a terse note from Roy.

Came by at one. Where were you? I'm your backup, remember?

R. R.

I called his house and left a message on his device, then went out for some crab claws at Guido's. I was back at the hotel again about four o'clock and found another note.

That's strike two. See you at 6:00.

After I'd apologized to him and promised never to do it again, Roy said, "We'll let it slide this once."

"Thanks."

He nodded.

"What'd Miles say about the house?" I asked.

"Said it was maybe arson and maybe not. We found the stove."

"Yeah?"

"Had a clock on it with a broken face, just like he said. But it was tipped on its back, with half the roof on top of it, which could explain why the glass was broken."

"No short wires?"

"Didn't find any."

"You talk to the witness?"

"Nah, the man you spoke to is in the hospital." When he saw my look, he said, "Wasn't anything like that. He went in for some tests, a woman told us."

I told him about my call to the F.B.I. and my visit to Jerry's house.

"Your friend, the fed, is afraid he'll get canned for talkin' out of school," Roy said. "And the Lamp kid sounds like a junkie."

"He's on something," I agreed.

"He can't make his loan payment; he's about to see his business go belly up; and there's a chance he might even go to jail. So, he decides to make a run for it and knocks over his old man's vault because he needs cash."

"And because it's his way of getting even with the Reverend."

"It listens," said Roy.

"I wouldn't be surprised if Jerry told his father what he'd done. After all, what good is vengence unless the victim knows?"

"You don't think the Reverend would turn him in?"

"And have his son go to prison? No, I don't think so."

"Maybe not," he conceded.

"Of course, it's possible that the Reverend's in on it, too. He used his influence to save the boy the first time. Maybe this time, he let him steal the money he needs to get away."

Roy said, "You like it better with the Reverend in it, don't you?"

"I don't care for the man," I admitted.

He nodded. "But, if Jerry ripped off the five million, why is he still here? And why's he hasslin' with this Research Center thing?"

"Maybe he thinks he can make even *more* out of the Center."

"How?"

"That's the question. There's twelve million in the building fund, but that's in escrow and . . . Hey, wait a minute."

Roy waited.

"Maybe that's it," I said. "If they *are* planning to take the building fund, maybe they can't do it as long as the money's in escrow. Maybe that's why the house was torched. Maybe Jerry figured that, with no house, the people would give up and let him have his land, so construction could begin, and the fund could be freed from escrow."

"You might have something there," he said.

"Trouble is, I still don't see how he expects to steal the money."

"Why don't you talk to your accountant friend?"

I tried Pete Shirmer at home and got his answering device. I left a message asking him how somebody could steal the Research Center's building fund. I said, if he had any thoughts on the subject, he should give me a call.

• • • • • • • • • • • •

Roy had just left when the phone rang. I thought it was Pete calling back with a brainstorm. Instead, a trembling voice whispered, "This is Jimmy McBride."

"Well, hello. Where are you?"

"Never mind that," he replied. "But we need to talk."

Recalling that Joe had said the same thing to me back at the start of this, I said, "Okay, where do we meet?"

"We don't *meet* nowhere," he said. "We talk *now,* on the phone."

"About what?"

"How we can help each other."

"How's that?"

"You tell the cops I'll give them Jerry and Bubba, if they give me immunity."

"Sounds fair enough. So, tell me something."

"After we got a deal."

"No," I said firmly. "If you expect me to trust you, you have to give me something. Something I can confirm."

After a brief silence, he said, "They found something at the

212

murder scene, something they haven't made public yet, something that ties the girl's death to another murder five years ago."

"What is it?"

" 'Born to burn,' " he said.

"What's that?"

"Just tell them that."

"How do I contact you?"

"You don't. I'll call you tomorrow night, same time. You talk to the police and give me their answer."

He hung up before I could agree.

I left messages for Puckett at home and at Homicide, then I phoned Roy.

"Things are startin' to break our way," he said thoughtfully.

"Then why do you sound worried?"

"It's Jimmy," he said. "We're gonna need him. And I'd feel a whole lot better if he was in custody right now."

"What does 'Born to burn' mean?"

He was silent.

"Roy?"

"It's a secret," he said.

"Are we partners in this, or not?"

"Yeah."

"Well, if it has something to do with the case, don't you think I should know about it?"

He sighed. "If I tell you, you gotta promise not to make it public, at least not till this thing is over."

"All right," I said impatiently, "you have my solemn oath. Now, what is it?"

"Five years ago, they found 'Born to burn' written on the forehead of a dead prostitute in a motel down on Navigation. It was never released to the press because the department was afraid a serial killer was starting up, and they didn't want any copy cats spoiling the trail. But they never saw it again. Just that once. I only know about it because I was partnered for a while with one of the detectives on the case.

"Anyway," he said, "this could cut both ways. Ahern was pitching for the Astros five years ago, wasn't he? Maybe Cobb and

Puckett figure he iced the first prostitute, too, and just now got around to repeatin' his crime."

"I don't believe it," I said.

"He didn't sound like the type," Roy agreed. "And he sure as hell doesn't fit the profile. But just remember that you promised not to tell anybody about it."

"I'll have to tell the cops."

"If Jimmy's right, then Cobb and Puckett already know about it. But you can't tell anybody else."

I regretted the promise already. "Okay," I agreed. "Until this is over."

"And I mean *all over,*" he said.

"All right," I said. "Agreed."

I was caught in a squeeze between my promise to Peg and the one to Roy. Here, I had evidence that might help me clear Joe's name, and I'd sworn not to reveal it to anyone. Not even to Peg.

Somehow, the lock and chain didn't seem strong enough that night, and in the end, I had to move the dresser in front of the door before I could get to sleep.

41

When the phone rang the next morning, I thought it might be Puckett, but it was Pete Shirmer returning my call.

"Sorry I didn't get back to you last night," he said. "Just got in."

"You accountants lead such wild lives." He chuckled. "Any ideas on my problem?" I asked.

"As long as the fund's in escrow," he said, "it's probably safe. But when it comes out—especially while the transfer is being made—it might be vulnerable. They'd need a high-class hacker and probably somebody on the inside, to furnish him with security codes. Unless their man's a super hacker. In which case, he might be able to bypass the security codes altogether."

Puckett had said that Wilmer Ott had a lot of fancy computer gear in his bedroom and claimed to be a free-lance programmer. A hacker, in other words. "Ever heard of Wilmer Ott?" I asked.

"No, but that doesn't mean anything. Pirate hackers often change their names, and some of the best are only known by their programming styles."

"Can you find out when the building fund comes out of escrow?"

"It's tomorrow," he said smugly. "The groundbreaking has been rescheduled for Monday."

"You've really been pounding away at this, haven't you?"

"Hell, it's all I've done since you called me. You've got my curiosity working overtime."

"Do you have a contact at the bank that handles the escrow account?"

"That's who told me the appeal for the restraining order had been dropped."

"You should tell him that somebody is going to try to steal the Energy Center building fund."

He was silent for a beat. "You're *sure* about that?"

"It's the only way this makes sense."

"Then I'll tell him," he said.

"Good."

"If you're right," he added, "you'll have some grateful friends at the bank."

"I'll be satisfied if we can just stop the bad guys on this one. It's time somebody slowed them down."

"Who are *they?*"

"I have some ideas, and I'll tell you about them as soon as I have some proof."

Puckett called, and I read him my notes on my conversation with Jimmy McBride.

"You sure it was him?" he asked.

"Who else would it be? Did you find 'Born to burn' written on Cordelia Mae's forehead?" When he didn't answer, I said, "I know about the other dead prostitute five years ago."

"You get that from Rodgers?"

"Don't worry. I promised not to say anything about it, not even to Peg. But do you honestly believe Joe was the killer?"

"He *could* have been. We checked it out, and the Astros were in town the night the first one was killed."

"Joe Ahern was no killer," I declared. "But what about Jimmy's deal? You buying it or not?"

"I'll get back to you."

"I'm going to be out today. I'll call you at noon."

. . . .

Bubba Lusby wasn't at home. A couple of the tenants were sunning themselves by the pool, but neither knew where he'd gone. I asked about Nivia, and after some discussion, they agreed that they hadn't seen Nivia or Bubba for several days.

Roy called Yancy Carpenter, the detective investigating the church robbery, who wasn't having any more luck at finding Bubba than we were. Roy suggested that he check the casefile on the poolhall killing in which Bubba had been a suspect, saying that it should contain a list of his hangouts. Yancy found the list, but he didn't want to read it out to us. He had to be reminded that it was Roy who'd told him about the file before he reluctantly gave us the list.

The information was three years out of date, but at least it gave us a place to start.

We began with a visit to a kicker joint out on Telephone Road, one with big yellow letters on the side hawking NUD DANCING and BEAUTIFUL G RLS. Inside, it was a big room with a long bar, a stage at one end, and maybe a hundred tables. At eleven o'clock in the morning, the place was almost empty and smelled of sour beer and stale smoke.

We took a seat at the bar and picked up a couple of cold Lone Stars and a terse "Bubba *who?*" from the potbellied Mr. Clean behind the bar. Not a hair on his glistening dome and only two tiny tufts of it, like reversed parentheses, where his brows should have begun.

A woman was asleep with her head on one of the tables, a young couple sat at the counter off to my right, and a skinny little weasel of a guy sat a couple of stools to Roy's left.

"Bubba Lusby," I repeated.

"Don't know him," the bartender said.

"Maybe you just don't know his name," Roy suggested. "He's a cowboy. Bigger'n you. Belly out to here. Head broad as a dinner plate. High squeaky voice."

The man thought about it all of a second and repeated, "Don't know him."

When I took out a five dollar bill, the bartender froze. He watched me fold the bill into a neat little square and slide it across the counter. "We just want to know where to find Bubba," I said.

As he made the five disappear and turned away, I said, "Hey!"

He turned back. "Yeah?"

"What about it?" I asked.

"What?"

"The information."

"What information's that?"

"About Bubba."

"Bubba who?"

"You took the money," I pointed out.

" 'Course I did," he said. "Man offers me money, I take it. It's a rule I live by."

The Weasel sounded like he was snorting beer through his nose.

"It was meant to be an exchange."

"Oh," he said. "What for?"

"For information about Bubba Lusby."

"I tole you," he said patiently. "I don't—"

"I know." I raised a hand. "You don't know him."

He nodded.

"Right," I said. "Keep the five. It was worth it for the conversation." I spun around on my stool and asked the room if anyone there had ever heard of Bubba Lusby.

The young couple agreed that neither of them had ever heard the name or laid eyes on the man we described. The young girl said she would like to see such a man, but her boyfriend didn't think that was such a hot idea. The Weasel's eyes didn't track. They moved independently, and neither looked directly at me. Like the couple and the bartender, he claimed to have never heard of Bubba Lusby, but he said he'd take a five if I had another one to spare. I took a last glance at the sleeper, decided not to disturb her, and told Roy, "Let's go."

We visited a bowling alley on Richmond, but nobody there had ever heard of him, either. Then we tried a pool hall on Shepherd— the same pool hall outside which a man had been beaten to death a few years before. The man who worked the cash register said sure, he knew Bubba. But after a few minutes of conversation, it became obvious that it wasn't the same Bubba. His was a smaller guy who

218

ran a sheet metal works in Galveston, and his name wasn't Lusby, it was Loveday. There was a distinct possibility that the man was putting me on, but I couldn't prove it.

After that, we broke for lunch, and I called Homicide.

Puckett said, "The DA's interested, but he wants to talk to McBride before he commits himself. If he believes the kid can deliver Lamp, then he'll make a deal."

"That may not be good enough," I said. "You lay on too many conditions, and he may just cut and run."

"It's the best the DA can offer. See what else you can get out of McBride."

"I'll let you know."

"You won't have to."

"Why not?"

"We'll be there with you, listening in. That's part of the deal."

42

There were seven people in my room that evening. The police technician, who installed the tap, the man from the phone company, who would direct the tracing of the call, plus Puckett, Cobb, Roy, the Assistant District Attorney, and me.

The night before, Jimmy had called a few minutes after nine, but the whole gang was there by six, just in case the call came early. By nine o'clock, the room was littered with heaping ashtrays and sacks of carry-out food.

By nine-thirty, the crowd was getting restless.

At ten-fifteen, the ADA shrugged and said, "Guess the kid got cold feet." He told the technician, "Keep the trace on here till eleven. I'll see if the hotel can give us an adjoining room and set up a listening post, just in case he tries later. We'll keep it on through the weekend."

By eleven-thirty, Roy and I were alone. The listening post had been set up in the next room, and somebody would be on duty there twenty-four hours a day until Sunday midnight.

I asked, "What do you think happened?"

"Wouldn't be surprised if Bubba got to him," Roy said. "A kid like that's bound to leave a trail. People don't forget somebody with pink hair."

The next morning, we went back to following our list. We drew blanks at a barber shop, a couple more bars, a newstand-lunchroom that Roy said was a front for a bookmaker, and a Mexican restaurant. After some of the greasiest burritos I'd ever tasted, I called Pete Shirmer to find out what had happened at the bank.

"Did they stop Ott?" I asked him.

"They did even better than that. They let him *take* it."

"They *what?*"

"It's a setup," he said. "With your warning, the bank had time to install shadow programs and were able to track the money as it was diverted into thirteen smaller commercial accounts—all of which, were opened within the last two weeks. But there's no money in those accounts now, just a whole lot of trouble for anybody who tries to withdraw any of it."

"Damn!" I laughed and felt like dancing. "We may have finally hit these people where it hurts. I owe you dinner for this. An expensive dinner."

"I'll pay for the dinner," he said, "if you'll just tell me what the hell is going on."

. . . .

That afternoon, Roy and I finally had some luck. Bubba was known to hang out with a guy named Humble Suggs, who ran a junkyard out west, off State Highway 6. Suggs had bought the place from a man named Redford Dokes, and it was still called Red's Auto Parts.

Red's Auto Parts and Garage Service was in an undeveloped area just across the city line. It occupied a newly renovated building on one side of the road, with the junkyard on the other. The yard was a big one, spread over a couple of dozen acres, surrounded by a high chain link fence covered with blue plastic sheeting to block the view. The entrance to the junkyard was offset about fifty yards down the road. As we drove past, I spotted Bubba leaning on the side of a silver Sedan de Ville in front of an unpainted wooden shed.

Roads ran on all four sides of the yard, so we could drive all the way around it. On the back side, I saw a lone oak tree with a limb hanging over the fence, and I coasted the pickup onto the verge.

As I switched off the ignition, I asked Roy, "You coming in with me?"

"Molly'd never forgive me if I let you go in alone." He checked his revolver, then got out and slipped it back into his hip holster. "But I'd feel better if you had a weapon."

"I do."

He eyed the Louisville Slugger as I pulled it out of the lockbox. "Not much range," he said.

I swished it through the air. "But plenty of stopping power."

Roy went first, going up the tree like a monkey. Not bad for a man with a bad ticker. Hanging onto the limb over the fence, he said, "There's a little patch of grass below."

I handed him my bat, and he tossed it over. He went after it, and with some difficulty, I followed. I was still sore from the beating, and the landing nearly finished me. When I was able to move, Roy helped me up and handed me my bat.

We cautiously wound our way through a graveyard of cars, trucks, buses, and even a bulldozer, through the stink of oil, dust, rust, and metal, all simmering in the afternoon heat. When we reached a large clearing near the front, we crouched behind an accordioned Chevy pickup and took a look.

There was a car crusher at the center, about fifty feet away. It looked like one of those long boxlike dumpsters you see at construction sites. Only this one was better than thirty feet long and fifteen feet tall, covered with rust like fuzzy red-brown moss. A crane was raised on steel supports at one end, with its arm tilted over the crusher and a huge electromagnet hanging at the end of the cable.

I could see Bubba's Cadillac, but nobody was in sight, so we made a dash for the gap between the crane's supports and the crusher. When I peeked around the corner, I saw Jimmy McBride standing in front of the unpainted shed. He was sandwiched between Bubba and another big man—the one we'd left handcuffed to a post in a house up in the pines. Humble Suggs, I assumed.

We were too far away to hear what they were saying, but it was evident that Jimmy wanted to leave and that Bubba wanted him to stay. Jimmy raised his voice a time or two in protest, but in the end, he let Humble lead him into the shed.

After Bubba drove off in his Cadillac, I left Roy at the crusher and went to call the cops. I climbed back over the fence and drove my pickup about a mile down the road to a pay phone at a gas station.

The officer who answered said Cobb and Puckett weren't there.

"Do you know when they'll be back?"

"No, I don't. Can I take a message?"

"You can beep them," I said impatiently. "And tell them, if they want to talk to Jimmy McBride, he's being held in the office of the junkyard across from Red's Auto Parts off State Highway 6 at Huffmeister and Springfield Road."

"Held against his will?"

"That's the way it looked to me."

"Did you see any use of force or a weapon?"

"No, but I could tell he didn't want to be there."

"That's Harris County jurisdiction, but I'll see if the sheriff can send somebody to take a look."

"I'd appreciate that," I said, "and so would the DA. He's looking for this guy, too, you know."

The County car arrived not long after I made it back to the crusher. The man I'd pegged for Humble Suggs came out to talk to the officer and, after a few words, led him into the shed. They were in there for five minutes or more, but in the end, they came out smiling.

As the officer got into his car, I asked Roy, "Should we try to stop him?"

He shook his head. "Wouldn't do any good," he said. "Just give us away."

"How could he not have seen Jimmy?"

He shrugged. "Don't know. But if he saw him, he wouldn't be leavin' ."

Watching the cop drive away, I wondered if the shed had a cellar.

43

Now that the County had come looking for Jimmy, I kept expecting Humble to get him out of there, but nobody left the shack. Maybe Humble figured he was safe, since the cops had already checked there, or maybe he was just waiting for orders from Bubba.

It was about eight-thirty when Bubba finally came back, and I figured our time was running out. After he disappeared into the shed, I told Roy, "I'm going to give Puckett another call."

"Go ahead," Roy said. "And tell them to hurry."

I spoke to a policewoman this time, who explained that the two sergeants had flown up to Austin this morning, but she said they should be back in town any time now.

"Why wasn't I told this before?" I asked her.

"Maybe the officer you spoke to didn't know about it," she said.

That didn't sound very likely to me. "Would you please tell them I called?"

"I'll do that, sir."

I got some more change from the filling station attendant and called the DA's office. A young man answered and said that everybody else was gone. When I explained the situation, he said he'd try to reach the DA. After that, I called Yancy Carpenter. He'd also left for the day, but the officer promised to beep him and pass on my message.

It was nearly nine and getting dark by the time I made it back to the junkyard. As I climbed over the fence, I heard the sound of a diesel engine. When I stopped to listen, it cut off. I carefully worked my way forward until I could see the crusher. A light-colored American sedan was hanging over it, still swinging slightly from side to side. In the dying light, I could see somebody in the driver's seat. I first thought it was Jimmy, but as the car swung back, the spotlight on top of the crane's control cab showed me a flash of a man with dark hair.

Roy. Goddammit! No!

I pulled back, dropped to my knees, and carefully peeked around the front of the accordioned Chevy pickup. I didn't see anybody else, but I knew they had to be watching. I also knew I couldn't leave Roy.

I was still trying to work it out when a voice behind me said, "Don't you move now."

I glanced back and saw Humble Suggs holding a shotgun on me.

"Tole ya not to move," he said with a grin and pumped his weapon. "Jus' put yer hands up."

I did, asking, "What've you done to Roy?"

"That his name?"

"Is he all right?"

"Don't worry 'bout him," he said. "You just git up and start walkin'. Man wants to talk to you."

Humble stayed right behind me, prodding me whenever I dawdled. We were heading for the shed, but we had to pass the crusher to get there, and my bat was leaning against the near end. If I could just get close enough . . .

With debris scattered everywhere, it looked fairly natural when I tripped over something and stumbled to my left. Humble moved in quickly and gave me a hard jab with the barrel of his shotgun, but not before I'd managed to put the end of the crusher between me and the shed. From here, it would be natural to take the gap between the crane supports and the crusher.

The closer we got, the more nervous I became. It was a lot like

225

the queasy feeling I used to get before a game. But in those days, I was only risking my career. If I didn't handle this right, I could die. On the other hand, I was convinced that Bubba wasn't going to let me live anyway, and this might be my only chance to escape.

I was two strides from the bat, and it was now or never. I picked now.

I stepped on one side of a pipe, slipped the toe of my boot under the other and stumbled into the end of the crusher with a dull clang.

"C'mawn now," said Humble. "No more a that shit."

As he moved in, I got both hands on the bat and spun with it waist high. His shotgun discharged as I knocked it aside. I raised the bat and chopped down on his hands. When he let go of the weapon, I swung at his head, but he threw up an arm to block it.

He went down with a groan, and thinking of Bubba, I took off in full flight back the way I'd come, still hanging onto the bat. Halfway across the clearing, I realized I should have taken the shotgun, but it was too late to go back for it.

I charged on, feeling like I had a target stenciled on my back and knowing I had only seconds before Humble got to his gun. When he did, it was an instant too late. I heard the blast and glass shattering behind me, then tucked my chin to my chest and kept going.

The problem was it was almost completely dark now, and the landmarks I'd used coming in didn't look the same. I managed to miss the bulldozer, took another turn, and ended up on the wrong path. When I found my way blocked ahead, I realized my mistake and had to backtrack.

I was passing the bulldozer again when I heard the shotgun blast. The pellets kicked up sparks as they struck the blade, and one caught me in the right thigh on the ricochet.

I went down in pain, stifling a yelp as I grabbed my leg. Hearing footsteps coming, I got a hand on the bat and pulled it after me as I crawled behind the blade.

When he scuffed to a stop, I stopped, too, and held my breath. I couldn't see him and didn't think he could see me, or he would have fired.

When I heard him move, I crawled around the back of the

226

'dozer. I squeezed between two wrecked cars, then slithered under the bed of a flatbed truck, and came out at an open lane that seemed to lead toward the rear of the lot.

I stopped for a moment and listened, but all I heard were the thrumming of cicadas and the distant whine of traffic. I pulled myself up the side of a car and started limping toward the back fence. The wound sent a jolt of pain through my thigh every time I put my weight on it, so I tried to use the bat as a crutch. It was too short for the job but better than nothing.

The fence was about forty feet away when I stopped for a breather. As I leaned on the front of a van, I spotted Humble through the glassless windows.

He stood very still, maybe fifteen feet away, head cocked as though listening, facing almost in my direction. I didn't think he'd seen me yet. I figured he'd heard me coming and was waiting for me to show myself.

Holding onto the van, I slowly bent down and felt around on the ground until I found a fist-sized rock. Then I stood up, again very slowly, and tossed the rock underhanded, arcing it over his head.

It was an old bit, but bits get to be old because they work. I'd never seen this one fail in a movie, and it proved to be as effective in real life.

The rock struck behind him with a clang and a clatter. I moved as he turned, coming up behind him as he snarled, "Come on out now, or I'll shoot!"

My foot hit something metal, and he heard it. I hit him as he turned. His shotgun discharged again, and I hit him a second time. He grunted and dropped his weapon, but he got a hand on me. When I brought the bat down hard on his shoulder, I heard a gasp, and this time he lolled onto his back.

I found his shotgun and took it with me as I hobbled on, keeping eyes and ears peeled for Bubba. I reached the fence and worked along it until I found a wreck pushed up against the chain links, then leaned the gun against the fence and painfully crawled onto the hood. Dragging my injured leg behind me, I forced myself up on to the roof before I had to stop. My vision was spotted with bright sparks and patches of blackness, and I was afraid I was going to pass out.

When my vision cleared, I got to my knees, then grabbed onto the fence and pulled myself to my feet. I swayed for a moment, too dizzy and weak to continue. But spurred on by the thought of Humble and Bubba behind me, I mustered the energy from somewhere to pull myself to the top of the fence. I threw up a leg and rolled over, but one of my pant's legs caught on a barb, and I slammed into the fence upside down. Then I heard a tearing sound as the fabric gave way, and I was falling again.

I landed flat on my back, knocking the breath out of me. Even after I caught my breath, I lay there. The bright sparks and black patches were back, and I had to give them a chance to clear.

Eventually, I managed to roll onto my belly. After a couple of tries, I made it to my knees. Then, by crawling up the fence, I got to my feet.

I stopped to look around, not sure where I was or which way to go, until I spotted the tree under which I'd parked the pickup. It was off to the left now, only about forty feet away, but it took me awhile to get there. I'd dropped the bat when I'd picked up the shotgun, and both were back in the yard now, so I had to use the fence for support.

My vision was getting spottier all the time, and I had to stop once to let it clear, but I finally drew even with the pickup. After another pause, I hopped across and pulled the door open.

The light came on to show me Bubba in the passenger seat, with another shotgun leveled at my chest.

He said with a wide, triumphant grin, "I knew that sooner or later the little bird was bound to come home to roost."

44

With Bubba holding his shotgun on me, I drove around to the junkyard entrance and parked beside his Sedan de Ville. For some reason, my vision had cleared up as soon as he'd appeared.

Humble limped over and jerked open my door, then heaved me out and took the opportunity to exact some revenge.

Bubba let him get a little of it out of his system before telling him, "Hold on there, Hum. I need to talk to the man 'fore you finish him off." When Humble paused in his pummeling, Bubba said to me, "Now, I want you to tell me everything you tole the police. And if I'm satisfied with it, I might even consider lettin' you live."

When I didn't respond, he let Humble work on me some more. Since I saw no point in letting him beat me to death, I finally told Bubba what he wanted to know.

After he'd clarified a few points, he shook his head and said, "You been real busy, ain't you?" He chuckled. "Man has to admire your persistence. But you'd've lived longer if you'd stuck to writin'."

"That mean we're gonna kill him?" asked Humble.

"Can't leave him 'round here, can we?"

"Can I do him?" Humble requested.

"Hell, no," said Bubba. "You'd take too long. You heard him say he's already called the cops, and they're liable to be here any minute. No, I think the best thing to do is put him in the wreck with the other one and let the compactor take care of both of 'em for us."

I told him, "You don't have to do this."

"Oh, yeah," he said, "I do."

Playing my last trump, I said, *"Anybody* could have killed Joe. But the cops and the DA both know that I saw you and Suggs out here with Jimmy. And if they find us dead, they'll know *you* did it."

"Hell," he said. "If they catch me, I'm up the creek anyway. And you know too damn much."

"I've learned my lesson," I said quietly. "I won't be any more trouble to you."

He grinned. "I believe that, son."

I would have got down on my knees and begged, if I thought it would have helped. But with Bubba, I knew it would only be a source of amusement.

Humble held a shotgun on me as Bubba climbed into the crane's control cab and fired up the engine. The wreck slowly swung our way, then began to descend. As the car touched down, Humble wrenched open the driver's door and, still keeping one eye on me, leaned in to shove Roy over.

Roy didn't resist or complain. He made a squishing sound as he moved and left a thick smear of blood behind him. When Humble gave him a final shove, Roy toppled onto his right side and lay still, now with his butt to me.

Humble stuffed me into Roy's place and cuffed my hands to the wheel. Then he slammed the door, waved to Bubba, and the car started to lift. Things were going too fast, and I was powerless to slow them down. When the car was high enough, Bubba swung it back over the crusher. And it was still swaying from side to side when it began to descend.

The only hope I had left was that Cobb and Puckett would show up in time to stop this. And *that* hope was running out.

I saw Humble hurrying away from the crusher toward the shed.

He went in and came out with Jimmy McBride in handcuffs. The last thing I saw before I dropped below the rim of the crusher was Humble half-dragging Jimmy toward my pickup.

I turned to Roy, but I could see no signs of life. In a flash of light from the spot on top of the crane, I caught a glimpse of closed eyes, and I figured it was just as well that he couldn't see what was coming.

"Sorry," I told him. Too late, but it needed saying. If he hadn't gotten involved with me, he might have lived to a ripe old age, in spite of his bum ticker.

The car settled to the bottom and bounced on its springs. Then the crusher's engine roared; metal screeched; and the side walls— great scarred paddles of steel—began to move inward.

At that point, adrenalin kicked in, and I started jerking on the cuffs, trying to rip off the steering wheel. I hardly noticed the metal edges tearing into my wrists. The urge for self-preservation, I rediscovered, was a powerful motivator.

The car jolted under the impact of the paddles, then shuddered and screamed as the frame began to buckle. I turned my head away as the windshield shattered. When my door started moving inward, I slid toward Roy, but that was no good, either, as his side of the car was also being pushed inward. I ducked at the sound of the rear window shattering and went on jerking frantically on the wheel.

When the paddles froze in place and began to pull back, I thought I was saved. But after they retracted to their original positions, they didn't stop. They started moving up the sides. When they were near the top, they swung from vertical to horizontal and moved together overhead, shutting me in darkness.

The engine roared again, and seconds later, I felt the crash as the paddles hit the top. Then the car gave up a piercing keen as they pressed downward.

As the roof caved in, I swung my right leg up onto the seat behind Roy and rolled him onto the floor. Dead or not, I didn't want to see him flattened. With my hands still cuffed to the wheel, I slid after him. Arms outstretched, I got down as low as I could, half-sitting up with my head and shoulders wedged under the dashboard.

Down the top came, to the wail of tortured metal. And by the time I felt the dashboard coming down on top of me, it was too late to do anything about it. I was stuck there and couldn't move.

As the dashboard continued downward, cutting into my chest and shoulders, I remembered my dream of being squeezed to death in the giant's fist. I swore that, if by some miracle I survived this, I would learn everything I could about the interpretation of dreams.

When I couldn't stand it anymore, I let out a scream—a roar of rage and challenge at the fate that had led me here. The scream filled my ears, going on and on, squeezing out every last micromilliliter of breath. It blotted out the engine's roar, the screech of metal, even the pain and pressure. When it ran out, I couldn't hear anything.

It took me a moment to realize there was nothing to hear. Nothing but a faint throbbing from the crusher's engine.

I didn't know what to think, wasn't thinking well in any case, but when the engine roared again, I prayed it wasn't starting over. I hadn't said a prayer in years—didn't even believe in God—but at that moment, I was willing to try anything.

The car crackled and popped as the paddles lifted off the squashed top. A moment later, a thin sliver of light leaked into my casket as the paddles parted above me. They retracted to the sides, then slid back down to their original positions, and the engine noise died.

I couldn't move and could hardly breathe. The pressure on my chest may have lessened slightly but was still far too intense. I had to hold my breathing to a shallow pant because anything deeper hurt too much.

When something crashed on the hood, I thought it was starting again.

Then a voice called, "Cochran? You in there?"

I tried to answer but found I couldn't make a sound.

"Cochran?"

I sucked in a deep breath, ignoring the pain, and got out, "Puckett?"

Somebody else said something—Cobb, I guessed—and Puckett

snapped, "Shut up. Think I heard something. That you, Cochran?"

"Yeah," I managed, louder this time.

"What's that?"

"Yeah!"

"You all right?"

"I'm alive. I think."

"He's okay," he called to Cobb. Cobb said something back, and Puckett asked me, "Rodgers with you?"

"He's dead."

A ragged voice whispered, "The hell he is."

"Roy?" I said.

Puckett asked, "What?"

"Shut up!" I snapped at Puckett. "Roy, is that you?"

"Yep."

"You're alive?"

"If *you* are."

"Puckett!" I yelled. "He's alive! Roy's alive!"

"Great," he said and called to Cobb, "They're both alive." He told us, "Just hang on, and we'll get you out of there."

"We'd appreciate that," I told him. To Roy, I said, "Why didn't you say something before? I thought you were dead."

"Just woke up," he said. "Thought I heard somebody screaming."

Puckett had made getting us out sound easy, but it wasn't. It took a long time. Much too long. The fire rescue team climbed into the crusher and went to work on the car with saws and torches. The closer they came, the harder it got for me to breathe. Roy said he couldn't move and couldn't feel anything below the neck. He kept fading out on me, and toward the end, I was convinced that we were both going to die before they reached us.

But we didn't.

45

They took us to the Ben Taub Trauma Center. Fortunately for Roy, it was one of the best in the country. The doctors soon transferred me to a less critical care unit, but they didn't let me go until Monday afternoon.

I was bruised and sore all over, had lost a good deal of blood from my thigh wound, had cuts and scratches from flying glass and two cracked ribs from the combined work of the car crusher and Humble's fists. I was hobbling on crutches, with my torso taped and a bandage on my thigh, but I was damn happy just to be alive.

On my way out, I dropped by to see Roy. He'd been shot twice with a .38. The first slug had nicked his lung, ricocheted off a rib, and lodged on his hip. The second had passed clear through his abdomen, punching ragged holes in his stomach and liver. But he was on a spinal ward because of the blow he'd received to the back of his neck, which had dislocated his fourth cervical vertebrae and pinched his spinal cord.

The doctors had immobilized his head in a complicated metal framework, while applying traction to relieve the pressure on his spine. He was taking his meals through one tube, relieving his bladder through another, and his bed had a built-in potty. The doctors were optimistic about his recovery, since the spinal cord was only pinched, not severed, but it hurt me to see him like this, and I couldn't help feeling responsible for his condition.

Roy whispered, "Don't look so down at the mouth." He took a slow painful breath. "Docs're givin' me five-to-one I'll be dancin' again someday." Breath. "Which's pretty remarkable." Breath. "Considerin' I never could before." He made a rasping sound that I took for laughter and ended with a deep racking cough and a groan.

"Don't talk," I said.

"Wanna talk," he insisted. "Tired of layin' here like a corpse."

"Okay. What do you want to talk about?"

"What's happening? They caught Bubba yet?"

I told him what I knew.

Puckett had come by the day before to deliver two pieces of news: the first was that Joe's and Dee-Dee's murder case had officially been reopened, and the department no longer believed it was murder-suicide; the second was that Jimmy McBride had been found dead under a tarp in the bed of my pickup. Pete Shirmer had called around noon today to say that Wilmer Ott had been arrested this morning at a bank in Georgetown on Grand Cayman Island. But Bubba, Humble, Nivia, and Jerry Lamp had all disappeared. I told Roy that Peg had visited twice, convinced now that Joe's name would be cleared. She'd wanted to thank him in person, but he'd slept through both of her visits. So, I read him the note she'd left.

. . . .

Molly was waiting for me in the lobby. She took my bag from the orderly, and we were crossing the sidewalk to her car when I saw Reverend Lamp.

I waited for him to climb out of his El Dorado, then called out, "Where's Jerry?"

"I don't know," he said, walking over. "I thought *you* might."

"No."

"Then he didn't have anything to do with what happened to you?" he asked.

"Oh, he was involved, Reverend. And you know that, or you wouldn't be here."

He stood there for a moment, glancing from me to Molly, not knowing what to say. Finally, he said, "Could I drive you somewhere?"

"No, thanks. I have a ride."

"I really would like to talk," he said.

"About what? You want me to help you cover up for him again?"

"Well, no, I—"

"Because it's too late for that."

"What do they think he's *done?*" he blurted. "Can you at least tell me that? They say he's implicated in serious crimes, but they won't tell me *what crimes.*"

"I don't know if I should—"

"Do they really think he had Joe Ahern killed?" he asked.

"I don't know what they think," I said. "I only know what I told them."

"Do you tell them *that?*"

"No."

"Well, if that's what they think, then they're dead wrong. My son would never have anything to do with killing anybody."

"I hope you're right," I said. Truthfully, I still didn't know exactly how Jerry was involved in the killings.

Molly took my crutches and stashed them in the back seat of her Celica, then helped me in and closed the door. She was climbing in on the driver's side when the Reverend appeared at my window.

I rolled it down.

"I wanted to . . ." He trailed off, shaking his head.

"Yes?" I felt a thin strain of sympathy for the man, seeing him standing there trying to find words for what he was feeling.

"I just wanted to clear up something," he said. "I know you suspected me—and perhaps you still do—of having something to do with Joe's death, because of my connection with Lusby. You were right that I hired him to keep an eye on Jerry, but that's as far as it went. I swear to you that I had no idea what he was up to."

I nodded. "I believe you."

"You *do?*"

"Now that I've seen Bubba in action, I can't picture him working for anybody but himself. But why'd you choose him to begin with, instead of some reputable firm?"

"I suspected that my son was involved in criminal activities," he explained, "activities that a reputable firm would feel compelled to report. So, I asked a friend to find me somebody who would overlook a few improprieties."

"Then you got what you asked for," I said.

"I suppose I did." He cleared his throat and added, "I just wanted to tell you that I'm sorry."

I didn't know if he was saying it to me or to Jerry. Thinking of Joe and Roy and Jimmy McBride, I said, "Yeah. Me, too."

. . . .

When I got home, I consciously put the investigation out of my mind. Letting my answering machine take calls from the press, I stashed my notes in a desk drawer and went back to my novel. Real life was too sad.

I picked up the story where I'd left off just over two weeks before, and by Wednesday evening, I had the climax in pretty good shape. Thursday and Friday, I moved on to the last chapter, working to tie it all together and bring it to a satisfactory conclusion. On Friday evening, Molly and I celebrated my rough draft with dinner at the Wentil Trap.

Saturday morning, three weeks to the day after I'd learned of Joe's death, I got out my notes on the investigation and took a look.

I knew, in general terms, what had happened. Dee-Dee had found out from Jimmy about the planned burglary at the church, or the attempt to rip off the building fund, or Jerry's use of Jimmy's talent for arson. She'd told Joe about it, and he'd started checking it out. Then, Friday night, on his way home from the game, he'd heard about the fire on the radio. Realizing it had to be Jimmy's work, he'd gone over to see Dee-Dee, maybe to talk her into going to the police with what she knew. But Bubba was waiting for him and killed them both.

Bubba had the means, the motive, and the opportunity. Unfortunately, *we* didn't have Bubba. Once again I'd let the culprit slip away, probably into Mexico by now. And to beat it all, we still had no proof he'd killed them. In the classic mystery, all the loose ends were always neatly tied up, but in real life, we always seem to be left with unanswered questions.

I spent the rest of the weekend with Molly, trying to take my mind off the case. I cooked dinner Saturday evening, then took her to a movie. We spent Sunday at the beach, picnicking and playing in the surf. Sunday night, we had an electrical storm for entertainment.

It was a real gulleywasher, complete with outlandish pyrotechnic spectacle and ear-splitting Wagnerian cacaphony. The storm marched on the island in trumpeting blares and clashing cymbals, then settled into a steady drumming downpour accompanied by periodic fanfares. Rising water chased islanders from low-lying areas and flooded stretches of Broadway. Lightning struck trees, one church steeple, one power transformer, and one clearly obsessive jogger. The jolt to the transformer cut off all the electricity to my part of the island, so Molly and I spent the evening in darkness and candlelight, enlivened by brilliant flashes of heavenly fury.

Monday morning, I got a call from Nivia Gonzalez.

46

"You still want the story?" she asked.

"You ready to tell it?"

"For a price."

"How much?"

"Ten thousand."

"Don't be ridiculous."

"Five, then," she said.

"Not five, either. To begin with, how do I know that anything you tell me is the truth?"

"You don't," she said. "But who else are you going to get it from? Bubba, maybe? Or Humble?"

"I have no reason to trust you."

"That's true," she agreed, unashamedly.

"Why'd you run away from me the last time?"

"I was scared," she said. "You can understand that, can't you?"

"Yes."

"I didn't want to go to Dallas, or anyplace else. I just wanted to get out of sight, and my people are in Houston. If I was going to disappear anyplace, it had to be there."

"We were only trying to help you," I said.

"I know that," she said. "But, to me, you looked like Laurel and Hardy, and I was afraid you'd get me killed. Besides, I didn't think I needed your help."

"But now you *do.*"

"I need money," she said.

"Why?"

"To get away."

"I thought you had to be in Houston to disappear."

"I can't stay there any longer."

"Why not?" I asked. "If you were safe there when Bubba *wasn't* being hunted, why aren't you safe there *now?*"

"Because he's been seen around asking questions."

"Around? You mean in *Houston?*"

"That's right."

That was news. "Where?"

"Not far from where I've been staying."

"Why's he after you?"

"Because he knows I saw him leaving Dee-Dee's apartment that night after the shootings."

"Why didn't you tell the police he was around?"

"I *did* tell them, but he was gone by the time they got there. But he'll be back. And sooner or later, he'll *find me.*"

"Okay, okay," I said. "Five thousand is out of the question, but I might be able to put together five hundred."

She hung up on me.

When the phone rang again, I answered it "A thousand's as high as I'm going."

She thought for a second and said, "All right, dammit. I'll take it."

"Where do we meet? You in Galveston?"

"I might be."

"Well, if you *are* in Galveston, you could drive over to my house, and—"

"No," she declared, "I'm not coming to your house. You say you don't trust me. Well, I don't trust *you* not to have the police waiting for me."

"Have you done anything criminal?"

240

"Not if you don't count concealing evidence."

Since I'd done some of that myself, I didn't bother to point out that it was a crime.

"I'll tell you where to come," she said. "You know that empty warehouse at the end of Rosenberg, just across Water Street, on the docks?"

"Yeah."

"I'll meet you there at midnight."

"Hold on," I said. "I don't like that."

"What?"

"Meeting on the docks at midnight."

"Why not?"

"Sounds too much like a trap."

She sighed. "Why would I want to trap you?"

"I don't know," I admitted, "but why does it have to be there?"

"It doesn't *have* to be there, but I can't think of anyplace better. It's private. I'll be able to see you coming and can tell if you're alone."

"No," I declared. "If you want the thousand dollars, you'll have to come up with a better meeting place. Someplace public, on Broadway or the Seawall, where there's light and people around."

She was silent so long that I thought I'd lost her, but she finally said, "All right. But I'm not giving you time to set anything up with the cops. I'll call you at a quarter of twelve and tell you where to go. And you better come *alone,"* she concluded. "If I see anybody who even looks like a cop, I'm out of there."

With that, she hung up, and I was left with another decision to make.

I wanted the answers she could give me, and if I managed to fill in the blanks about Joe, I thought Peg would consider it worth a thousand dollars. Besides, I felt okay about the meeting place, and I really couldn't think of any reason why Nivia would want to trap me.

My pickup had been impounded by the Houston police, and I'd had to rent a car. I'd had my heart set on a 'Vette or a Camaro, but after looking at the rental rates, I'd settled on a "sporty" Ford

Escort. I drove it down to the bank and withdrew the thousand dollars.

Molly came over at seven to fix dinner, after which I pleaded exhaustion and said I wanted to go to bed early. She offered to join me, but I told her I really just wanted to sleep. I could see she was confused by the rejection, and I hated doing that to her, but I knew she'd never let me make my rendezvous alone. At the very least, she'd insist on going with me, and Nivia had made it plain that, if she saw anybody else, I'd never get my answers.

• • • • • • • • • • • • •

Nivia called back at a quarter of twelve and agreed to meet me at the Sonic Drive-in on Broadway. After she hung up, I left a message on Molly's answering device, telling her where I was going. I wasn't really worried, but telling Molly seemed like a sensible precaution. Since she was pulling an all-night surveillance and might not check her messages before morning, it was more of a gesture than anything else. After that, I slipped the business envelope containing the thousand in twenties into the back pocket of my jeans, then hobbled out to the car. I'd been getting around the house without a crutch, but I took one along for this outing. Like the message to Molly, it seemed like the sensible thing to do.

I was reaching for the car keys when somebody kicked the crutch out from under me. I landed hard, and the jolt to my cracked ribs brought out a gasp, but I cut it off as something cold jabbed me behind the ear.

"Don't make a sound," said Humble. " 'Cause there's nothin' I'd like better right now than to blow your head clean off. You hear?"

I nodded.

"All right," he said. "You can get on up, but make it real slow."

I did as he said, stifling my groans as I pulled myself up the side of the car.

When I was on my feet, he told me, "We're just gonna stand here a minute like ole buddies chewin' the fat." He held the .38 at waist level between us, looking all too eager to use it. He was even more unkempt than before and had a wild look to his eyes, as

242

though being a fugitive didn't agree with him. "And you're not gonna try anything smart now, are you?"

I shook my head.

"That's good," he said.

His eyes were nervous, trying to look everywhere at once, but they never strayed from me for more than half a second at a time. Regrets were useless, but I couldn't help wishing I'd brought the police in on this. I thought I'd covered all the bases, but it never occurred to me that they'd be waiting as I left the house.

When the silver Sedan de Ville pulled to the curb, Humble handed me my crutch and shoved me toward the car.

Bubba powered down the driver's window and said with a grin, "We decided the Sonic was a little *too* public after all."

Humble opened the back door for me, pushed my head down, and crammed me inside. When I turned back, he was right behind me, covering me with a new shotgun and shoving the .38 into his waistband.

Nivia peeked around the front passenger seat headrest and said, "Sorry. He found me. I had no choice."

"It's true," Bubba said, as he pulled away from the curb. "She wanted to live."

He made a left, another left at Broadway, and a right onto Rosenberg, where the Texas Heroes Monument stands in the middle of the intersection. He drove past City Hall, which hid the police and fire stations behind it, past the Post Office, and a couple of blocks down, the Moody Railroad Museum.

The road ended at Water Street, and the warehouse where Nivia had wanted to meet was across the street. It was east of the grain elevators and containment loaders, a dark, cavernous former cotton warehouse, with a huge FOR SALE OR LEASE sign out front. The building was set well back from the street, behind a muddy loading area under the tracks of an overhead crane.

We stopped at the corner, and Nivia got out. She looked both ways, then jogged across Water and dropped the chain that blocked the entrance. I figured they must have broken the lock earlier.

Bubba eased across and stopped to pick her up, then headed up the drive. Weekdays, Galveston mostly shuts down by eleven, even in summer, and only one car passed behind us. The drive was rutted and irregular, and Bubba spun his tires a few times in the soft patches left over from last night's rain. The main door of the warehouse was a square of blackness ahead.

We drove into the blackness and turned left past a tall stack of pallets, giving me headlight flashes of a great empty space. Then Bubba turned off the engine and said happily, "Everybody out."

Humble opened the door, waved his shotgun at me, and I slid after him.

A dim light toward the back of the warehouse revealed a great open space supported by towering girders. Bubba set off toward the light with Nivia, and Humble nudged me along behind them.

We made a racket crossing the floor, our footsteps kicking up echoes that doubled and redoubled against the distant ceiling and walls, until the four of us sounded like a regiment.

When we reached the light bulb, which was attached to one of the girders, Bubba turned, and I caught the glare off his fancy red and black cowboy boots. "You bring that thousand, Bull?" He took it from me with a grin, then gave Nivia an unwelcome hug. "I tole her you'd never buy her sob story unless she asked for money." He laughed. "She's a purty little thing, but she can't help bein' just a little bit mercenary. Can you, sweetheart?" When Nivia pushed away, he let her go and turned all his attention on me. "You know, I like you, Bull, cause I get to kill you so many times. Too bad this'll be my last chance." He told Humble. "Get him movin'."

As Hum gave me a shove, I heard a scrape to my right and saw Puckett step out from behind another stack of pallets. Humble spun with his shotgun, but before he could bring it to bear, Puckett shot him twice.

As Humble fell back, I knew I was saved. Other cops would appear now, riot guns leveled, and take Bubba into custody. I knew it was going to happen because I'd seen it before.

But not this time.

This time, Bubba said to Puckett, "Forgot to tell him 'bout you." He looks down at Humble. "Oh well, saves me havin' to deal with him later on. C'mon." He jerked his chin at me. "Bring him. We gotta get outta here."

As Bubba pulled Nivia toward the back of the warehouse, Puckett nodded for me to follow them.

"What are *you* doing here?" I asked him.

"Let's go," he said.

"Tell me."

"Just *go!*" he growled.

I went, hobbling on my crutch across the sandy concrete floor toward an open loading-bay door in the back wall. Beyond it, we stepped onto a crumbling concrete wharf, and Puckett helped me down into a boat.

It was a sleek, white, thirty-foot cabin cruiser. A rich young man's weekend plaything. Jerry Lamp gave me a guilty glance from the wheel, then turned back to the controls.

Puckett helped me to a bench at the stern, and Bubba shoved Nivia after us. "Go sit with the dead man," he told her and laughed. Then he slapped Jerry on the back and said, "All right, hotshot, let's move it. Gettin' late."

In spite of the warm evening, I could feel Nivia shivering. As for me, I was neither hot nor cold, more numb than anything.

Jerry eased us out into the channel and headed west up Galveston Bay. Galveston is the largest barrier island in the world, and it took us an hour to reach the westernmost tip. As we passed beneath the San Luis-Vacek Bridge, Jerry stuck the boat's nose into the Gulf and steered due south.

Her nose lifted as she accelerated, slapping across the waves, then leveled out as she reached cruising speed. After that, she seemed to glide along, with little more than her screw touching water.

47

The numbness was passing, and fear was on the rise. With fear, came adrenalin, and with adrenalin came the shakes and the churning stomach. I tried to think of a way out, but the best I could come up with were all "what-if" fantasies, centered around the slim possibility that Puckett or Nivia or maybe even Jerry was actually a covert operative of some state or federal law enforcement agency, and that Bubba was now blindly fleeing into their trap. In these scenarios, speedboats would come roaring out of the night at any moment, with sirens wailing, spotlights flashing, and loud hailers blaring. But a more logical part of my mind told me it was too late for the cavalry. If a trap had been set, they would have sprung it before we left Galveston Bay.

I needed distraction and tried to start up a conversation with Nivia, but she was too busy gnawing her nails to talk.

We were beyond the outermost coastal oil rigs when Bubba came back to check on us.

Speaking over the engine's drone and the hiss of the wind, he asked Nivia, "How's it goin', honey?" When she didn't reply, he turned to me. "Would you believe, Bull, that this purty young thing actually tried to blackmail me?"

"How'd she do that?"

"Tole me she put the whole dang story down on paper and give it to her attorney, to be released to the press if anything happened to her."

"Sounds smart to me."

"Would be," he agreed slyly, "if it was true."

"It *is* true," Nivia declared.

"Maybe so," said Bubba, "maybe not."

"So, *that's* why she's still alive," I said.

He chuckled. "Ain't it a pisser?"

"Can you blame her?"

"Guess not," he conceded. "What about you? Can I git you anything?"

"You can let me go."

He smiled. "Keep dreamin'."

"Then you can answer a few questions?"

He threw back his head and cackled. "You're not still after a story, are you?"

"It's what I came for."

He grinned and sat down on the gunwhale next to Nivia. "Mister Writer, I'll give you a story. I coulda been a writer myself, you know. Got a million stories. Which one you wanna hear?"

"Why don't you start by telling me where we're headed."

"Well," he said with a wink, *"our* first port a call will be in a sleepy little village down in the Yucatan, where the girls are cheaper than the booze. But we'll be dropping *you* off along the way."

"This boat can go that far without refueling?"

"No," he admitted. "Even with the oversized tanks, it's only got a range of about three hundred miles. But we got it set up to refuel at an oil rig on the way down. Paid a man to leave a pump unlocked for us."

"You really expect to get away?"

"Why not?" he said. "We got the money for it. And we got new names and passports waitin' for us down there."

"Then what?"

"We disappear."

"Just like that?"

"They'll have to go to a hell of a lot of trouble to bring *me* back, I'll tell you that much."

"Reverend Lamp hired you to look out for his boy, didn't he?" He glanced toward Jerry, who was concentrating on the controls. "The Preacher'd just finished bailin' him outta one mess and wanted to make sure he wasn't gettin' hisself into another one."

"Was he?"

"Course he was. Had this Energy Center scam in the works when I come along."

Jerry spun around. "It wasn't a *scam!*"

"Shut up, boy!" Bubba snapped. "And stick to your drivin'!"

"It wasn't a scam," Jerry repeated, quieter this time.

Bubba turned on him slowly. "You hear what I said?"

As Jerry ducked his head and looked back at the controls, Bubba admitted with a grin, "He's right, you know. He really believed in his Energy Center. Thought he was out to save the world. 'Course, at the same time, he was into a few other little scams here and there, and he was still takin' dough from the bad guys. So, he wasn't what you'd call goin' cold turkey with this virtue thing."

"At least he was trying," I said.

Bubba shook his big head. "Pitiful, ain't it? But I made him see you can't be a little bit dirty any more'n you can be a little bit pregnant."

"Better to be *all* dirty?"

"Yeah!" Bubba said. "Lot more fun. Not to mention more profitable."

"What'd you tell his father?"

"That his little Jerry had seen the light and was now walkin' the straight 'n' narrow. But I tole him, if he was still worried, that I could keep an eye on the boy for a modest monthly fee."

"And he's still paying you?"

"Oh, yeah," he said smugly, "ever' month."

"Meanwhile, you talked Jerry into making you a partner?"

"Just made him see he needed me."

"To keep quiet about his other scams?"

"That and other things."

248

"Did you steal the building fund?" I asked.

"Well, we tried. Or Wilmer did." He looked at me. "Wilmer Ott?"

"I remember him."

"To tell you the truth, all this computer garbage is way over my head, but Ott was s'posed to know his stuff. He was inside the system when the money come outta escrow, and he was s'posed to shift all that dough into a bunch of smaller accounts without anybody knowin' about it until they tried to withdraw the money."

"And where is it now?"

"That's where the trouble comes in. The money was s'posed to be wire transferred to banks in the Cayman Islands, and Wilmer and a friend of mine were s'posed to fly down there and withdraw the cash and wait for us with it in Mérida. Only they run into some trouble, and Wilmer was arrested. But," he said casually, "I guess you know more about that than I do."

I didn't say anything.

He smiled. "It was *you* that sicked the law on Wilmer, wasn't it?" When I still didn't answer, he said, "Hell, you should be proud a yourself—taking that twelve million away from us all by yourself like that."

Given the situation, I didn't feel much like gloating.

"What about the five million you took from the church?" I asked.

He nodded toward the cabin. "We got that with us."

I glanced at Puckett, who hadn't said a word. "How about *him?*"

"The Sergeant's been in it even longer than me, since back when the F.B.I. was on Jerry's ass the first time. He stumbled over evidence that Jerry was laundering money for some spic drug dealer, and he took a bribe to keep quiet about it."

Before Puckett could object, Bubba added, " 'Course, he'll tell you he needed the money for his wife's cancer. But the truth is, he saw easy money and grabbed him some." Puckett was stewing, and Bubba was loving it. "After Jerry and I went partners, he tole me about the Sergeant, and I suggested we should invite him back on the payroll. I figured we could use somebody on the police force."

"Did you jump at the chance?" I asked Puckett, who was sitting sideways in the bucket seat next to Jerry.

Bubba answered for him, "He took some persuadin', but he finally come 'round."

"What'd he do?" I asked Puckett. "Threaten to tell the department about the bribe?"

Bubba said, "I tole you he took some persuadin' ."

"But if the story of the bribe had come out," I said, "wouldn't it have finished Jerry, too?"

"Might've at that," Bubba agreed.

I asked Puckett, "Why're you here now? You got away with it, didn't you?"

"I made him come," said Bubba. "Said I'd tell the cops all about him if he didn't. Figured if I have to go into exile, then so does he."

"What'd the Sergeant do for you?" I asked him.

"Well, he was s'posed to keep his eyes 'n' ears open and try to make sure the other cops didn't look our way."

"So, what happened?"

"With what?"

"Your plan?"

"Hell," he said and shook his head. "Everything went just hunky-dory until Cordelia Mae found out what her darlin' brother was up to. When some useless wino got hisself burned up in one a Jimmy's fires up in Austin, she begged the boy to stop. When he wouldn't, she called up Joe Ahern. Guess it was on account of he was into that Energy Center with Jerry. Reckon she wanted him to put a stop to it all by exposin' Jerry, but she didn't want to turn her dear brother in, and she wouldn't go to the cops about it. So, Ahern started lookin' into it and makin' a nuisance of himself."

"What happened that Friday night?"

He squinted at me. "You want it *all,* don't you?"

"Why stop now? We're just gettin' to the good part."

"Yeah." He grinned. "What the hell, right? So, anyway, I went up to Cordelia Mae's that evenin' to give her a little talkin' to, and your buddy comes waltzin' in like he was King Jesus and orders me to leave her alone. I tell him we're just havin' a little talk, if he don't mind. He says he *does* mind. Says he knows we stole the Salvadoran

Relief Fund. Says he heard about the fire and knew it was one of ours. Says we made the mistake of pulling *him* into it, and now it's all over."

"So," said Puckett, tired of hearing him talk, "this asshole shoots the man."

"What was I supposed to do?" Bubba asked him. "He was gonna ruin ever'thing."

"And what do you think *you* did?" snarled Puckett.

"I saved your ass, that's what."

"How? By makin' me an accessory to murder one?"

"No gratitude," said Bubba to me.

I asked him, "What does 'Born to burn' mean, anyway?"

He was surprised. "Where'd you hear 'bout that?"

"Jimmy told me."

"Shit," he said. "Tell Humble Suggs one little secret, and the whole fuckin' world knows."

"What does it mean?" I repeated.

His little eyes glassed over for a moment. "Just' somethin' my momma used to say."

"Your momma?" I asked.

"All God's children are born to burn, she used to say, but I had a head start on the rest on account of I was too much like my daddy. The Devil was extra strong in us, she said, and it took extra strong whippin' to drive him out."

"Maybe that explains it," I said.

"What?"

"I know about the prostitute, but I bet there were others that nobody knows about."

"You're right there," he said with a grin. "You think my momma drove me to it?"

"Slapped you in the right direction, anyway."

He smiled. "Well, if she did, I reckon she paid for it."

"How do you mean?"

He chuckled to himself. "There's a funny story 'bout that, Mister Writer. See, my momma was the first one I done, back when I was fourteen years old. She caught me goin' through her bag and pulled down her whippin' belt. She screamed that she was gonna call the police on me, and she was just raisin' that belt to the ceilin' when I shot her with Uncle Buford's twenty-two pocket gun. Took three shots to put her down, too. She was a tough ole bird.

"Funny part is, they 'lectrocuted a nigger named Briney Muldoon for the crime. He was picked out of a lineup by two of our neighbors, who swore they saw him sneakin' around the house the day I shot her. And the prosecutors brought in another nigger who said he'd seen Briney flashin' a twenty-two pistol just like the one I used on momma." He cackled. "Now, ain't that a shame! Pore ole nigger dyin' like that for a crime *I* committed. There just ain't no justice in this world, is there?"

"Did you write 'Born to burn' on your mother's forehead, too?"

"Nah." He shook his head. "I only done it that once before, to that whore. And I only thought about doin' it again 'cause Cordelia Mae was a whore, too."

"No, she wasn't," Nivia declared.

Bubba ignored her. "It come to me like a inspiration." He got a sort of mystical look on his cramped features. "Like somebody whispered in my ear that, if I put the words on Cordelia Mae, it might look like Ahern done that other whore, too. To tell you the truth, I'd always felt stupid about writin' the words on the first one. You hear about killers leavin' their mark like that, but it always struck me as real dumb, unless you just wanta get caught. 'Cause sooner or later, it's bound to catch up with you."

"How many people have you killed?"

Trying to look modest, he said, "I'd say the total is better'n twenty now."

"How does it feel when *you* kill?"

He grinned as widely as his little mouth would allow. "Great." Then he squinted at me. "Why? You ever killed anybody?"

"Two people."

"Were you close enough to see the fear in their eyes?"

"No."

"Too bad," he said. " 'Cause, let me tell you there ain't nothin' in the whole wide world like that look a holy terror that comes over 'em when they finally realize it's really gonna happen."

"Did you see it in Joe's eyes?"

"No," he admitted. "I wanted to, but with him bein' a ballplayer and all, I was afraid he might be too quick for me. So, I had to shoot him when he wasn't lookin'. And to tell you the truth, not being able to look him in the eye did kinda take some of the pleasure out of it."

"I imagine you made up for it with Cordelia Mae."

"Oh, yeah," he agreed cheerfully. "Had a good time with her. I knew the cops could tell if Ahern had actually fired the gun, so I picked him up, put the gun in his hand, and tole her, if she made a sound, I'd make him shoot her. I shot right past her ear, just to give her a little scare, and tole her, if she resisted me, I really would shoot her. After I played with her some, I tole her I was gonna shoot her *anyway.*" He hooted. "She was just openin' her yap to scream when I gave her the bullet."

"So, we had two dead people," said Puckett with disgust.

Bubba shrugged. "Hell, she saw me shoot Ahern. 'Sides, it was her fault we were in this pickle."

"Her fault, huh?"

"You don't think so?"

Puckett just shook his head and turned away.

Bubba stood up and stared at him for a moment, but Puckett refused to turn back. Finally, Bubba gave up and walked past him without a glance, taking the ladder down to the cabin.

48

The night was clear, with only a few wisps of cloud against a cobalt sky. Stars glittered like pinpoint jewels, and the quarter moon picked up platinum highlights in the Gulf.

Puckett and Jerry were up front, staring silently ahead. Nivia sat beside me on the bench. She occasionally glanced my way but didn't risk drawing attention to herself by saying anything.

I thought about escape, of course. My hands were untied, and I could swim for it if I wanted, but I knew it would only get me wet. They were sure to miss me and come back to pick me up. Puckett and Bubba had guns; I had my crutch, and the only other weapon in sight was a baseball bat secured by flexible clamps to the port gunwhale. Used to subdue boated sharks, I assumed. I liked the idea of having a bat on hand, but I doubted its effectiveness against two men with guns.

I'd come close to death several times while hunting Juice Hanzlik's murderer and, more recently, in the car crusher, but on all of those occasions, I'd believed that help was on the way and that it was only a question of whether it arrived in time. Here, I didn't believe that. Here, I had only myself to depend on, along with the unhappy alliance between Bubba and Puckett.

• • • • • • • • • • • • •

That came to a head when Bubba climbed out of the cabin with his shotgun and said something to Jerry. The engine died to an idle, and the boat wallowed as it slowed. "Time for the Writer to hit the drink," he announced. "I figure we're far enough out now that the current should carry him down to Mexico." As our wake caught up with us, lifting the boat on its swell, Bubba latched onto the back of Jerry's seat to steady himself and added to Nivia, "Better move out of the way, hon. Don't wanta get blood splattered on your clothes."

Nivia glanced at me, then got up and moved to the starboard gunwhale. "You've escaped now," she said to Bubba. "Why do you have to kill him?"

"Like the man said, honey, 'cause I *like* killin' people." He cackled. "Besides, the sonofabitch cost us twelve million dollars. If that ain't worth killin' over, then I don't know what is."

"It ain't a good 'nough reason," Puckett said from behind him. Bubba ignored him. "Get up," he said to me.

I did and stood with feet spread, leaning on my crutch to hold my balance in the chop.

"You hear me?" said Puckett. "I said that ain't a good 'nough reason for killin' a man."

When Bubba turned. Puckett had his revolver out, not leveled at him, just resting on his knee. Keeping the shotgun pointed at the deck, Bubba asked, "What do you want me to do, let him go?"

"Why not?" said Puckett. "You got a rubber dingy, don't you? Why not set him off in it before we hit land?"

As though explaining it to a retarded child, Bubba said, " 'Cause he will tell somebody, and they will come after us."

"Not if we drop him off far 'nough out." Puckett insisted. "We could be outta reach by the time he paddles ashore."

"Not good enough," said Bubba.

"Why not?"

"It's a loose end," he said. "And if there's one thing I hate, it's a loose end."

255

"Well," said Puckett, *"I* don't like killin'. And I've seen all of it I want to."

"Then close your eyes."

Puckett shook his head.

Losing his sense of humor, Bubba snapped, "Who the hell do you think you *are,* anyway? An officer of the *law* or somethin'? You ain't no police sergeant no more. You're just a bad cop on the run."

"Thanks to *you,"* Puckett growled.

"You're blamin' *me?"* Bubba snarled back.

"It wasn't *me* started shootin' people."

"No," said Bubba. "Matter of fact, I can't see that you done much of anything."

"I made your murder-suicide gag work."

"Yeah, you did such a good job that *he"*—jerking a thumb my way—"found out everything."

"Bullshit!" snapped Puckett.

They stared at each other for a beat, then Bubba pumped the shotgun and dropped it back to his side. "If you don't want to see no more killin', you just step on down to the cabin till it's over?"

"I told you, no."

For a minute, neither of them moved or said anything. The sea grew quiet, and a curtain of cloud drew over the moon. I leaned to my left so I could see Puckett around Bubba, but his face told me no more than Bubba's back.

"Aw, hell!" Bubba finally cried. "Rich as we are, I reckon we can afford to be generous."

Puckett relaxed a little—not much—just let his gun barrel dip slightly. What happened then, happened so fast that it was only later that I was able to put the pieces in order.

Bubba's shotgun came up, but Puckett saw it coming.

The blast missed Puckett but blew the hell out of the back of his seat.

Puckett fired as he rolled across the desk, missing Bubba as well.

I dropped the crutch and hit the wet deck in a dive, feeling a sharp jolt of pain as something snapped in my chest. Probably one of my previously cracked ribs finally breaking. I slid up to the

256

gunwhale and tried to ignore the pain as I jerked the bat out of the clamps.

Bubba and Puckett fired at the same time, Puckett taking it in the leg, Bubba in the belly.

As I struggled to my feet, Puckett hit Bubba again, this time just above the groin. Up now, I brought the bat down on Bubba's shotgun, which discharged into the deck.

Bubba backhanded me almost over the side, and Puckett shot him in the chest.

Bubba stumbled back, pumping and firing another blast into Puckett.

When I swung the bat at Bubba's head, he saw it coming and took it on the shoulder.

He blew a chunk out of the gunwhale as I dove aft. Then he turned, pumped again, and took careful aim at me, as I cowered against the stern seat. But the shot, when it came, came from behind him. It caught Bubba in the back of the head just as he was squeezing the trigger, and his blast went high.

Puckett's slug exploded out of Bubba's face, showering me with a fine mist of blood, bone, and brains. But Bubba stood there for a beat or two afterwards, rocking with the chop, before realizing he was dead.

· · · · · · · · · · · · ·

Nivia was already with Puckett when I got there. He was still alive, but not for much longer, it appeared. His blood was thick on the deck, mingling with Bubba's.

Nivia told me, "Hold him up while I go find some bandages."

I didn't figure bandages would do him much good, but I didn't argue. I sat down on the deck with him, put my back to the edge of the hatchway, and let Puckett lean against me.

He twisted his head around so he could see me. "You tell Peggy Ahern I didn't have nothin' to do with killin' her husband."

"I'll tell her," I said.

He nodded. "Almost shot Lusby on the spot when he tole me what he'd done. The sonofabitch tellin' me he shot my favorite pitcher." His back arched, and he grunted in pain.

"Just hold on," I said.

He grabbed my hand and said, "I really *did* need that money for Allison."

"I'm sure you did."

He nodded and let go of my hand. "Her dyin' like that—" Another grunt of pain cut him off.

"I know," I said.

Nivia showed up, complaining, "What kind of boat doesn't have a first aid kit? All I could find was a clean sheet." She handed it to me, then started unbuttoning Puckett's shirt. She gasped unconsciously at the sight of the wound, and he looked down at it.

"Goddam," he said, "will you look at that." To Nivia, he added, "Wouldn't waste a clean sheet on that, ma'am."

"Give it to me," Nivia snapped at me. She took the sheet, folded part of it, and gently laid it over the wound.

Puckett put his head back on my shoulder and licked his lips.

"You thirsty?" Nivia asked. "I'll get you something."

"No," he said, as she started to rise. "Just sit here with me."

Nivia glanced back at Jerry, who hadn't moved from the wheel. "Go get some water."

Jerry just stared at the blood soaking through the sheet until she snapped, "Go! Now! Water!"

As Jerry dove down the stairs into the cabin, Puckett coughed, groaned, and wiped his mouth.

Coming away with bloody foam on his hand, he stared at it and said, "Lung shot. Damn." He shivered. "Feel cold."

"Get a blanket, too!" Nivia yelled down the stairs.

"Fuckin' Lusby," Puckett muttered, sounding drunk. "Shoulda shot him a long time ago."

"Yeah," I said.

"Sonofa—"

Jerry stood at the top the stairs, holding out the blanket and water. After a moment, he asked, "Don't you want them?"

Nivia got up and walked to the port gunwhale, and I lowered Puckett's head gently to the deck.

When the fact of death sank in, Jerry just stood with his mouth open and stared.

49

Jerry finally turned us back toward Galveston, though he didn't want to at first. When I threatened to shoot him with Bubba's shotgun, he reminded me that I couldn't kill him because I needed him to drive the boat.

"Maybe so," I said, "but you don't need feet for that." When I pointed the shotgun at his left topsider, Jerry obligingly spun the wheel back toward home.

I couldn't have actually shot him in the foot, of course, if he'd called my bluff. But Jerry didn't know that, and he'd spent too much time with people who wouldn't have hesitated for an instant.

I sat with him for a while after that, making sure he didn't change course. I didn't know much about boats, but I could read a compass, and as long as the needle pointed northward, I figured we were headed in the right direction.

It appeared that I had nothing to worry about. Once the decision was taken away from Jerry, and a new course established, he seemed to have no more fight left in him. He'd made his gesture of resistance, been soundly trounced, and had relaxed back into himself.

He stared placidly ahead, hands resting lightly on the wheel, doing what little steering that was necessary with a small part of his consciousness, while the rest retreated within. I wondered where he was in his mind, what amazing structures were taking shape there. I knew the pleasure of putting together a story in my head, but Jerry seemed to have gotten lost in his, lost to the point where real life had no "reality" for him.

It made me angry that he should escape so easily, made me want to reach out and shake him, to force him to confront what he'd done and the consequences of his actions. But I also knew he didn't get this way on his own, and I couldn't help wondering what kind of upbringing would lead to the development of a defensive mechanism like his. Maybe all it took was a father who thought of himself as a conduit for the word of God. That might be enough.

Maybe Jerry caught some of that, because he turned and asked, "Did you say something?"

I opened my mouth, then shut it and shook my head. "No, nothing."

. . . .

Nivia had gone back to the rear bench, and I eventually went back to join her, stepping around Puckett and over Bubba along the way. They lay where they'd fallen, covered with blankets we'd found in the cabin.

"You all right?" I asked.

"What do *you* think?" she snapped back.

"Just curious."

"That's you all the way, isn't it? Curious to the end."

"That's me," I agreed.

When she sighed and looked away, I asked, "How'd you get into this? How're you connected to Bubba?"

"I wasn't connected to *him* at all," she said, kicking his boot with her toe, "until this started."

"Then how?"

She sighed. "My only *connection,* as you put it, is that I was Lamp's mistress."

I glanced toward Jerry.

"Not *him,*" she said with a laugh. "The *father.*"

260

I was more than a little surprised. "What do you know?"

"Hardest work I ever did," she said. "The man was a ferret in the sack."

"So, you moved out on him."

"Right."

"How'd you happen to pick Bayou View Apartments?"

"I met Dee-Dee at a party about a year ago. After that, we went out to lunch now and then. When I left the Colonel, I called to ask if she could put me up for a day or two. I needed a place to stay, and there was a vacancy."

"Did you know Bubba before you moved in?"

"Saw him once with the Colonel, but I never spoke to him."

"How did Dee-Dee end up there?"

"Her brother was living there when she moved in. But they had a fight, and he left a couple of months ago."

"Did you—"

Cutting me off, she asked, "Don't you *ever* run out of questions?"

She was right. Soon as one was answered, another popped up. It was getting to be downright obsessive. I was tired and hurting and figured I'd earned a rest, so I decided to take one. I crossed my arms on my knees and put my head down. Not to sleep—I didn't trust either of my shipmates enough for that—just to rest my eyes for a moment. But I really *was* tired, and in spite of my aching ribs, it was everything I could do to fight off sleep.

I was on the verge of losing the fight, when Nivia said, "I got up after the third shot that night and walked into the living room. When I looked out the window, I saw Bubba pulling the door shut to Dee-Dee's apartment. I didn't see a gun, but I knew Dee-Dee was afraid of him. Right after I moved in, she told me to look out for him, said he was capable of anything. She said he'd come into her bedroom one night and was just standing there at the foot of her bed when she woke up.

"So, when I saw him coming out of her apartment, I was scared for her. I thought of all the awful things he might have done, but I didn't *know*. After he disappeared down the steps, I called the cops, but I didn't tell them about Bubba or what I'd seen, just that

I'd heard some shots. I wasn't sure what had happened, and it could've been nothing. When I went over to check it out, her door was shut, so I knocked. Getting no answer, I tried the door, and it wasn't locked. I opened it a few inches and called her name, then I pushed it open the rest of the way, and there they were.

"Like I told you before, I wasn't sure they were dead at first, then I realized they were. I saw the gun and knew Bubba must have shot them. But when I turned to leave, he was standing there. He took me back to my apartment and stayed with me all night. I was sure he was going to kill me, but he was just weird, sitting there humming old hymns to himself, drinking one beer after another. I kept hoping he'd get drunk and fall asleep, but he didn't. About nine-twenty in the morning, he told me to call the police. He told me what to say and stood beside me as I said it. Then he took the keys to my Blazer, pulled my phone cord out of the wall, and told me not to try to leave or he'd kill me. He told me I was messing with something big, involving powerful people and lots of money. He said I might be able to get him arrested, but if I did, they would kill me.

"On Sunday, a woman who'd bought one of my paintings came to see me. She wanted to commission me for a mural, and when she couldn't get me on the phone, she got my address from the gallery and dropped by. She managed to get in without Bubba seeing her, and I thought about telling her everything. But I couldn't do it. I was afraid Bubba would kill her, too, and I didn't want that on my conscience.

"He saw her leaving and came up to check on me. I told him she was my lawyer and fed him that story about Dee-Dee telling me everything and me putting it all down and giving it to the lawyer in a sealed envelope for her to open and release to the press if anything happened to me. I wasn't sure he ever believed me, but he didn't kill me. After that, he installed Humble in the next apartment to keep an eye on me."

When I didn't say anything, Nivia asked, "Are you asleep?"

"Yeah," I said and raised my head. I stretched and looked north to where a faint gray glimmer sat on the horizon. "Like you said, I ask too many questions. To be honest, I don't know if you're telling me the truth or not. It sounds all right. Roy would say it listens. But that doesn't make it true, only plausible. It's also plausible that a woman who just broke off with her lover might be in the mood for revenge. Such a woman might consider stealing the El Salvadoran Relief Fund an appropriate method. But," I added, "at this moment, I don't really care. Bubba's been taken care of; Joe's reputation is safe; Peg can sleep a little easier now; and I have an ending to my story. Even the name of Briney Muldoon will finally be cleared. What more could I want? If you're hiding something, so what? Somebody else can dig it up."

She nodded. "Wonder how long *that'll* last."

I shrugged. "Who can say?"

She gave me her up-from-under look, then smiled and looked away.

It was just a smile. Nothing wrong with it. But to be on the safe side, I decided not to turn my back on her till I was back on dry land, with a cop in sight. One I trusted. Molly.